Half Baked

Half Baked

Maddie Baker Mystery #3

Denise Grover Swank

DGS

Chapter One

Maddie

My stomach churned as I stood in front of St. Vincent's Village on a cold late Tuesday afternoon in January. I'd only been living with my Aunt Deidre since last September, and I was already seriously considering moving her here. I felt like I'd failed her.

Still, there was no denying her dementia had gotten progressively worse over the past few months. Yesterday, I'd taken her to Nashville to see her doctor, and he'd forced me to face some cold hard truths. It was becoming more and more dangerous for her to stay at home, despite all the precautions we had taken. It would be safer for her to live somewhere with twenty-four-hour care.

I'd cried a good part of the two-and-a-half-hour car ride home. Thankfully, my best friend, Mallory, had driven us. Mallory had decided to stay in Cockamamie, and she'd even found a new remote job that gave her the freedom to help out with my aunt occasionally. To say I was grateful was a massive understatement. Having her around was keeping me going. Because my aunt was the only family I had left, and she rarely remembered me. And Noah, the man who'd pledged himself to me before Christmas, had visited his family for the holidays and returned a changed man. He'd told me he had to take a break from our relationship. He still had issues he was working through, and he wasn't as far along with them as he'd thought. It had seemed to torture him to say it, to mean it, but he'd gone and done it anyway.

I hadn't seen him since.

I'd never felt more alone in my life.

But standing outside in the cold feeling sorry for myself wasn't going solve anything. The pity party was over. Time to deal with reality.

I squared my shoulders and opened the front door, reminding myself of what Mallory had said before I'd left to come here. This was only a cursory visit to check things out. It didn't mean that Aunt Deidre had to come here.

But we both knew that she probably did. Especially since she'd gotten out of the house twice last week. That and it was the only residential care facility in town qualified to take her.

A receptionist greeted me at the front counter with a warm smile. "You must be Maddie. I'll let Ms. Farrow know you're here."

"Thanks." I turned to study the photos of some of the residents on the wall—all smiling and having fun. I doubted Aunt Deidre would feel that way. Then again, she likely wouldn't even know where she was most of the time. Most of the time. She still had lucid moments, and what kept me up at night was thinking about how she'd feel about all of this in those rare moments when she remembered everything—and knew I'd plucked her from her comfortable home.

"I see you're studying the photos," a voice said from behind me.

I turned to see a woman who looked like she was in her forties standing next to the receptionist's desk.

I offered a weak smile, still in disbelief it had come to this so quickly. "Guilty as charged."

"I admit they're propaganda," she said with a self-deprecating smile, "but our residents really *do* love it here." She extended her hand. "I'm Ms. Farrow, director of St. Vincent's Village. I understand you're looking for help with your aunt?"

I swallowed the lump in my throat and forced out, "Yes."

She gave me a sympathetic smile. "I know this is a difficult decision, not to be made lightly, but hopefully we'll settle some of your fears on your tour of the facility."

"It's not that I don't want her at home," I said, frustrated by the way my voice caught. "But her doctor says her dementia has progressed too rapidly..."

She stepped closer and lowered her voice. "There comes a time when you're actually doing your loved one a favor by moving them to a facility. You're fortunate that we have an available bed. We have a very attentive staff here that's on duty twenty-four hours a day. There are safeguards that just aren't realistic for you to employ at home." She patted the side of my arm. "But no decisions are being made at the moment, right? You said you were just here to tour."

"Yeah."

"Shall we get started?"

The facility was clean, bright, and cheery. I'd been to depressing nursing homes before, so that made me feel better. Ms. Farrow showed me the game room, the cafeteria, the outdoor courtyard, and then the memory care unit.

While some residents lived in actual apartments, others had private rooms. The memory care unit was undeniably impressive, with its own cafeteria, courtyard, and fitness facility.

"We find that keeping their bodies active is good for their minds," Ms. Farrow said, which started a new cascade of guilt.

Should I have kept Aunt Deidre more active?

"This is the room we have available," she said, moving down the hall toward an open door.

The room had a living area, a small bedroom, and a bathroom.

The living area and bedroom faced a landscaped bed filled with a mixture of evergreens and bare deciduous plants. It was...nice.

A phone rang, and Ms. Farrow slipped it out of her pocket and glanced at the screen. "I need to take this. Feel free to continue looking around; I'll be back in a moment."

I nodded. "Thank you."

She walked away, and I moved around the room, trailing my finger over the back of the gray vinyl sofa. This place was the polar opposite of Aunt Deidre's home, where she'd lived her entire life. I couldn't imagine sending her to live here alone. She'd hate the décor—she loved her vintage furnishings, and this place was very modern—plus she'd be incredibly lonely without me, Mallory, and her next-door neighbor Margarete.

Then again, half the time she thought I was the live-in help my deceased uncle had hired. Two weeks ago, she'd thought I was a burglar and had called 911 to report a break-in.

No, Aunt Deidre wouldn't be lonely for me. She'd be lonely for Uncle Albert, and my mother, and a whole host of family members who were long since dead. My aunt's mind was burrowing deeper and deeper into the past, and no matter where she lived, she'd be lonely for the people who couldn't be there.

Tears burned my eyes, and I hurried back into the hallway. I had known this would be hard, but not this hard. Mallory had offered to come, but she'd already taken off the day from work yesterday. I hadn't wanted to ask her to take a couple of hours off this afternoon too.

Noah should be here with you.

I shut that thought down immediately, both because Noah had made it crystal clear that he was wrapped up in his own issues and because visiting a residential care center wasn't something you did with your new girlfriend. It was something you saved until you had at least exchanged I love yous. Which we hadn't.

Even if I *did* love him.

That's what hurt the most about the whole situation. While he'd warned me that he ran when he got scared, I'd figured he might need a few days to get himself together, not weeks. Still, I was giving him his space, hoping his therapist would talk some sense into him.

In all honesty, Mallory might knee him in the balls if and when he came back, but that was a worry for later.

I needed to stop thinking about Noah. This visit was about my aunt, which was causing me enough pain. I didn't need to borrow more.

I started down the hall toward the reception area, taking in the décor. I could have been walking down the hallway in an apartment building. There were wreaths and decorations on the doors, name-plates, and doorbells. One door was open, revealing a man on a recliner who was staring at a blank TV screen. His head swiveled to face me, and he shouted, "Hey, you! Girl! Come in here!"

He was rude enough that I almost walked away, but I reminded myself of how rude Aunt Deidre could be at times and decided to ignore it. "Do you need help with something?"

"I can't get the damn TV to turn on."

I almost told him that was because he was trying to turn it on with a cell phone. Instead, I walked into the room, picked up a remote control off the end table, and clicked the power button.

"How'd you do that?" he asked, shaking the cell phone.

I handed him the remote. "You needed this one."

His brow furrowed as he looked down at it, then stared at the home screen on the TV with a frustrated expression.

I sat on the edge of the sofa next to him. "What would you like to watch?"

"I wanna watch the damn football game," he grumbled.

I suspected there weren't any live football games playing on a Tuesday afternoon, but my ex-boyfriend Steve had watched old games on ESPN. I searched for an ESPN channel, found an old college game, and turned it on. "How's that?"

His face scrunched. "I wanna watch the Falcons."

"They've got a bye week," I said, proud of myself for knowing what that meant and using it correctly. But I continued my search and found an old NFL game. "How about the Cowboys?"

He didn't answer, just made a face and sank back into his chair.

I took that as a yes and left the TV on that channel. When he seemed as satisfied as was likely possible for him, I stood. "You have a good rest of your day, Mr...." I let the sentence trail off since I didn't know his name and realized he might not know it either. Something to get used to in the memory ward, I guess.

"That's Detective to you," he snapped. "Detective Bergan. Show a little respect."

My jaw dropped, but thankfully he didn't seem to notice my reaction.

Howard Bergan was the detective who had investigated my mother's murder. From what I'd learned, he'd bungled it. It had been a cold case until November. After joining the police force last summer, Noah had tried to reopen it, but no one had managed to find the file. He and his partner Lance suspected Bergan had taken it. Detective Bergan's wife had let them search his old home office, but it hadn't turned up. Nor had they found it in their search of a storage unit that had contained multiple other official files. Noah and Lance had closed my mother's case because they'd found evidence indicating a recently murdered high school teacher/sexual predator had killed her. But they were wrong, because soon afterward, I learned that Martin Schroeder had an alibi for the night my mother was murdered. Noah and Lance knew, but they'd been tied up in other, more current murder cases, so they hadn't done anything about it yet. That meant her case was in limbo. Officially closed, but unofficially unsolved.

And the answers might be locked in this man's brain.

"Do you know who I am?" I asked, barely above a whisper, but it was loud enough for him to hear me.

He looked up and scrunched up his nose. "The afternoon nurse who'd rather wander the hallways than do any damn work?" he asked in a snotty tone.

"I'm Andrea Baker's daughter."

I wasn't sure why I'd told him. I doubted he'd remember her name, let alone her murder. It was widely known that he had early-onset dementia, which, of course, was why he was in the memory care unit. So I wasn't prepared for the recognition that washed over his face, quickly replaced by fear. "I haven't talked. I swear."

My heart slammed into my rib cage, and I took a deep breath to remain calm before slowly sitting back down. "Haven't talked about what, Detective Bergan?"

"I never told anyone about the eagle."

My heart thumped painfully fast. What eagle? No one had ever mentioned an eagle in connection to my mother's murder.

"That's good," I said reassuringly, scared I was going to say the wrong thing. I could only wing it and hope Bergan didn't shut down. "Your secret is safe with me. I swear."

"If you know, you're not safe," he said, starting to panic. "No one is safe."

"I'm okay, Detective," I said, reaching over to pat his hand.

He jerked away, his eyes wild. "They're gonna come looking for me."

"Who's going to come looking for you?"

He struggled to get out of his recliner. "I have to run. They'll get me."

"Who will get you?"

"The skinny man," he said, trying to stand up.

I shook my head. Had his terror been sparked by a memory, or a dementia-induced hallucination? One thing was clear—he was terrified. I stood and reached for his arm to help him up, but he shoved me away.

"Get away from me! You're cursed now too!"

"Who cursed you, Detective Bergan?" I asked with a shaky voice.

Hearing his official name flipped a switch, sending him from panic to calm.

"The skinny man."

The skinny man? He sounded like an urban legend, but Bergan was truly terrified.

I held his gaze, which looked slightly less cloudy. "Tell me where the skinny man is, and I'll end the curse," I said evenly. "I'll save you."

"No one can save us now."

A young man wearing scrubs showed up in the doorway and said in a soothing tone, "Hey, Howard. What seems to be the problem?"

"That's Detective Bergan to you," the older man grumped. He was standing in front of his recliner. I was in front of him, closer than I should have been, but the aide didn't seem concerned.

"I saw his door open, and he was having trouble with his remote," I said, feeling the need to explain myself. "I came in to help him."

"Don't you worry about it," he said, coming close enough that I could read his name tag—Alan. "He gets agitated for no reason at all these days. It's been getting worse since last November."

It didn't require any mental gymnastics for me to remember that Martin Schroeder had been killed in early November. I wasn't ever likely to forget it, because I was the Uber driver who'd driven him to his murder. That's the kind of thing that makes an impression. He'd been a science teacher at the high school where my mother had taught English. The high school where she'd been murdered. And the two of them hadn't gotten along.

Had Bergan heard about Schroeder's death? Noah and I had discovered the former detective had protected scores of people for profit. Come to find out, Schroeder had been one of them. He'd been suspect number one in my mother's death. My mother had suspected him of molesting female students, and according to her fellow teacher and friend, she'd planned to confront him the night of her murder. But Detective Bergan had buried the connection—and other molestation accusations as well.

Maybe hearing Schroeder's name in the news had caused Bergan's paranoia to resurface. Or it could have just been the disease eating his brain away. Aunt Deidre had moments of paranoia; as far as I knew, nothing in particular triggered those. So, yeah, the onset of his paranoia around the time of Schroeder's death could be coincidental. Still, if I were prone to betting and had the money to do so, I'd bet a hundred bucks that Detective Bergan was worried his sins would come to light.

Which led me back to the question at hand—

Were his fears the babblings of a man with dementia, or the valid concerns of a man who had protected some evil people?

I was going with the latter. And if that were true, then Bergan still remembered something about my mother's murder—something that might solve it once and for all.

I stepped to the side while the aide tried to get Bergan settled down. I knew I should leave, but it was hard to walk away from the person who had the answers I'd been looking for since the night the cops had shown up at our front door nearly nineteen years ago to tell me the person who'd been my world was dead. Still, I couldn't exactly interrogate him while the aide tried to settle him down. They would likely deny Aunt Deidre the available bed and ban me from ever seeing Bergan again.

Except...could I really put my aunt in the same facility—hell, the same *hall*—as the man who'd failed to find her sister's killer?

Did I have a choice?

"I should probably go back out to the hall," I said, thumbing toward the door. "Ms. Farrow was taking me on a tour and got called away."

"She's still up at the front entrance if you want to head that way," Alan said, leading Bergan toward the bedroom. "Just press the button on the wall by the door, and they'll buzz you through."

"Thanks." Still, as I walked out of Bergan's living room, I scanned it for anything that might give me some direction. I nearly laughed out loud at my own folly. It wasn't like a paranoid man was going to leave evidence of his wrongdoing from almost two decades ago out in the open.

No, I suspected whatever Detective Bergan knew was locked up tight in his diseased brain.

I buzzed the front desk, and they let me through the door.

Lisa, the receptionist, gave me an apologetic smile. "Ms. Farrow is still dealing with the situation that called her away, and she's the one who does our financial rundowns. Unfortunately, you'll need to reschedule an appointment to discuss your aunt's assets and what secondary insurance she might have. I'm so sorry."

"I don't think she has secondary insurance," I said with a frown. "She's on Medicare."

Sympathy covered her face. "Ms. Farrow will get into all of that with you on your next appointment. Would you like to schedule that now?"

Her talk of assets and secondary insurance made me nervous. So did the idea of housing my aunt under the same roof as Detective Bergan. "I know you can't tell me how much it would cost to put my aunt here because of all the variables, but can you give me a ballpark figure? Just so I know what I'm dealing with?"

She made a face and leaned closer. "I'm not supposed to tell you this, but it costs around eight thousand."

I breathed a sigh of relief. "A year?" I asked to clarify.

She released a soft chuckle. "Oh my. No. A month."

A month? Where did people get eight thousand a *month*? I hadn't even made that much at my middle school librarian job in Nashville.

Lisa must have seen the panic on my face. "But there are multiple options to pay for your aunt's care," she continued sweetly. "I'm sure there's real estate you can sell, and many older folks have investments."

Uncle Albert had done some investing, but truth be told, he'd sunk a lot of money into the house over the last decade. There was enough money in her accounts to pay for a little over half a year, then we'd have to sell the house. It might be a tall order to find an interested wealthy buyer who wanted to hold property in Cockamamie.

"Thank you," I muttered, feeling overwhelmed. I wished I had someone here to help me deal with all of this. My mind couldn't stop fixating on Noah, but I didn't need a man to solve my problems. I could solve them myself.

The thing was...I didn't want Noah to solve my problems. I wanted Noah to share my life.

Enough.

Okay, so Noah had bowed out. I still had Mallory.

"Would you like to go ahead and set up that appointment?" Then she added, "Ms. Farrow is really sorry she had to go."

"Let me get back to you," I said, trying to keep the defeat from my voice. "I want to bring my friend, so I need to check her schedule."

"Don't wait too long, now," she said. "We have someone else interested in the room. We'll only hold it until next Monday for you before we move on to them."

No pressure.

Feeling discouraged, I walked outside, surprised to find it colder than when I'd gone in. I tugged my coat tighter and then found my next surprise.

Lance was standing at the end of my car with his hands stuffed inside his coat pockets and a grim expression on his face.

My heart skipped a beat, and I froze in place in the parking lot several feet from him. Why was Lance here? We were friends, but not close enough that he would know about the nursing home tour. I could only think of one reason he would come here to see me, and the thought made my blood run cold.

"Noah," I said, my voice sounding strangled. "What happened?"

His face remained grim as he took a step forward. "Maddie, I don't want you to panic."

"What happened?"

"Noah's been shot."

Chapter Two

Noah

Two hours earlier

I sipped coffee from my insulated tumbler, savoring the rich aroma. Six months ago, I would have drunk anything wrung from coffee beans. Now, thanks to Maddie and my exposure to her barista job, I'd turned into a coffee snob. My partner, Detective Lance Forrester, found it hilarious.

Maddie. I missed her so much my chest ached.

"Did you just sniff your coffee?" he asked with a snide look from the passenger seat of my car. We were parked about half a block away from the mechanic's shop we were surveilling.

"*No,*" I scoffed, sitting upright in my seat.

Amusement danced in his eyes. "Okay." He turned slightly to face me. "There's no harm in enjoying your caffeinated beverage. I can tell from here it's better than the gas station swill you used to get before Maddie taught you the benefits of a good brew."

I knew he'd thrown Maddie's name out as bait to start yet

another conversation about what an idiot I was. I already knew I was an idiot. I didn't need him piling on.

But he wasn't joking about the coffee. I'd since bought a French press and was now learning the art of the pour-over.

My father would surely call me a pussy if he found out, but there was little likelihood of that ever happening. After my trip home for Christmas, I'd decided never to speak to him again. Ever. But I hadn't told Lance that or anything else about the conversation we'd had two days after Christmas. I hadn't told anyone—just like I'd promised. My father might think I was worthless, but I could keep a personal confidence. So instead of becoming vulnerable with my friend, something my therapist was not so gently suggesting I do more of, I focused my attention on the shop down the street.

Early this morning, one of my informants told me she'd heard that one of the cars from a recent string of thefts was going to be delivered to George's Garage. We had nothing else to go on, so Lance and I were on a stakeout, hoping to see it delivered. We were fairly certain George Dempsey, the garage owner, was a middleman. If we caught him with stolen merchandise, we hoped we could convince him to give up the people above him.

"That really sucks about Aunt Deidre," Lance said, taking a sip of his own coffee. I'd found that most of Maddie's friends called her Aunt Deidre, as if she were their aunt too. When the woman's mind wasn't clouded with her disease, she seemed to bask in it.

He cleared his throat, keeping his gaze through the windshield. "Did you hear that Maddie's touring St. Vincent's today? She and Mallory took Deidre to the doctor up in Nashville yesterday, and he told Maddie it was time."

Shock ran through my body, followed by grief for Maddie. That had to be killing her. Then I got pissed. "You *know* I wouldn't have heard that Maddie was touring St. Vincent's."

He shrugged. "Maybe you *should* know."

"Cut the shit, Lance."

He turned to me, anger flashing in his eyes. "Maybe you should be the one cutting the shit."

"We need to focus on this stakeout. Not my love life."

"So you admit that you love her?" he countered.

"It's a *saying*, Lance. Let it go."

"It's hard to let it go when Maddie's heart is breaking not only for her aunt—which is unavoidable—but because you dropped her like a hot potato after going home at Christmas. What the hell happened, man?"

I shifted in my seat, but it didn't make me any more comfortable with this conversation. He'd danced around it plenty, but he'd never flat out asked me like this before. "That's none of your business. And I didn't drop her. I told her I needed to take some time to sort things out in my head."

"Even *you* have to realize how ridiculous that sounds," he said snidely.

He wasn't wrong.

Every day I woke up with the terror that Maddie would grow tired of my bullshit and find someone else who was more worthy of her. Someone who wouldn't ask to be with her, then tuck tail and run. I knew I was an idiot—I knew it better than anyone else. But my father had done a pretty damn good job of pointing out one last time what a fuckup I was. And while part of me knew I didn't deserve Maddie, the selfish part of me wanted her anyway. Even if I was ignoring her at the moment.

"Mallory says she has an appointment at one."

My chest tightened. "Is Mallory going with her?"

"Nope," he said in a breezy tone. "She took off yesterday, so Maddie refused to let her ask for more hours off today."

"What about Margarete?" She'd been Deidre's next-door neighbor for decades and was more like family. She often took care of Deidre when Maddie needed help.

He turned serious. "She's going alone."

That was like an arrow to my heart, but I also knew there was a purpose to this discussion other than an FYI. "Are you suggesting I go on the tour with her?"

He jutted back his head and lifted his hands. "I never said that."

"That's what you're hinting at."

He turned to me, all joking gone. "Look, I know your family did a number on you at Christmas, and it messed you up again." He tilted his head toward me. "But by distancing yourself from Maddie, don't you see that you're letting them win?"

"You don't know what you're talking about." But his suggestion hit closer to home than I would have liked. "She can do better than me."

"Yeah," he said, back to his amused tone. "I *know* she can. But for some damn reason, she wants *you*. And seeing how she's a grown woman, perhaps you should let her decide what's good for her, not *you*."

I sat back in my seat, mulling over his words.

"You can make it on time, you know," he said, lifting a foot and propping it on my dashboard. "You have about an hour to get there on time."

I shot him an irritated look, for both the foot and the suggestion. "I'm the last person she wants to see."

"Don't be so sure about that."

"She's got to be pissed at me." Not that I could blame her.

He sighed and dropped his foot. "Not pissed, Noah. Disappointed. Hurt, but not pissed." He grinned. "If anyone's pissed at you, it's Mallory. The next time you see her, I can't promise you'll leave with all your parts."

A lump filled my throat, not because I was terrified of Mallory's rage—which I was, by the way, any smart man would be. I found myself saying something I never would have admitted to him two months ago. "I don't want to hurt her any more than I already have."

He turned to me and gave me a sad smile. "Dude, you're your own worst enemy. Quit overthinking it and just be with her."

"We still have things we need to work out. Like having kids. I'm still not sure I want them, and she definitely does."

"So work them out as you go. You admitted that you're open to reconsidering that." He paused. "I'm not trying to tell you what to do—"

I snorted.

He held up his hands. "Okay, I guess I am. But it comes from a place of love. For both of you."

He sat back in this seat and stared out the window again.

We watched the building in silence for several seconds before I said, "Seems like you need to take your own advice."

He burst out laughing. "Are you talking about Mallory?"

"Who else?" The two of them had spent New Year's Eve together, and they'd promptly stopped talking. I wasn't sure what had happened, only that something had. "I thought you two weren't speaking. How'd this conversation about Maddie take place?"

He shrugged, looking nonchalant. "She keeps me informed about important things."

"So there's nothing between you two?" I didn't usually get involved like this, but I figured it was fair game since he wasn't going easy on me either.

He shrugged and said lightheartedly, "I'm ready for a relationship with her. The next move is hers."

"What happened after you two spent New Year's Eve together?"

He waggled his eyebrows. "A gentleman never kisses and tells."

"Hmm." I'd wanted to ask Maddie about it, but it hadn't seemed like a good idea after I'd asked her for space. I had to admit that all this space hadn't stopped me from thinking about her nearly every second of the day. Or remembering kissing her and holding her in my arms and wanting so much more. Lance was right, it was patronizing of me to insinuate she was incapable of making decisions about what was best for her. Still, that wasn't the only reason I was staying away. My father's words at Christmas kept ringing in my ears.

"We both know we're not planning to make a bust today," Lance said. "This is a fact-finding mission."

I looked around the car in an exaggerated manner. "I already know this. Who are you announcing it to?"

"Just reminding you, is all." He lifted a shoulder into another lazy shrug. "*If* you were thinking about taking off early to meet Maddie at the nursing home."

He was full of shit. We'd been chasing the stolen car parts ring for weeks, and this was our first big break. What if we had to follow someone? A lot could happen while I was gone.

He gave me a pointed look. "Look. Noah. We both know—*shit*."

I caught movement down the street—a middle-aged man heading toward the garage. He was probably in his late forties, early fifties. He had salt-and-pepper hair, beefy arms, and an air of confidence that almost begged someone to challenge him. I'd never met him in person, but I'd seen plenty of photos.

"What the hell is Joe Kipsey doing here?" Lance asked in disbelief.

Joe Kipsey was the owner of a bar called Cock of the Walk at the edge of town. Everyone and their dog knew both the bar and the Brawlers, a group of drug dealers who hung out there, were trouble. But no one on the Cockamamie force or the Wayfare County Sheriff's Department had ever been able to find enough proof to nail anyone of significance to the wall.

From what little intelligence we had, the Brawlers were strictly in the drug business. They never mixed in anything else. But Kipsey was a new player. He'd swooped in about six months ago and taken over the bar and somehow the drug business. The previous owner had retired, hopefully to a beach somewhere and not a shallow grave. Before showing up here in town, Kipsey had been locked up for a decade, and he had a record littered with assaults, batteries, and attempted murders. In short, he was bad news. Maybe he was looking to expand the Brawlers' range.

"Having his car worked on?" I asked with plenty of skepticism.

Lance grabbed the binoculars from the center console and held them up to his eyes. "It's him, all right."

"I thought Kipsey didn't typically leave his property." There was a residence attached to the bar, which made it easier for him to hole up in his newfound kingdom.

"He doesn't," Lance said, his voice tight.

Now, my interest was really piqued. "Can't be a coincidence." Still, it didn't make sense that he'd turn up in person to oversee the delivery of a stolen car. Why risk his freedom for something so minor? Had our intelligence been wrong?

Kipsey disappeared into the building and then headed to the back of the garage, out of view of our prying eyes.

"Dammit," I grumbled. "What I wouldn't give to have a bug in the place."

"Or listening ears," my partner said, unfastening his seatbelt.

"You're not seriously considering going in there, are you?" I asked in shock.

He shrugged. "There's nothing wrong with me asking about an oil change."

I shook my head. "You won't hear anything. They'd never talk that close to customers."

"Maybe, maybe not," he said, reaching for his door handle. "But I can scope the place out. See if the employees are skittish about Kipsey showing up on the property. Or if they look like they're used to having him around."

"Still," I said. "They might not appreciate a cop showing up at the counter when a known bad guy is in the back."

"Good thing I don't look like a cop." He was right. He was dressed in jeans and a pale blue button-down shirt.

"What if someone recognizes you?"

"I don't know anyone there. Don't worry so much."

"But if someone knows you're a cop, it could blow the whole thing."

Lance opened the door. "That's not likely to happen. The risk is low in comparison to the possibility for reward." He nodded to me. "Text Maddie that you'll meet her." He got out and shut the door before I could answer.

I watched him head down the street, my stomach tightening with nerves. So many things could go wrong, but I had to admit that most of my worst-case scenarios weren't likely to happen. My thoughts drifted to Maddie. Would she be upset if I showed up at St. Vincent's after weeks of silence, or would she be relieved? Because Lance was right. He was perfectly capable of watching the place without me—as long as he promised not to go poking around after I left him alone. Still, it was crazy to go, but my father had always put work before anything in his personal life, including his wife and kids. If I chose Maddie over work—especially something important—then maybe it was proof that I could prioritize something or someone else over my job.

We could make this work.

Lance was about to walk into the garage office, so I picked up the binoculars, giving him my undivided attention. He entered through a glass door. Through it, I could see the waiting room was empty except for a few vacant plastic chairs. He approached the unmanned counter, and a guy came out of the back a few minutes later. Going off body language, he and Lance carried on a relaxed conversation for a couple of minutes.

Movement next to the building caught my attention. I noticed Kipsey walking out of the door he'd entered, heading toward a newer-looking, decked-out pickup truck. He looked pissed.

I held up my phone and took several photos as he exited the building, walked to his truck, then drove away.

Lance walked out of the building as Kipsey drove down the street. When he got back into the car, he said, "That was helpful."

"What did you learn?"

"Not a whole lot, but as I was wrapping things up, I could hear Kipsey talking to an older man. He told the guy he'd be in touch, but it wasn't in friendly way."

"That's it?"

"I learned that if I start getting my oil changed there, the tenth one is free."

"About the case?" I asked with a sarcastic sidelong look.

"The guy at the counter didn't seem all revved up because Kipsey was there. I could see some mechanics in the back, and they didn't seem overly concerned either."

"So they either didn't know who he was or didn't care."

"I'd go with the latter," Lance said. "Did you text Maddie?"

"I was too busy making sure you weren't murdered."

He placed a hand over his heart, making mooney eyes at me. "Nice to know you love me."

"I can't let you get killed," I grumped. "With budget cuts and all, I have no guarantee the chief will get me a new partner. Besides, now that Kipsey's dropped by, we need to stick around and see if the stolen car shows up."

Lance laughed. "If I weren't here, you'd do this alone. So if you insist on staying, you're saying you don't trust me to watch the place by myself. That true?"

"No, of course not—"

"The only exciting thing that's likely to happen, already has. And as we already established, we weren't planning on busting anyone today. Just observing. I know how to do that." He gave me a pointed look.

"We're driving my car."

"That's easily resolved." He pulled his car keys out of his pocket and tossed them to me. "Walk a few blocks away and have a patrol car pick you up and take you back to the police lot. You can borrow my car."

I glanced down at his car keys. "If I didn't know any better, I'd accuse you of trying to get rid of me."

He scoffed. "If I wanted to get rid of you, I wouldn't be subtle."

I couldn't hold back my laugh. "Yeah, that's for damn sure."

I glanced at my phone, nervous about leaving Lance. Nervous about upsetting Maddie. Ever since Christmas, I'd been nervous about everything, thinking every step I took was in the wrong direction.

"I'll be fine, Dad," Lance teased.

"I know," I said, turning serious. "I don't want you to think I don't believe you can do this."

"It's all good," he said with a grin. "I know you're a control freak who has trouble letting go."

His words caught me by surprise. Was that an accurate assessment? If so, that made me more like my father than I cared to admit. Then again, hadn't my father pointed out the very same thing a few weeks ago?

Lance picked up his phone and tapped on the screen. A second later, he looked up and said, "Neil's gonna pick you up at the convenience store on Vesper in about five minutes."

I shouldn't go. I was no less fucked up than I'd been after getting back from that trip, maybe more so, because I'd realized that Maddie helped settle my restless mind. I found a peace just by being with her that I'd never had with anyone else. But in the end, my own need to see her and offer support won out.

Before I could change my mind, I wrapped my fingers around his keys and got out, stopping myself from giving him any advice. He could handle this.

The walk to the convenience store was quick, but I'd had coffee and water that morning and hadn't used the bathroom in several hours. I texted Neil that I had to pop into the store and would meet him in the parking lot.

I went in and waved to Jeremy, the cashier, an older teen I'd gotten to know when I used to stop in regularly for coffee.

"Hey, Detective Langley," he said in a friendly greeting. "Long time no see. Where ya been?"

"I refined my coffee palate," I said with a laugh. "I'm gonna use the restroom. I'll be out in a minute."

"Sure thing."

I headed to the restroom, and when I came out a few minutes later, I walked over to a cooler to grab a prepackaged sandwich for lunch. Just as I closed it, I heard a man in the front of the store say in a menacing tone, "Give me all the money in the register, and everyone gets out of here alive."

I ducked behind the shelf and looked up at the mirror in the corner. A man with a hoodie and jeans stood at the counter, pointing a gun at Jeremy, who was staring at the weapon in shock. A quick glance around the room, using the mirrors in the corners, told me no one else was inside. I reached for the Glock in my holster under my jacket and pulled it out, pointing toward the ceiling. My heart began to race as my mind caught up with the situation.

Was Neil outside? If so, he obviously wasn't in front of the store.

I peered around the corner.

"Did you hear me?" the robber shouted, thrusting the gun at Jeremy. He was an average-sized guy, and the hood was pulled low over his head. His back was to me, so I couldn't see if his face was covered too. If not, it was less likely he'd let the kid live. "Empty the cash register!"

Jeremy jumped at the order and started punching buttons on the register. His gaze lifted toward the coolers.

"What are you lookin' at?" the robber demanded, sounding even angrier.

I jerked behind the shelves, looking back up at the mirror. The robber took a step down the aisle in my direction, pointing the gun in front of him. He had a red bandana wrapped around his face, covering most of his nose, mouth, and chin.

"Who's back there?" he demanded.

My pulse pounded in my head, and I forced myself to take slow, deep breaths. I couldn't let my nerves get the best of me. My life and Jeremy's depended on it. And anyone else who might walk through the door.

"No one needs to get hurt," I called out in a calm tone, still watching him in the mirror. I quickly glanced at Jeremy, who seemed frozen behind the counter...except for his violent shaking.

"If this fuckin' cashier would give me the money, then nobody would." He turned back to the counter. "*Where's my money?*"

Jeremy flinched, and the robber pointed his gun at him and shot. The kid shouted and dropped behind the counter.

I didn't hesitate. I rounded the corner and took a shot, aiming it at the robber's center mass.

The gunman turned as I pulled the trigger, pointing his gun at me, and fired.

Chapter Three

Maddie

N*oah's been shot.*

I couldn't seem to draw in enough air.

"What happened?" I repeated.

Lance ran a hand along his jaw. "We were on a stakeout, so he left and walked to a convenience store to wait for Neil—you remember Officer Erickson?—to pick him up. He wanted to be here with you for your tour. But someone came in to rob the store while he was there. Noah tried to stop him and got shot."

Lance was a talker, but even in my dumbstruck state, I could tell he was babbling. One thought stuck out to me, though.

Noah had been coming to meet me?

I could feel my hysteria building, but I needed to get more information before I let it completely take over.

"Is he *okay*?" I shook my head. What was I thinking? He'd been shot. Of course he wasn't okay. "I mean, how bad is it?"

When he'd been shot last year, he'd nearly died. Could a person be shot twice in less than a year and survive?

Lance must have realized how badly I was spiraling because he walked over and grabbed my arms as though to keep me from falling over. "I don't know. By the time I got there, he was already in the ambulance and on his way to the hospital."

He'd told me how upset his mother had been after his last on-the-job injury, and how she'd begged him to quit the Memphis police force. Instead, he'd moved to Cockamamie, partly because of its supposedly low crime rate. She was going to be devastated. "Has anyone called his mother?"

Lance shook his head, his usual confidence gone. He looked utterly helpless. "I don't know."

The numbness was wearing off a little, and I started to cry. "I have to see him, Lance."

He pulled me into a hug. "I know. That's why I'm here. I'm heading there now. I figured you'd want to come with me."

"*Thank you.*"

He released me and motioned to his car. "Get in."

My hands were shaking so hard it took two tries for me to get the door open, but as soon as I was in, Lance backed out of the parking space and sped out of the lot. I pulled my phone out of my purse with shaky fingers and called Mallory to let her know what was happening. She promised to take care of everything at home and asked me to give her an update as soon as I had one.

Lance was on the phone with God knew who, trying to get information, but all they would tell him was that they were evaluating Noah in the ER.

"He's been shot before and pulled through," Lance said, giving me a reassuring look. "He'll be okay."

"Yeah." As the news set in, a new thought occurred to me. I hoped to God he'd be okay physically, but would he be okay emotionally? I knew part of the reason he'd distanced himself from me in the past was because of the trauma of his previous injury. Would he distance himself from me even more?

What was I thinking? He was already taking a break from me.

That was a hair's-breadth away from breaking up. This might push him over the edge.

"Will he want to see me?" I whispered to myself, but Lance heard me.

He reached over and placed his hand on mine at the edge of the seat. "Of course he'll want to see you."

"Things have been weird with him lately," I said, and this time I was very aware that I was the one who was babbling, telling him things he must already know. "We're not together right now. He said he needed some space, and—"

"Maddie, I promise that he cares about you. A lot. I know something bad happened when he went home for Christmas, but he's refused to talk about it. I take it he didn't tell you what happened either?"

"No. Only that he needed to take a break and sort some things out."

Lance released a long sigh. "We both know he's kind of a mess, but I know he's crazy about you." He cracked a sly grin. "And now I sound like I'm in middle school. I promise, though. He's going to want you there. He was really upset when he found out you were taking that tour on your own."

Lance didn't have sirens on his car, but that didn't stop him from speeding and honking his way through stop signs and red lights until we reached the hospital.

We were lucky enough to find a parking space by the entrance, and we barged in and rushed to the counter, both of us driven by the same sense of urgency.

Lance pulled out his badge and showed the receptionist, who sat behind a plexiglass window with a small opening at the bottom. "Detective Lance Forrester. I'm here to see Detective Noah Langley."

She gave him a sympathetic look. "You need to wait in the waiting area."

"Doesn't he get to have someone back there with him?" I asked.

"Not right now," the receptionist said. "The team is still working on him, but I'll be sure to let them know his colleagues are here."

"But she's not his colleague," Lance said, wrapping an arm around my back and drawing me closer to the counter. "This is his fiancée, Maddie."

My gaze jerked over to him, but then I tried to look natural. I wasn't sure how Noah would feel about me calling myself his fiancée right now. Then again, when I'd been shot, he'd let the hospital staff think he was my husband so he could see me, and we hadn't been together then either.

The receptionist eyed me over. She must have decided I didn't look like a cop, because she gave a short nod and said, "I'll call back and see if they'll let her in."

"Thank you," I said, fresh tears springing to my eyes. They'd finally stopped leaking right before we got here and they felt swollen and puffy, probably helping sell the fiancée story. I'd been prepared to sneak through the double doors after someone came out if forced to it. But the goal was to *stay* with Noah if he'd let me, not have security drag me out, so I impatiently waited.

The receptionist picked up the phone on her desk and placed a call. She glanced up at me and said something I couldn't hear into the phone. Then she hung up and leaned forward, saying through the small opening, "They say you can go back, sweetheart. He's in Room 5."

"Thank you!" I glanced at Lance, feeling guilty he couldn't go with me.

He gave me a wave. "Go. Text me as soon as you know something."

"I will. I promise."

The double doors began to swing open. I hurried through as soon as I could squeeze through the crack, then made my way down the hall to Room 5. The door was partially closed, and I carefully pushed it open, terrified of what I'd find. I didn't expect to see Noah sitting upright in the bed, fussing at the nurse.

"I'm fine," he said in frustration. "It's barely a scratch."

"Detective Langley," she said, sounding exasperated, "you may not need surgery, but you still have a bullet hole in your arm. You'll get an infection if you don't let us clean it properly."

"Already giving them trouble," I said, relief cascading through my body. This obviously wasn't a life-or-death situation.

Noah glanced over to me in surprise, worry filling his eyes when his gaze landed on my tear-stained face. "Maddie. What happened? Did things not go well on the tour? Lance told me you were going. I wanted to meet you there, but..." He glanced down at his bloody left arm.

I must have looked worse than I thought. "I'm not upset about the tour, you fool," I said, starting to cry again. "Are you okay?"

He reached his right arm out toward me, and I rushed to him, burying my face in his neck as he held me close to his side.

"I'm okay. I swear," he murmured in my ear, his voice heavy with emotion. "I'm sorry I scared you."

All of my pent-up anxiety released, and now that I'd started crying, I couldn't seem to stop.

"I'm finished," the nurse said. "I'll give you two some privacy, but the doctor will be in soon to stitch you up."

"Thanks," Noah said over my head as he still held me tightly.

I heard the door close, and Noah spoke into my hair. "It's okay, Maddie. I'm okay."

I realized I hadn't given Lance an update. "I have to text Lance," I said, my voice sounding like I had cotton stuffed up my nose. "He's worried sick."

He kissed my forehead, then gave me a sad smile. "Text him now. I would have texted him sooner, but they took my phones."

I tapped out a message to Lance, telling him Noah had been

shot in the arm, and the nurse had declared it minor and said he wouldn't need surgery. He immediately wrote back.

Thank God

The door opened and another nurse walked in and set a medical kit on the counter.

"Have you heard anything about how the suspect is doing?" Noah asked her in a tight voice. "Or Jeremy? The clerk?"

She looked up in surprise, then sympathy filled her eyes. "Last I heard, the shooter is in surgery. And the clerk is fine other than the lump on his head from when he fell dodging a bullet. He hit his head on the counter."

"Thank you," Noah said, and I could tell a weight had been lifted off his shoulders.

"From what I heard, you probably saved his life," she said, then left the room and closed the door behind her.

A troubled look crossed Noah's face, and I grabbed his hand and squeezed. "You don't think you saved the clerk's life."

His eyes widened, then he frowned. "I didn't."

"How can you say that?" I asked in shock. "You stopped the robber."

"But he shot at Jeremy first. The only reason Jeremy's still alive is because that asshole had bad aim."

I shook my head. "Once he realized he'd missed, he would have shot at him again, Noah."

He looked lost in thought, then something shifted in his eyes and he asked, "How did the tour go?"

"Forget the tour," I said in exasperation. "You were just shot."

"Which is becoming a frequent occurrence," he said unhappily. "I'd rather not dwell on it. So tell me about the tour."

I narrowed my eyes. "Lance said you were planning to come with me. Why?"

He started to talk, then stopped, confusion in his eyes.

"Never mind," I said, feeling like a first-class bitch. This wasn't the time to dig for information about his feelings for me.

Time and place, Maddie.

But it occurred to me that in every relationship before this one, I'd put my own feelings on the back burner to smooth over disagreements. I wasn't doing that anymore. Things were weird with Noah, but I was going to be truthful. Even if it hurt.

"I don't really know where we stand, Noah."

He gave a sharp nod.

"But I obviously care about you," I continued. "I was terrified when I heard you'd been shot, and I even lied at the front desk to get back here."

His eyebrow cocked and the corner of his mouth lifted. "Lied?"

Cringing, I said, "I told them I was your fiancée."

A grin spread across his face.

"Stop that!" I said half-heartedly, my heart skipping a beat. When Noah smiled at me, it made me forget everything else. "You broke up with me."

"I didn't break up with you," he said, looking contrite. "I want to be with you, but I need to get my head screwed on straight."

"Because of your father."

His brow shot up, then he scowled. "You've been talking to Lance."

"I'm not an idiot, Noah. We were happy before you went home, and I know the man's a first-class asshole. It wasn't hard to piece it together."

"I don't want to talk about him. Now tell me how you feel about the place for your aunt."

I wanted to push him on his father. We hadn't resolved anything. He was merely sweeping the past few weeks of silence under the rug. But really needed to tell someone about my mixed feelings about putting Aunt Deidre in St. Vincent's, and I wanted it to be him.

Maybe I *was* an idiot.

But it occurred to me that I could also tell him about Howard Bergan and his cryptic words. "I don't know." I shrugged. "I have reservations. The cost to put her there might be enough to dissuade me. The receptionist says it could be about eight thousand a month."

"Eight thousand?" he asked in disbelief. "What about insurance or Medicare?"

"I have to talk to the director about the financials. She got called away for a meeting. I'd probably have to sell my aunt's house to pay for it, but Noah, something happened while I was there. I saw—"

The door opened, and a woman in scrubs and a white lab coat entered the room. "Detective Langley, I'm Dr. Donahue, and I'm here to stitch up that wound." She turned to me and narrowed her eyes. "You look familiar. Have you been in the ER recently?"

I cringed.

"Maddie was shot back in December," Noah said.

"You two must live life on the edge," she said with a chuckle.

"My life is usually very, very boring," I insisted. "I was trying to find a missing..." I let my voice trail off. I had to admit the story didn't sound very boring. "I usually live a boring life."

The doctor laughed. "I'm not here to judge. Detective Langley has a dangerous job, and what you do on your own time is your business, I suppose." She took a look at Noah's bicep, examining both sides. "You're lucky it went clean through. A half inch to the left and it would have struck bone. All you're going to need is a few stitches."

Noah kept giving me worried looks as the doctor worked on him, and I had to wonder what was going through his head.

A few minutes later, Dr. Donahue examined the stitches on

both sides of his arm, then put a bandage over the wound and said the nurse would be in with the discharge paperwork soon.

As soon as the door closed behind her, I asked, "What did the doctor say that made you look so worried?"

"Do you know how many times I've been shot at, Maddie?"

"However many times it's been is too many."

The corners of his mouth ticked up. "True, but still, it's more than most officers exchange gunfire."

I couldn't help but feel guilty that several of those instances were because of me.

Noah must have read my mind. "Maddie, the times that involved you have nothing to do with you and everything to do with the situations you were caught up in." He shook his head. "How did you feel when you found out I'd been shot?"

"Terrified."

"Exactly." He paused. "I can't help thinking I'm some kind of magnet for gunfire. I don't want to continually put you through that."

I recognized this for what it was—another excuse to pull away, and I was tired of being on this roller coaster.

"I know the risks of your job, Noah. I'm walking into this with eyes wide open." I lifted my chin. "When we started this, you told me that you run when you're upset, but you'll always come back. Well, it's been weeks since Christmas, and you still haven't come back to me. I've been patient, but I can see that this is about to make everything worse." I swallowed the lump in my throat and asked the question that had kept me up for weeks. "Are you giving up on us before we even really got started?"

His jaw set. "No. But it's not fair for you to constantly worry about me."

"You're not the only cop in a relationship. Lots of cops have significant others."

His brow rose. "And do you know the divorce rate for cops?"

"For asshole cops with an ego complex? I'm sure it's pretty high, but you never struck me as one of those guys." I pinned him with a sharp gaze. "Are you?"

His shoulders stiffened. "Of course not."

"Do I know your job is dangerous? I met you on a dangerous case. So don't treat me like I'm a fool."

He started to say something, then stopped.

It had been a crappy day and I needed to deal with my aunt, not my confusing feelings for a man who wasn't ready to commit to a relationship. "I think I should go."

His face softened. "Maddie, I only want to protect you."

"Are you sure about that, Noah? Or are you protecting yourself?" I drew in a breath and headed for the door. "Take some time to think it over."

Only later did I realize I'd never told him about Detective Bergan and his ominous message.

Chapter Four

Noah

I may have gotten discharged from the ER, but my afternoon had just begun. There were interviews with my chief as well as the Arkansas State Police. They'd already interviewed Jeremy and viewed the security footage. The robber was out of surgery and in the ICU but expected to make a full recovery. Unofficially, they'd declared me in the clear of any wrongdoing, but it was still exhausting. It didn't help that all I could think about was Maddie and the look of disappointment and hurt on her face as she walked out the door.

I couldn't shake the feeling that I'd fucked up again, but the fact that I kept messing up made me think she was better off without me.

But I also couldn't stop thinking about the fact that she was wearing the heart necklace I'd given her for Christmas. I'd told her I was giving her my heart both literally and figuratively. The fact that she was still wearing it had filled me with more hope than I had a right to. Especially since I'd been the one to back off.

It was well past dinnertime by the time I'd filed the last bit of paperwork. Lance had stayed close to my desk for hours, and I could tell he was exhausted too.

"I say we call it a day," I said as I turned off my computer.

"Good call," he said. "Do you want to go by the tavern for dinner? I'm sure my mom's heard about the shooting. She's bound to cook something special for her favorite son."

I couldn't help laughing. "I can't help it if your mother likes me better than you."

Grinning, he held his hands out at his sides. "No complaints. It takes the pressure off me and my love life."

Lance's mother, who ran Lucky's Tavern, had pretty much adopted me. Before I'd started dating Maddie, I'd spent many nights at the tavern, and she'd taken me under her wing. Before Christmas, I'd spent most of those nights with Maddie, but after...it was fair to say I still saw more of Lance's mother than he did. And she gave me plenty of grief about Maddie too.

The lidocaine the doctor had injected had begun to wear off, and the ibuprofen I'd taken barely touched the throbbing in my arm. "I think I'm gonna take a raincheck. I'm pretty beat."

Worry filled his eyes. "What are you gonna do for dinner?"

I noticed he didn't ask if Maddie would be taking care of me. I suspected he knew she hadn't left the hospital on a good note. He'd driven her to the hospital, but apparently Mallory had picked her up.

"I have some leftover meatloaf and potatoes your mom made for me a few days ago. It should still be good."

"Suit yourself, but don't be surprised if Mom calls to check up on you."

I grimaced and glanced down at my phone. "I might actually answer that call."

"How many times has *your* mom called?"

"Ten."

His eyes flew wide. "Jesus, Noah. You should answer one of them and tell her you're okay."

"I texted that it was nothing, and whoever called her was an idiot." I pinned him with a hard stare.

"To be fair, I didn't call her. Neil did. But only after Maddie got upset that no one had notified her. And to be fair to *Maddie*, she thought you might be mortally wounded. We hadn't gotten an update, and she was pretty freaked out."

"And who freaked her out?" I asked, my irritation rising.

"All of us were freaked out. There was a lot of blood, and the paramedics weren't talking."

I groaned. "Yeah. Sorry. It's just that my mom's going to make a big deal out of this, the same way she does about everything, and it's nothing."

"Sorry. But maybe you should call her anyway. Get it over with."

"And have her try to convince me to give up police work and move back to Memphis? I think I'll pass." I'd had an earful of that at Christmas, along with everything else. I stood and started to reach for my coat off the back of my chair, then remembered it was bloody and in a bag in my car along with my dress shirt. If it weren't for the spare shirt I kept in my car, I would have been forced to go home to change before returning to the station.

Lance started to say something, then stopped. "Whatever you think is best."

I could only imagine what Maddie would say. She'd insist I should call my mother. They were both right, but I had to psych myself up to do it. "I'll call her tonight. After I get home."

Lance shrugged on his jacket. "No judgment, man."

Yeah, right.

We headed for the exit, and I was surprised to see Chief Porter still sitting at his desk.

"Noah," the chief called out. "Come in here for a moment."

Lance gave me a questioning look, but I waved him off. "You go on ahead. I'll see you tomorrow."

He nodded, then headed out while I walked into the chief's office.

"Shut the door," he said, motioning to it after I'd walked inside.

I did as he asked, my stomach clenching. He had an open-door policy, which he took literally. He rarely closed the door...unless he was discussing something private. "Should I be worried?"

"Nah, this is just a formality." He waited until I'd settled into a worn chair in front of his desk. "First, I want you to know I don't think you've done anything wrong. The state police agree, even if they can't give a formal statement yet."

"Why do I feel like there's a but in there?" I asked, my nerves on edge.

"I wanted to warn you that there's going to be an editorial in the local newspaper. A piece about you."

I resisted the urge to shake my head and clear my ears. "Wait. Did you say there's going to be an editorial about *me*?"

He pressed his lips together, looking grim. "Yeah. I got a heads-up from a friend of a friend that they're questioning the number of shootings you've been involved in since coming to Cockamamie." He made a face. "They're mentioning the shooting in Memphis too."

I sat back in the chair, my head feeling light. "Why?"

"It's a slow news day?" he said with a shrug. "Who knows. I suspect they're struggling to accept that crime's moving into their smug little town." He shifted in his seat. "That fact is, crime has always been here; the criminals have just done a good job of hiding it, and before you got here, we didn't do a good job of unearthing it. Hell, it's a badly kept secret that the Brawlers are doing God knows what just outside of town. They tend to keep it on the down low so the citizens can pretend the town's safe. But there's no denying that *you've* brought those things to light, and they think it takes some of the shine off the town..."

"You mean I'm digging up the dirt they want to ignore, so they're blaming me for its existence."

He made a face. "Something like that."

"I had nothing to do with the fact that some whack job was murdering people during break-ins last fall," I protested. "I stopped him."

He held up his hands in surrender. "I know. You're preaching to the choir, Noah. But the editorial's still coming out."

"Okay," I said, then realized his body posture hadn't relaxed. In fact, he seemed even more tense. "So, what else do you need to tell me?"

"I know we planned to put you on desk duty, but with the editorial and all, I think we should put you on administrative leave."

My eyes widened. "You said the state police informally said they were finding me innocent. They viewed the video and took the clerk's statement. They said my quick action stopped the perp from killing the clerk. Desk duty is the protocol."

"I know, and I'm not firing you. Hell, Noah," he said in frustration, motioning to me. "You were injured. Just call it sick leave."

"But it's not sick leave. It's administrative leave."

He gave me an exasperated look. "It wouldn't kill you to take some time off. You've been busting your ass since you got here."

"But Lance and I are working the car thefts."

"Lance can work it with Cuso if he needs help. But I think he'll be okay on his own for a bit. It'll be good practice for him."

"Lance is a new detective."

The chief lifted his brow. "Are you insinuating he isn't cutting it as a detective?"

"No, of course not. But..." Anything I came up with would look contrary to what I'd just said, so I stopped. "How long am I on leave for?"

"Let's say two weeks for now, and we'll reevaluate next week."

"You mean after you gauge public opinion around the piece."

He shrugged. "You know how these things go. There might be outrage for a few days, but things will settle down and everything will return to normal."

I leaned forward. "I did everything by the book. I always do."

"I'm not disputing that, Noah. No one in this department is, and every single one of us will stand behind you. But you have to admit that you taking a couple of weeks off might help the situation blow over quicker."

"And make me look guilty." I could only imagine what my father would say when he found out. He'd had plenty to say at Christmas about everything else in my career.

A pleading look filled the chief's eyes, and he suddenly looked older than his sixty-some years. "I'm doin' the best I can here, son."

I let out a breath and sank back into the chair. "I know."

"So go home, sit tight, and enjoy your time off. You've earned it."

I took that as my cue that we were done, so I stood. "Yeah. Thanks."

Half expecting to find protesters, I headed out to my car, but the parking lot was dark and quiet. I approached my car and stopped next to the driver's side door. Everything in me wanted to get inside and drive straight to Maddie's house. I needed her, and I wanted to tell her that I was sorry for pulling away from her, especially since I wanted her more than I wanted anything in my life. But I didn't, because I could hear my father's words still ringing in my ears, telling me I was incompetent and incapable of doing the right thing.

After today, I couldn't help wondering if he was right.

My father had told me his terrible secret, followed by an ultimatum, and I'd let it stew inside me like a festering wound. My therapist had helped me realize I was giving him power over me, but I didn't know how to stop, and I was disconcerted by how much one discussion had screwed up my progress. I needed to break free from him again, for good, so I could become the kind of man worthy of Maddie.

So instead of giving in to my impulse, I got into my car and headed to my small rental house about a half mile away.

All I wanted was a beer and Matilda's leftover meatloaf and

mashed potatoes, followed by sleep, but as soon as I approached my house and saw the car parked at the curb, it became apparent I wouldn't find any peace over the next few hours, possibly days.

I parked the car and got out, preparing to meet my doom.

The car door opened, and the woman exited and walked over to me. I found myself staring down at my mother.

"Noah Alexander Langley," she snapped, her eyes blazing. "You have a hell of a lot of explaining to do."

Chapter Five

Maddie

"What an asshole," Mallory said as we cleaned the kitchen after dinner.

"You can't call a man who just got shot an asshole," I protested weakly.

"The hell I can't," she countered, vigorously washing a pot. Water was flying everywhere, so I took a step back.

"I'd rather him be honest than pretend he wants to be with me."

She turned to face me. "Any man who lets his family sway his decisions isn't worthy of you, Maddie. You deserve a man who will stand up for you, not cave."

I groaned. "We don't know that's what's happening." But I had to admit to myself that it sure looked that way.

She propped a soapy hand on her hip. "Even if it's not, you know how I feel about how he's been handling things. Or not handling them."

"I think he's scared," I said. "He's been hurt before."

"So have you, and *you're* not emotionally stunted."

I gave her a sly smile. "He's a man, Mal."

"Big fucking deal. It's no excuse."

I pushed out a sigh. "You're right."

"All I'm saying is you deserve someone who loves you with everything in him."

"Whoa..." I said, holding up my hand. "No one said anything about love."

But the truth was, I'd already fallen for him. Everything had felt right—so very right—before he'd left for Christmas. He'd given me a heart necklace, and it had felt like he'd given me his own heart with it.

Or maybe this was just one more instance of me being stupid with men.

She rolled her eyes. "You know what I mean."

I did, and she was right. "Look, I probably shouldn't have pressed him about the relationship stuff. For heaven's sake, he'd just been shot. And he was shot on his way to meet me at St. Vincent's. He wouldn't have been in that convenience store if not for me."

"Oh, no," she said, pointing a soapy finger at me. "Don't you dare blame yourself for him getting shot."

"But—"

"Nope! Not discussing something that's blatantly untrue." A scowl covered her face, and she turned back to the sink to wash a casserole dish. "*Speaking of St. Vincent's*," she said, changing the subject. "What are you going to do?"

I'd told her all about my tour. Well, everything except for seeing Detective Bergan. I still wasn't sure what to do with that information.

"I guess I have to get a solid answer about how much it will cost to have her stay there. Then I'll make my decision."

"I should have gone with you." She handed me the casserole dish to dry. "Do you want me to come with you when you go back?"

I considered it for a moment. "No. The facility is nice, although I'm not totally sold on it." In part, because it might set Aunt Deidre off if she saw Detective Bergan in the hallways. If she was having a clear moment, she'd remember him. Still...we could place her somewhere else. The real question was where? St. Vincent's was the best residential care center in town, which meant I'd have to leave Cockamamie, and I wasn't ready to do that yet.

Fool that I was, I wasn't ready to close the door on Noah.

"I'll look into all my options and how much they cost before making a decision." I leaned my hip against the counter. "Aunt Deidre has *at least* a good decade left. After we sell her house, whatever residential home I put her in will probably plow through whatever money I get from the sale. What if they use it all before she...?" I couldn't bring myself to say before she died. "What will happen to her then? Better to hold off as long as we can before we put her somewhere."

Mallory's eyes flew wide. "You'll have to sell the house?"

"She has enough money to pay for the first six months or so, but after that?" I shrugged. "They'll go through her other assets, which includes her house."

Alarm covered her face. "Where will *you* live?"

"Where will *we* live?" I shrugged. "Maybe you shouldn't sell your condo in Nashville after all."

"That's a done deal. Besides, Nashville's gotten too crowded for me. I like quieter places, although Cockamamie is maybe a bit too quiet." She lowered her face and held my gaze. "You could move to Chattanooga, Maddie."

I frowned. "Not unless I find a better residential situation for Aunt Deidre there."

Her face lit up. "You could look for a librarian job."

Guilt squashed the spark of excitement that lit up in me. "She wouldn't want to leave this place, Mal."

She pulled me into a hug. "I know, Mads, but it might not matter to her anymore." She must have seen the look of dismay on my face because she quickly added, "But we don't have to think about any of that right now. We need more answers first."

Defeat seeped into my pores. "But we can't keep her here like this either. It's not a tenable situation. She left the stove on the other day."

"We'll just be more diligent," Mallory said with a forced smile. "Maybe we'll hire an evening aide. That has to be cheaper than St. Vincent's."

I started to thank her for being here for me when a knock at the front door interrupted me.

A satisfied gleam filled Mallory's eyes. "I suspect that's Detective Asshole here to grovel." She grabbed a towel to dry her hands. "Don't go easy on him."

I shot her a wry look. "The man was just shot, Mal. He was *shot*."

"Okay," she conceded. "So don't go *too* easy on him."

Rolling my eyes, I headed for the door, Mallory on my heels, probably preparing to gloat. But when I opened the door, I saw Lance waiting out on the porch.

"Well, lookie who's here," Mallory said in a snippy tone. "Officer Hotshot."

"Mallory," he said in a neutral tone as he nodded toward her.

I cast a warning glance at her, but she'd already begun stomping upstairs. Her attitude toward Lance had taken a 180 right after New Year's Eve. She'd had a crush on him, and he'd seemed pretty interested in her too, but after they'd gone to a New Year's Eve party together, she'd started giving him the cold shoulder and refused to tell me why.

His gaze followed her before he turned back to me.

I tried to decipher the look on his face. There was no malice or sorrow. There was definitely interest, but he didn't look like he was about to run past me and demand she talk to him.

Maybe I could get the story out of him.

I tilted my head and gave him a wry look. "What happened between you two?"

"You should ask Mallory."

"I did, and she refused to tell me."

He shrugged and turned serious. "I'd like to talk to you about Noah if you have a minute."

I tried to bury my disappointment. *Lance* was here to talk about Noah. I would have preferred to talk to him directly. I took a step back and motioned down the hall toward the kitchen. "Come on in. I planned on making a cup of tea. Would you like some?"

"I'll pass on the tea, but I'd take a glass of water."

"Sure."

He followed me back and slipped off his jacket. As I filled my electric kettle, it occurred to me that I could tell Lance about my visit with Detective Bergan.

"So go on," I nudged as I put some ice into a glass for him. "Say whatever it is you came to say."

After hanging his coat on the back of a chair at the small kitchen table, he sat and leaned toward me. "Something's going on with him, Maddie."

"You mean other than getting shot?" I asked dryly as I poured water from a filtered pitcher into the glass.

"Something's eating him, and we both know he's not one to share his feelings."

I set the glass on the table in front of him. "I was hoping that Noah would come back to me, but he tried to push me away at the ER again. Maybe I should take the message. I'm not begging any man to stay with me, Lance. I've already had my share of emotionally distant men." Angry tears stung my eyes. "I suppose I brought it on myself. I *knew* he wasn't ready for a relationship."

Lance's jaw set. "Bullshit. He *was* ready. Something spooked him."

Like his family.

I leaned my head back and sighed in frustration before I leveled my gaze on him. "I've got my hands full with Aunt Deidre. I don't have the time or energy to figure out Noah's shit too."

"I know, but I'm asking you to be patient with him a little longer."

I shrugged, because I didn't want to discuss it to death. Neither of us knew anything, and if Noah refused to talk or engage, there was really nothing to discuss.

"That's not the *only* reason I came over," Lance said, picking up the glass and taking a drink. "How did the tour at St. Vincent's Village go?"

"As well as could be expected," I said, heading back to the counter and finishing my preparations for the tea. I carried my cup to the table and sat across from him. "I have some decisions to make, but something else happened while I was there that I'd like to get your opinion on."

His brow shot up. "*Me?*"

"I'd ask Noah, but he's too busy wallowing in angst."

He laughed. "So I'm second choice?"

"Consider it second best," I said with a smile, then blew across the surface of my tea. "Or maybe first."

"I'll take it. What's up?"

I took a breath. "When I was touring the memory care unit, the director got called away, and I walked past a room in which an older man was struggling with his TV remote." I held his gaze. "Lance, it was Detective Bergan."

Surprise washed over his face. "I guess I knew he was in there because of dementia, but I hadn't really connected the dots. I heard he's totally out of it. Did you talk to him?"

I narrowed my eyes. "Sort of? He seemed pretty delusional, but when I mentioned that I was Andrea Baker's daughter, he got really paranoid."

Lance cocked his head. "How so?"

"He looked scared and swore he hadn't talked."

"Talked about what?"

"An eagle."

"An eagle? What does that mean?"

I made a face. "I was hoping it might be some code word or something and you'd know. In any case, he told me neither one of us was safe because he'd told me. No one who knew was safe. He said they were going to come looking for him."

Lance leaned closer. "*Who* was going to come looking for him?"

"The skinny man, but he also said, 'She shouldn't have done it.' He never made it clear what she shouldn't have done, though."

"Do you think he was talking about your mother?"

I shook my head. "Honestly, I don't know. It could have all been in his head, but I don't want to dismiss it either."

"You know Noah and I want to re-investigate your mother's case," he said slowly, watching me. "We just haven't had time, and since her file is missing, we have to start from scratch. Kind of hard to do on an eighteen-year-old cold case."

"Almost nineteen, and I know," I said, giving him an appreciative smile. "Especially since you were so certain Martin Schroeder was her murderer."

"You still won't tell us who provided his alibi?"

I took a sip of my tea and gave him a pointed look.

My best friend from high school, Colleen Nichols, had told me that Martin Schroeder had molested her. But she'd also said that he'd been with her at the Bluebird Inn the night my mother was killed. She had a family now and claimed to have put all of that behind her. Her husband had no idea it had happened, and she didn't want him to find out. So I'd promised to keep her secret, especially since I didn't think it would help us find my mother's killer.

Lance gave me a stern look. "You do know that the person's memory could be faulty. Especially after all this time."

"And we both know that everyone in town knew where they were the night my mother was killed. It was Cockamamie's own version of the Kennedy assassination."

He didn't argue because he knew it was true. He could tell me without hesitation what he'd been doing the night my mother was murdered.

"So let's say Bergan's ramblings were about your mother. Do you have any idea what he was talking about?"

"None whatsoever."

Lance sat up straight. "I think we should go back and talk to him."

"I have to work at the coffee shop tomorrow, but I get off at three."

He let out a short laugh. "When I said we, I meant me and Noah. Not you."

My indignation rose. "She was *my* mother, Lance."

He sat back in his chair. "This is an official investigation. You need to let us handle it."

"And fit it in when you can?" I asked, my brow raised. "I have a right to know what happened to her."

"I'm not disagreeing. We'll tell you everything we can as we learn it."

"Which means you'll leave things out."

Lance groaned. "Maddie. It's an official police investigation."

"Actually, it's not. It's a closed case, remember?" I asked haughtily. "And even when it was an official investigation, it was dropped like a hot potato. Forgive me if the label of official police investigation doesn't fill me with warm fuzzies."

He looked stricken for a moment, then his eyes softened. "I understand where you're coming from, and I know Noah has his head up his ass, but I'd hoped you'd at least trust *me*."

I leaned my head back, then looked back at him. "I do, Lance, but you've admitted it's not your first priority. You've got active cases you need to work on. Besides, I'd planned to go back and talk to Bergan again anyway. Why not take me with you?"

"Maddie."

I set my mug on the table. "Fine. Do it your way."

His gaze narrowed. "Why do I feel like you caved too easily?"

Because he was right—I had no intention of letting this go. I knew Lance wasn't lying to me. He'd follow the lead I'd given him, but he and Noah were working on a case that required their attention. I couldn't expect them to dedicate time to my mother's murder investigation. What harm would there be in me asking questions?

But I wasn't going to admit to any of that. Instead, I gave him a demure smile. "You're the professional. I need to leave it to you and Noah."

Lance started to protest, but his phone rang. He pulled it out of his jeans pocket and looked at the screen. "I have to take this, and it could be a while. How about we talk about this tomorrow after you get off work?"

"Sure," I said, knowing he wouldn't sway me.

He stood and grabbed his coat, looking like he wanted to say more, but his phone continued ringing. "I'll meet you at Déjà Brew after you get off."

I didn't answer, not that I needed to. He answered his phone as he headed toward the front door, his coat still in his hand. I followed him and watched while he walked to his car with a serious expression on his face.

My mind was working fast, chewing over the problem. Aunt Deidre's memory was slipping by the day, which meant Detective Bergan might not be able to tell me anything the next time I talked to him. I had to talk to him ASAP. Plus, with all the uncertainty in my life right now, I needed something productive to focus on.

I'd do this on my own if I had to.

Chapter Six

Noah

"Mom," I said, still dumbfounded. "What are you doing here?"

Anger filled her eyes. "You get shot, and you can't even bother to tell me? I had to find out from someone in your department. And when I tried to call you, you sent a text. A *text*, Noah."

I cringed. "It's nothing. Barely a scratch. In fact, I left the ER and went back to work."

She propped her hands on her hips. "You *what*?"

"I told you. It was nothing."

She pushed out a couple of breaths, then tears filled her eyes. "You scared me half to death, Noah."

My defensiveness melted. "I'm sorry."

"I don't know if I'll survive it if something happens to you like what happened last year." She swallowed and said in a tight voice, "Or worse."

I pulled her into a one-armed hug. "I'm sorry. Mom. Really. I guess I thought you'd know it wasn't very serious since I didn't call you back. It was stupid and thoughtless."

"How is it you're walking around? Let me see where you got shot."

"It was my upper arm, and I'm fine," I said, even though my whole left arm was still throbbing. "Come inside." I gestured toward the front door. "You haven't seen my house yet. I'll show you around."

She looked like she was about to protest, but then she turned to face the front of my house and frowned. "It looks smaller than the photos you sent."

I laughed. "It hasn't shrunk. Do you have a bag in the trunk?"

"I threw a few things into a suitcase and left as soon as I could." She walked over to the car and clicked her key fob. The trunk popped open, and I lifted her suitcase out of the back with my good arm, surprised by how heavy it was.

"Noah, you shouldn't be lifting that!"

"I got hit in my left arm. I'm fine. Although it seems like you packed half your wardrobe."

"I didn't know what I'd need or how long I'd stay. But since I've never seen where you moved to, I thought I could get a look at your house and your new town."

I bit my tongue to keep from telling her that she could leave tomorrow. I loved my mother, but ever since my near-death last year, she'd become an extreme worrier, suffocating me with her obsessive concerns. It was part of the reason I'd moved to Cockamamie five months ago—to put a few hours' distance between us. But now there was the additional, unmentioned confrontation with my father. While she knew it had happened, I wasn't sure she knew what we'd discussed, and I suspected she either planned to find out or wanted to discuss it during her visit. Neither option appealed to me.

"Well, my chief gave me a few days off to recover, so I'll get a chance to show you around." I forced a smile. "Not that there's much to show you."

"Let me be the judge of that."

I let her into my two-bedroom bungalow and turned on the light. Thank God I'd picked up the night before. I wasn't a slob, but after a long day at work, I was known to leave empty plates and glasses on the coffee table.

My mother stood at the doorway and silently surveyed the place for several seconds before declaring, "It's cute."

"Thank you."

She turned to me in surprise. "You decorated?" Then her eyes narrowed. "Or was it the mystery woman your sister told me about?"

I swallowed the groan rising in my throat. I regretted telling my sister about Maddie while I'd been home for Christmas. "Maddie's never been here."

Her brow rose. "You're dating a woman who's never been to your home?"

"It's nothing serious, Mom." Which I supposed was technically accurate—I'd put the brakes on things after Christmas, after all—but I felt like a liar and an asshole for saying so. "And I usually go to her place. She cares for her aunt with dementia, and it's hard for her to get away in the evenings."

She frowned. "Seems like a burden you don't need in your life."

"You sound an awful lot like Dad," I said dryly.

She gave me a pointed look. "Your father's right more often than you give him credit for."

I drew in a breath to keep my anger in check. My father was a self-serving asshole, and while my mother had always been a Leonard Langley apologist, she'd never before tried to convince me he was implicitly right. Maybe she *did* know his secret.

Rather than contradict her and possibly start an argument, I took her on a tour of the house that lasted all of twenty seconds before we ended up in the kitchen.

"Have you had dinner yet?" I asked.

"No. I was too eager to get to Cockamamie and see you with my own eyes." Her gaze traveled up and down my body as though looking for wounds I hadn't admitted to yet.

"I haven't had dinner either, but I don't have much to eat here. I get dinner at Lucky's Tavern several nights a week. I was going to eat leftovers tonight."

Her frown of disproval returned. "That's so unhealthy, Noah."

"Matilda makes sure I get plenty of vegetables if that's what you're worried about."

"Matilda?"

"Lance's mother."

"But you're eating at a *tavern*." The way she spat out the last word made it clear she questioned my judgment. Then again, my mother had plenty of opinions about what was and wasn't proper.

I was too tired to have this argument. "I have some chicken nuggets and French fries in my freezer."

Mom rolled her eyes. "Let me see what else you have, and I'll come up with something." She scrounged my pantry and miraculously came up with the ingredients to make a modified version of spaghetti carbonara.

After she got everything going, she insisted on checking out my stitches, then frowned for the next five minutes while I sat at the island, watching her cook in silence.

Finally, she turned to look at me. "Are you going to tell me what happened with your father at Christmas?"

And there it was. I held her gaze, my jaw setting. "No."

"Noah—"

"What happened at Christmas is between Dad and me."

She sighed in exasperation. "That's what he said, but obviously it hasn't been resolved."

"I doubt it ever will be."

"He's your father, Noah."

My eyes widened. "You're taking his side?"

"How could I take his side if I have no idea what you two fought over?" She shook her head as she stirred the spaghetti noodles in the pot. "Look, I know you two have never seen eye-to-eye, but he's not getting any younger."

"So he gets to be a shitty father and husband the entirety of my life, but somehow it's on me to fix it?" I asked, getting more pissed by the minute. "Unbelievable."

Anger flashed in her eyes. "I won't deny he wasn't the best father while you were growing up, but don't you dare presume that he was a shitty husband."

My mother was so stuck in her delusions there was no hope of making her see the truth. "Your marriage is your business, but I don't see why I'm expected to repair something that never existed. He's treated me like crap my entire life."

"Not your *entire* life."

"The parts I remember."

Her anger faded. "I also won't deny that he's always put his job before us, but he loved you in his own way."

I started to tell her that was no excuse, and I had no interest in *his way*, but my cell phone rang. I was grateful for the distraction, so I slipped it out of my pocket and saw Lance's name on the screen. I nearly didn't answer it, but I needed an excuse to end this conversation with my mother.

"I've got to take this, Mom," I said as I moved into the living room, answering the call. "Hey, Lance. What's up?"

"I stopped by Maddie's house after I left the station."

Another meddler. Why couldn't people just leave me alone? I suddenly felt beyond exhausted.

"I don't want to talk about Maddie."

"Too damn bad," he grunted. "If you'd made it to the tour, you would have had a chance to talk to Detective Bergan."

"So? I hear Bergan's dementia is worse than Deidre's."

"Maybe so, but he said some really interesting things to Maddie this afternoon."

That got my attention. My grip tightening on the phone, I said, "Like what?"

"Maddie told him she was Andrea Baker's daughter, and I guess he got totally paranoid. He said he wasn't supposed to tell anyone about the eagle, and the skinny man would have it out for both of them if he knew."

"Sounds delusional to me."

"Maybe, maybe not, but Maddie wants to talk to him again and see if she can get more information."

I groaned. "She's getting her hopes up over nothing."

"Like I said...maybe, maybe not. I told her you and I would look into it, but she countered that the case is closed, and we'd make it low priority. She's right, of course, and we can't stop her from talking to him, but I don't think she should go alone. So...you're going to go with her, aren't you?" he asked, making it clear he expected the answer to be yes.

The answer was *hell* yes. Bergan's ramblings were probably the workings of his diseased mind, but I owed it to Maddie to help her sort through it. The case wasn't open, so I could unofficially investigate it even though I was on leave. Admittedly, it was a pretty gray area, and I liked to keep things black and white, but there was no hesitation. I wasn't going to let Maddie do this on her own. This was something I could give her. This was my way to show her how much she meant to me, even if I couldn't get my act together. "Of course. Besides, I've got plenty of time."

"What does that mean?" he asked in confusion.

I glanced back at my mother in the kitchen, then headed out through the front door and stood on the porch. I told him about the editorial piece coming out in the paper and how the chief had put me on administrative leave.

His frustration was palpable. "That's *bullshit*, Noah."

"I know, but I can see where he's coming from. Besides, this will give me a chance to work on Andrea Baker's murder case." And my chance to prove to Maddie how much I cared about her, despite the fact I'd screwed everything up. She needed closure for her mother's murder, and I would do everything in my power to give it to her.

Plus, it helped me out of another tricky situation. "And it also gives me a chance to escape from my mother's very attentive gaze," I said.

"What?"

I told him about my mother's surprise visit. "I love my mother, but the thought of spending twenty-four/seven with her indefinitely is enough to make me pull my hair out."

"I want to meet your mother," he said, suddenly sounding chipper.

"You can, but don't mention the leave, or I'll never hear the end of it."

"As long as you're investigating the Baker cold case, my lips will be sealed shut." His tone sobered. "But don't talk to Bergan without Maddie. For one thing, I've heard he doesn't do well with men, which means she has a better chance of getting him to talk again."

"And what's the other thing?"

"She acted like she was good with us investigating this without her, but I know better. She'll kill us both if either one of us talks to him without her."

Chapter Seven

Maddie

Wednesday dragged on despite how busy we were at Déjà Brew. My boss Petra could tell I was out of sorts, and my coworker Chrissy, by far the saltiest of all of us, shot me dirty looks when I screwed up a few orders. The truth was, my head wasn't in it. I was too busy trying to figure out how to question Detective Bergan. I knew Lance was probably going to try to convince me to back off, but I'd decided I wouldn't. I couldn't. The way I saw it, the police had had nearly nineteen years to solve my mother's murder. It was time for me to take the lead. Even if Lance was interested now, he'd be pulled onto another case soon enough.

Since I'd been expecting Lance at the end of my shift, I was surprised to see Noah walk through the door at 2:55. Then again, it was just like Lance to try to throw Noah at me. He seemed almost as concerned about our relationship status as I was.

Still, I couldn't say I was upset to see him. I wasn't sure I liked what that said about me, but there was no denying he looked downright sexy in his jeans, navy blue thermal T-shirt, and brown leather jacket. My heart skipped a beat, and confused butterflies twisted in my belly.

Chrissy had left for the day, so I was alone at the counter as he walked up. He stopped in front of me, sadness in his eyes. "Hey, Maddie."

"Hi," I said, barely above a whisper, my emotions roiling.

"I'm sorry about yesterday." The sincerity in his eyes convinced me he meant it.

"Emotions were high. Today's a new day. But I thought Lance was coming, probably to make sure I don't pay a visit to Detective Bergan on my own."

"About that..." He grimaced. "I know he was supposed to meet you, but I'm on administrative leave, which means I have a whole lot more time than he does right now."

My eyes flew wide. "Are you in trouble? How can getting shot be *your* fault?"

He cracked a smile. "No one in the department thinks it is. The public, on the other hand..."

"*What?*"

"You haven't read the paper?"

"No..."

"There's a piece about me in the editorial section. But that's not why I'm here right now. I'm here because I have a lot of free time, and I can finally devote the attention to your mother's case that it deserves."

I frowned. "If you're on administrative leave, doesn't that mean you're not supposed to be working?"

He leaned closer and lowered his voice. "It's still a closed case. As long as I don't question people under false pretenses, I should be fine."

"False pretenses?"

"Introducing myself as a cop to get people to talk. Like I said, I should be fine."

Should be fine. I stared at him in disbelief. Noah Langley followed the rules. I found it hard to believe he'd buck them to help me. Then again, he'd put his life on the line multiple times to protect me. Maybe he was worried it was dangerous and didn't want me to do it alone.

I glanced at the espresso machine while I sorted out my feelings. "Would you like an Americano?"

"Yeah," he said, pulling out his wallet.

I waved a hand at him and grabbed the largest cup we had. "You know Petra says your money's no good here." At least it hadn't been before Christmas. As far as I knew, he hadn't been in for coffee since.

He pulled out a five-dollar bill and stuck it in the tip jar.

I made his drink as he stood watching me from the other side of the counter.

"Does your arm hurt?" I asked when I stopped grinding the coffee beans.

"Not too much. Nothing ibuprofen can't handle." He grimaced. "My mom came to town last night."

That caught my attention. His mother had never been to Cockamamie. "Your mom's here?"

He nodded. "She pulled up in front of my house as I got home last night. I texted her from the ER that I was okay, but she wanted to see for herself."

"I can't say I blame her," I said. "We're not even really together, and I had to see you immediately. She's been your mother for thirty-seven years."

"True..."

"So why are you here to help me instead of at home with your mother?"

He reached up and scrubbed the back of his neck. "That's a complicated answer."

"You don't want to see her?"

"I do, but she's a hoverer. Especially after I got shot last year."

"Again, I can't blame her there either, but I can also see your side. I'm not a fan of hovering."

A smile lit up his eyes. "I know."

"How long is she planning on staying in town?"

He laughed. "Your guess is as good as mine. She says she wants to get to know the town I've moved to, but I suspect there's an underlying purpose."

"Like what?" I asked as I put a lid on his cup and handed it to him.

"After this shooting, I suspect she's here to full-court press me into changing professions and coming back home."

Home being Memphis, not Cockamamie, not that I could blame him for his word choice. He'd been born and raised in Memphis. He'd only been here five months.

I felt a stab of pain. While he was adamant he wasn't moving back, something had changed when he was home for the holidays. Who was to say his mother wouldn't be successful in her mission to get him to move home?

He shifted his weight and his gaze seemed to settle at the base of my throat where the heart necklace he'd given me for Christmas hung before he lifted his eyes to mine. "How long do you have before you get off?"

I glanced down at my watch. "Technically, now, but I'm waiting for Trista to show up for her shift. She's often a few minutes late."

"And Petra puts up with that?"

"Good help is hard to find these days."

He looked nervous as he said, "In case you haven't already guessed, I want to go with you when you talk to Howard Bergan again."

"When you say *go with me,* do you mean I get to sit and watch you interrogate him, or will I be an equal partner?"

"This is an unofficial investigation," he said. "So we'll talk to him together."

I still felt a tinge of excitement, but I told myself not to get my hopes up. "Let me go check if Trista's here."

Noah walked over to a table in the empty seating area and sat down, stretching out his long legs while I headed to the back.

Trista was clocking in, so I found Petra in her office and told her I was heading out for the day.

I grabbed my coat and purse and headed out to the front. Trista was standing at the counter, ogling Noah, not that I blamed her.

When he noticed me coming around the counter, he stood and smiled, and I could hear Trista groaning and muttering, "Why are all the good ones taken?"

"Ready?" Noah asked, his gaze firmly on me. If he'd heard Trista, he was doing a great job of ignoring her.

"Yeah."

"I thought we could ride together in my car, in case we need to follow up on something. I'll bring you back to your car when we're done."

"Sounds good."

We walked outside in silence. He put his hand on the small of my back and steered me toward his personal car, a Jeep Grand Cherokee, and while I welcomed his touch, I felt like a yo-yo, bouncing back and forth—he wanted me; he didn't want me. If he was going to help me with this, I wanted him to help me without distractions.

He opened the door for me, and I turned to look up at him. "Look, I know you're dealing with something, and I've never been one to make demands, so for the sake of working together, I think we should just do this as friends."

Surprise filled his eyes. "Yeah," he said, his head bobbing. "Right."

"I know when we started this thing, I told you I'd be patient when you ran, but honestly, I hadn't expected it to happen so soon or for so long. And if I'm honest, I'm still struggling to correlate the you before Christmas with the you now. So for the sake of this investigation, this seems best."

He looked stricken. "Maddie, I'm sorry I've been an ass lately."

I shrugged, trying to act more casual than I felt. "We both have a lot on our plate. The timing's just wrong. But there's no reason we can't work together as friends."

He looked like he wanted to protest, then stopped. "Yeah, you're probably right."

I climbed up into the SUV. "I made an appointment for another tour at three-thirty. We better get going, or we'll be late."

He got in the driver's side, and as he started driving, I asked, "What's your mom doing while you're doing this with me?"

"She's reorganizing my kitchen." He laughed. "It's not as bad as that sounds. My gunshot wound scared her, and when she's scared, she cleans."

I cringed. "Sorry. I insisted they call her, but in my defense, Lance thought you were really hurt when he came to see me."

"Given the circumstances, it was the right call. She'll get over it."

It was a short drive to the care center. After Noah parked, we got out and met in front of his car. He reached for me, then seemed to think better of it and let his hand drop to his side as we silently walked inside.

The receptionist smiled when we approached the desk. I couldn't help noticing that her gaze lingered a little longer on Noah than necessary.

"I see you brought a friend today."

Noah nodded. "Noah Langley."

The receptionist glanced back at the office behind her then back to me. "Ms. Farrow is ready to talk about the financials."

"Before we do that," Noah said, resting his left forearm on the counter, "is there a chance I could look at the room you showed Maddie yesterday?"

She frowned. "Ms. Farrow can't get away from her desk. She

barely has time to go over the financials. In fact, she's currently on a call."

"That's okay," Noah said, giving her a warm smile. "Maddie took the tour yesterday, so she can show me around."

The receptionist's expression wavered. "I'm not sure that's a good idea. We like visitors to have a chaperone."

"But you said Ms. Farrow is busy," Noah pressed, then leaned closer and lowered his voice. "And if it makes a difference, I'm a detective with the Cockamamie Police Department. I'll make sure nothing happens."

So much for not mentioning he was a police officer. I had no problem with it, but did he? The confident look on his face suggested he didn't.

Her eyes flew wide. "You're the officer who got shot yesterday."

Noah stiffened, probably waiting for her disdain, but instead she fawned over him. "Are you okay? That had to be so scary. My friend knows Jeremy, the guy the robber shot at, and he said you saved his life. You're a hero."

Noah's cheeks flushed, and he patted his left elbow. "I'm no hero, and I wasn't hurt that badly."

"Thank goodness," she breathed in relief, then glanced at the double doors. "*Of course* you can go back, Noah."

She pulled a flat card with a lanyard out of a drawer and handed it to him, then pointed to the doors. "Just use the key card to go through. I trust Maddie remembers the way."

"I do," I said. "And if I get lost, it will be good practice for if Aunt Deidre moves in here."

Her face brightened. "We'll be glad to have you as part of our family."

I led Noah toward the communal living room for the nursing home and started toward the hallway that led to the memory care unit.

"Wait," he said, "give me the tour."

"We're here to see Detective Bergan."

"I suspect he'll still be there in ten minutes. You still need to make a decision about your aunt, so give me the tour I would have gotten if I'd made it yesterday."

I shook my head. "Even if I wanted to put her here, I'm not sure I can. Not with Bergan here. It might set her off. I could never forgive myself if it did."

His eyes widened slightly. "So what are you going to do?"

"I don't know yet. More in-home help? Look for a residential center somewhere else?" I sighed. "One issue at a time."

I pointed out features the director had shown me while we headed to the memory care center, but I was too nervous to tell him much. As we got closer to Bergan's room, my stomach started to churn.

"I think you should be the one who asks questions," he said in a hushed tone as we walked down Bergan's hallway. "Lance said Bergan's not very receptive to men."

"The nurse who helped him yesterday was a man, so I'm not sure if that's true."

"Still, let's try it this way."

While that was what I'd thought I wanted, I was suddenly consumed with doubt. The pressure of getting it right felt crushing. "Are you sure? I barely got anything out of him yesterday."

"You did better than you realize. But keep in mind that he's not well. It might not have meant anything. He could say even less today or contradict himself. I don't want you to be too disappointed if we get nothing because I plan to investigate your mother's murder no matter what he tells us. Okay?"

A lump filled my throat. "Thank you."

He nodded. "I'm just sorry I haven't done this sooner. So let's start with Bergan. You take the lead, and I'll hang back and feed you questions to ask if you get stuck."

I drew a deep breath. "Let's do this."

When we reached Detective Bergan's door, it was closed.

"Now what do we do?" I asked, worry creeping into my voice. "His door was open yesterday."

"We could knock," Noah said, then lifted the key card. "Or we could see if this works."

"We can't do that," I protested. "It's an invasion of his privacy." I narrowed my eyes. "Not to mention it seems illegal for a police officer to enter an apartment without a search warrant."

He grinned. "Looks like someone has been doing some homework on police procedure. But I'm not here to collect evidence or arrest him. And even if I wanted to question him myself, it wouldn't hold up in court. This is a fishing expedition. I hope it will point me in the right direction to start looking." He lifted the card to the reader next to the door, and the lock clicked open. "Maybe just push it open a crack and call out his name."

"Okay," I said reluctantly. While I wanted answers, I didn't want to get in trouble—or to get Noah in trouble.

I pushed the door open and peered inside. Detective Bergan was exactly where I'd left him the day before. The only difference was that he was wearing a fresh shirt. "Howard?" I called out, deciding it was better to use his first name.

He didn't respond. Instead, he kept his gaze on the TV screen, which was airing another football game.

I pushed the door open wider. Remembering how annoyed he'd been when the aide had called him mister, I said, "Hi, Detective Bergan. It's Maddie."

He swung his gaze over to me, confusion on his face. "Who?"

"Maddie." I stepped into the room. "I stopped by yesterday, and I thought I'd visit you again and see if you need more help with your remote."

His face scrunched up as he turned his attention back to the TV. "I don't need any visitors, and I don't need help with my remote."

"I hope you don't mind me coming in and sitting for a minute anyway," I said, my heart beating rapidly against my ribcage. This wasn't off to a great start. "You have such a lovely view of the courtyard." I sat on the sofa beside his chair, my back to the view. Noah stood in the doorway, then slipped in. He stayed by the door, letting it close behind him.

We sat in silence for several long seconds before I started asking questions.

"Detective Bergan, do you remember who I am?"

"You just told me your name is Maddie," he snapped, his gaze still on the TV. "I may have dementia, but I can still remember plenty."

"But do you remember me coming in yesterday?"

He turned to look at me, confusion and recognition fighting for control. "You look familiar."

I took a deep breath to calm my nerves and flashed him a smile. "We talked about my mother."

Confusion flickered in his eyes. "Who?"

"My mother. Andrea Baker."

The confusion in his gaze was chased out by fear. "I don't want to talk about her."

I leaned in closer. "I need to know what you know about her."

He shook his head, his eyes wide. "No."

"Detective Bergan," I pleaded. "Tell me about the skinny man. Did he kill my mother?"

"That man is dangerous," he said, a moment of clarity returning to his eyes. "You need to stay far away from him."

"If he killed my mother, then for all we know he killed other people too. Did he blackmail or threaten you to keep you from naming him as a suspect?"

Surprise washed over his face. "What do you know?"

It had been a lucky guess, but I didn't gloat. "I need you to tell me who he is."

"I don't know his name. He just told me to stall the case, or he'd kill my entire family."

"Why did he kill my mother?"

"I don't know. Maybe she discovered something about him, and he killed her to keep her quiet. I took his threat seriously."

"So you stalled the case and lost the file," Noah said, stepping forward.

Detective Bergan looked up at Noah with alarm, then must have realized the buff man standing across from us didn't fit the description of a *skinny man*. "Who the hell are you?"

"Detective Noah Langley. I'm here to clean up your mess." Then he repeated, "Like stalling the case and losing the file."

He glared in defiance. "I did what I could to protect my family."

"You could have called the state police."

Bergan shook his head. "They couldn't protect us forever."

"Why'd you call him the skinny man?" Noah asked.

"Because he was skinny," Bergan snapped. "Seems pretty self-explanatory."

"The threat can't have been all that serious if he was skinny," Noah countered. "You're not a small man. You could have taken him."

"He may have been skinny, but he was tall and lanky and had a crazy look in his eyes. He was someone you didn't want to piss off." A new wave of panic hit him, and he tried to get out of his chair. "He's gonna kill me for talking to you."

"Andrea Baker was killed almost twenty years ago," Noah said. "He's probably long since forgotten about you."

Bergan shook his head again. "A man that cold will never forget."

"Maybe he's dead," Noah said.

"He must have been in his twenties," Bergan said. "So he ain't all that old now."

"Then maybe he's moved on. Either way, it's unlikely he'll ever know you talked to us. Maddie's here because she's considering moving her aunt into St. Vincent's. He'd never make the connection." Then he added, "Besides, most people think you're deluded with dementia. I'd dismissed talking to you about the case because I was told you're never coherent enough to hold a discussion."

His brow furrowed. "A couple of years ago, I started talking about things I shouldn't. I have too many secrets from the job, and I didn't want them to get out. Some of the things I did could piss people off. They might take it out on my family. It was safer this way."

I bit my tongue to keep from pointing out we already knew that he'd taken multiple bribes over the years.

Noah kept a straight face and didn't say anything either.

"My wife and I agreed putting me in here was the best move," Bergan continued. "To protect all of us."

"What happened to Andrea Baker's file?" Noah asked.

Detective Bergan shifted his gaze to Noah's. "I burned it. If you're smart, you'll stay away from that case."

"Well, consider me stubborn because I'm not letting this go. Maddie and Deidre Saunders deserve to know what happened to their mother and sister."

"If you press this, you'll get them killed."

"Over twenty years later?"

"The guy wasn't working alone. He was working for someone."

Noah walked over to the sofa and sat beside me. "Andrea was looking into Martin Schroeder's pedophilia. Was the skinny man part of that?"

"I have no idea. But I'm guessing she got too close to something that he or his boss were involved in, and it made them nervous. Other people were killed soon after, bad people, so I had a right to keep it quiet. The threat was real."

"Who?" Noah asked.

"You think you're hot shit. *You* figure it out," Bergan sneered.

"You didn't know who this skinny man was?" Noah asked. "He wasn't on your radar?"

"I'd never seen him before, but some of the backwoods people don't hang around town."

"Was he a backwoods person?"

"I don't know."

"Take a guess."

"He seemed to know the lay of the land. But like I said, I'd never seen him before...and I never saw him after."

"That you remember," Noah said dryly.

Bergan grimaced in acknowledgment as he shrugged.

"You must remember *something* about him that would help me find him."

Bergan's eyes widened again. "He said he'd kill me and whoever I told if I ever talked. He meant it. He knew my wife and kids' schedules, from baseball to dance classes to when my wife took her lunch break. He said that if I talked he'd kill every one of them and make sure they suffered. He killed Andrea Baker, and it was brutal." His gaze turned to me, and his eyes went glassy. "You look a lot like her. I'd hate for you to end up like the woman I saw on that classroom floor."

I gasped.

"That's enough of that," Noah grunted, looking about ready to pounce on the older man.

"I didn't know Andrea Baker personally," Bergan said with a sigh, "but I'd heard of her. Everyone loved her." He paused, then sighed again. "Look. I wish I could have proven the skinny man had something to do with her murder, but I had to think about the town's safety."

"You mean your family," Noah said bluntly.

Bergan's eyes hardened. "I would do anything—*anything*—to protect my family." His gaze lowered. "Wouldn't *you*?"

Noah's hand clenched at his side, but his face remained neutral.

"Give me something to follow. Some kind of lead. You know *something*. Otherwise you wouldn't have burned the file."

Bergan's jaw set, and I was sure he was about to tell Noah to go to hell. Instead, he lifted his chin and held Noah's gaze. "Andrea was holding a gold necklace when she was found. We were sure she'd pulled it off of whoever had killed her."

"No one ever mentioned a gold necklace," I said in shock.

"That's because we never made it public."

"Did it have an eagle on it?" I asked, the eagle comment suddenly clicking into place.

Bergan's eyes widened. "How did you know? Only three of us know that."

"You told me yesterday," I said bluntly.

Bergan looked like he was going to be sick. "Shit. I'm getting worse."

"Lucky for you, the women playing bingo down the hall don't give a rat's ass about your ramblings," Noah said. "Who else knows about the necklace?"

"Only three of us and the other two are dead."

Noah's brow rose in question.

Bergan waved a hand in dismissal. "Natural causes. After my visit from the guy, I made the necklace and a few other things disappear."

"And no one noticed?" Noah asked.

"Sure, months later. We attributed it to carelessness."

"Where's the evidence now?"

"I burned it all with the file."

"I call bullshit," Noah sneered, sitting back on the sofa. "You kept the evidence of all your other cases like trophies. Hell, you might as well have built a shrine to all your subversion in that storage room you rent. So there's absolutely no way you'd destroy the hidden evidence connected to the biggest case of your career."

Bergan swallowed, suddenly looking nervous. "You found all that?"

"Yep," Noah gloated. "Maybe you should have burned all that stuff too before moving in here. But you didn't. Which tells me you didn't destroy Andrea Baker's stuff either." He leaned forward, resting his forearms on his thighs, his voice dark and threatening. "So where'd you store it, Bergan?"

Bergan's face paled. "I can't tell you."

"The fuck you can't," Noah growled. "You owe Andrea Baker justice."

"She's dead. She doesn't give a shit whether she gets justice or not."

Noah sat up and snorted in disgust. "How the hell were you ever a detective?"

"What about me?" I asked, frustrated that this man had answers and refused to give them up. "*I* deserve to know what happened to my mother. You treated me like shit when I was a kid. I was orphaned, and you had absolutely no sympathy for me. You wouldn't tell me anything about your case."

Guilt crossed his face. "I was protecting you too."

"The hell you were," I sneered. "You made it pretty clear that I annoyed you when I asked questions. You weren't subtle about not wanting to deal with me."

"Could her killer have been part of the Brawlers?" Noah asked.

Bergan scoffed. "The Brawlers weren't a thing back then. They started up later."

"How soon into the investigation did the man show up?" Noah asked. "How did he approach you?"

Bergan's upper lip curled, and I was sure he would refuse to answer again. So I was surprised when he said, "About three days into the investigation. We quietly asked questions about the necklace, and I guess the guy found out. He cornered me outside my house. Told me that my wife and kids were inside watching TV, and if he'd been inclined, he could have gone in and murdered all of them just like he'd murdered that teacher. Then he told me everything he knew about them and made his threats." He paused, then looked me dead in the eyes. "I did what I had to do. I refuse to apologize. For any of it."

Pain stabbed me in the heart, but anger burned it away. "If you don't tell me where to find the evidence of my mother's murder, I'm going to walk out of here and tell everyone who will listen that your dementia is all an act and you've been hiding in here to escape charges for suppressing evidence. I'll also tell everyone in town, including the newspaper, that you told me you suppressed evidence and information regarding my mother's case. We'll see if the skinny man's alive or not then."

His face turned red. "You wouldn't."

I clenched my jaw so hard my teeth ground painfully. "Try me."

"So either way, you're gonna kill me and my family," he spat.

"No," Noah said, "if you tell us where you hid the evidence in the Andrea Baker case, we'll keep your secret."

Bergan drew in a breath, his chest rising as he stared out the window to the courtyard. He looked pissed, but at least he seemed to be considering my threat.

"Fine," he grunted, swinging his gaze between us. "But you can't let anyone other than my buddy know I told you anything."

"If anyone asks, I'll say I found something in the boxes from our house when my aunt and uncle packed it up after it was sold," I interjected before Noah could say anything. "After a while, it became clear to me that you and the other assholes weren't taking the investigation into my mother's murder seriously," I said bitterly. "That you were more concerned with padding your pockets than solving crimes and keeping Cockamamie safe, I decided to start my own investigation." I narrowed my eyes. "All of which is true."

"It's easy to paint me out to be the bad guy when—"

"Enough of the self-justifications," Noah snapped. "Either tell us what you know, or we'll get up and head straight to the newspaper."

"I really do have dementia," Bergan seethed.

"I believe that," I said. "My aunt has it too. She has very lucid days, then days when she thinks I'm a stranger breaking into her house. I believe you were having an episode when I saw you yesterday, but I know in my gut that you're as clear as a bright sunny day right now. So tell us what you know and where you hid the evidence, and we'll leave you in peace."

His jaw worked for several moments before he said, "I gave what I had to a buddy of mine in Galena. Stewie Pitcavage. Tell him that Howie sent you, and I told him to give it to you."

Noah's gaze narrowed. "Don't bullshit us. He's not going to just hand it over."

"Not to mention he probably thinks you're out of it with dementia," I added.

Bergan's shoulders sank, making him look resigned. "He knows I have my good days and bad. But if he questions you, tell him I said he could go fuck a duck. He'll know I really sent you."

"Do you have an address for this guy?" Noah asked.

Bergan gave him a sneer. "If you're as good as you think you are, you'll be able to find it on your own." He sat back in his recliner. "Now get the fuck out of here because I'm not telling you another word." His eyes hardened as he looked at Noah. "And if anything happens to my family, I'm breakin' out of this place, and I'm coming for *you*."

Chapter Eight

Maddie

Noah and I didn't waste any time leaving Bergan's room and heading toward the front desk.

"Ms. Farrow's ready to meet with you now," Lisa said as I handed her the keycard.

"I'll have to reschedule," I said, glancing at Noah for confirmation. He gave me a slight nod. "Something came up at home. I'm sorry to have to leave like this..."

Sympathy filled her eyes. "Don't say another word. We understand the difficulty of having dementia patients in a home setting, which is why we're eager to help."

Noah and I didn't say anything until we were sitting in his SUV. "I'm going to drop you off at your car, then head to Galena."

"What?" I cried out in dismay. "That wasn't our agreement."

"I know, but for all we know, Stewie Pitcavage will greet us with a shotgun."

"It's not like you're on duty, Noah," I countered, my anger rising. "Do you even have a gun with you?"

"Of course I have a gun with me," he shot back. "I'm a police officer. I carry one just about everywhere I go."

Which I knew from experience. I'd seen the piece he carried strapped to his ankle. "I thought you were on administrative leave."

"I am, but I'm still allowed to carry." He gave me a pointed look. "I know how to handle things if he starts shooting. You don't."

I lifted my chin. "I've been shot at multiple times and survived, so don't you dare tell me I don't know how to handle myself. I'm going, Noah, whether you like it or not."

He grumbled, then said, "Maddie, that's not the same thing."

"Just shut up and drive," I said, knowing I'd already won. "We don't want to be looking for this place in the dark. Not in Galena. It's a mountain town and more than a little rough."

He turned to face me. "We don't have an address."

"Then I guess we start by looking this guy up."

Scowling, Noah pulled out his phone and started tapping.

"You're Googling it?" I asked.

He kept his gaze on the screen. "I'm texting Lance."

"So does this mean you're not going to fight me about going?"

His gaze lifted. "Would it do any good?"

"No."

"Then there's your answer." He set his phone in the cup holder in the console and backed out of the parking space. "Do you know Galena very well?"

"No, but take Highway 23 out of town. It's about twenty miles to the northwest."

"So let's head in that direction and hope Lance gets back to me before we hit the city limits." His gaze met mine and held it. "Talk to me. How are you doing after that?"

Some of the tension eased between my shoulders. "I can't believe Bergan never looked for my mother's killer at all. I get that he was worried about his family..."

"It doesn't matter," Noah insisted. "He took an oath to uphold the law. He could have called the state police. They would have protected his family. It was more dangerous for him to let the guy go. Now, we're practically at square one." He shook his head. "Bergan's description of the guy was so vague it could be just about anybody. Let's hope Pitcavage has something helpful."

"And if he doesn't?"

"We've still got other avenues to pursue. I'll look into other deaths around the time of your mother's. We'll interview all the teachers your mother worked with and even some of her students if we can come up with a list." He glanced at me before turning back to the road. "Ideally, we'd ask the school to give us anything they have, but since I'm on administrative leave, I'm technically not supposed to be doing this."

"You don't *have* to do this while you're on leave, Noah," I protested. "The last thing I want is to get you in trouble."

"I'm not worried about the chief. I'm more worried about optics if the public catches wind of what's going on." He held onto the steering wheel. "Think you can get off work for the next few days and help me with this?"

I gasped. "Are you serious?"

"Yeah. If anyone catches wind of what we're up to, I'll just say you're asking questions—which you have every right to do—and I'm tagging along."

"But you don't like to break rules."

A sly smile lifted the corners of his mouth. "It isn't the first time I've broken the rules for you, and I suspect it won't be the last."

"Okay," I said with a half-laugh. "Who are you, and where is Noah Langley?"

He laughed with me. "It's me. Maybe I'm feeling rebellious."

He'd never struck me as the rebellious type. Then again, maybe this was some latent teenage rebellion. His mother was currently reorganizing his kitchen, and he and his father were at odds.

I tried to sound natural as I voiced a question that had been burning in my chest since he'd first mentioned his mother was in town. "So...how is it having your mother here?"

He talked about his mom for the rest of the drive, telling me about growing up with his mother and sister and his rarely present father. His mother was active in their lives, signing up for room mother activities and PTA. I knew he was frustrated that she'd popped up unannounced, but there was plenty of affection in his voice.

"Does she know about the editorial?" I asked.

"No, and I'm hoping she doesn't find out."

"I didn't know anything about it. What did it say?"

He spent the next few minutes telling me what the paper had written about him. The editorial claimed he'd brought the violence he'd encountered in Memphis to our town, citing the recent robberies, rapes, and murders.

I was pissed on his behalf. "That's the most ridiculous thing I've ever heard! Those crimes had nothing to do with you, Noah. You're the one who *caught* the bad guys!"

"I know," he said with a defeated sigh. "But the chief thinks we need to give it time to blow over. In the meantime, I'll be on paid leave. On the plus side, I can work on your mother's murder investigation."

While he'd said before that he'd investigate her murder, he'd done some cursory digging then put the case on the back burner. Now he was on administrative leave, which meant he wasn't supposed to be working. Was he helping me because he was a workaholic who lived for his job and couldn't stop, or was he doing it for me? When it came to solving her murder, it didn't matter the reason as long as he helped me find the killer. But in regard to a relationship between us, it made all the difference in the world.

"I really hope Bergan wasn't blowing smoke up our asses."

I gave him a nervous smile. "I guess there's only one way to find out."

We were approaching Galena when Lance texted back with Stewie Pitcavage's last known address. I plugged it into Noah's map app. Pitcavage's home was located at the base of one of the mountains, ten minutes from our location.

We grew silent as we got closer, and anxiety bubbled in my stomach. I'd waited nearly nineteen years for some kind of information about what happened to my mother. But we had nothing if Bergan's friend didn't have the evidence or wouldn't hand it over.

Noah slowed down on the narrow two-lane road as we approached the location on the app. It was darker now, and we had to search the trees to find the house. The brick ranch home was set back about fifty feet from the road. Several lights illuminated the front of the house and a flagpole with an American flag. A narrow gravel drive led from the road to the house.

"I want you to stay in the car," Noah said in a low tone as he turned onto the driveway, the gravel crunching under the tires. "At least until we're sure he's not going to try to shoot us."

I nearly told him he was overreacting, that we wouldn't get shot for approaching a house, but this was Galena, so it was an actual possibility. "Yeah. Sure." Getting shot once was enough for me. "But what about you?"

"I'll be fine." He parked in the driveway and left the car running. "Just in case we need to make a quick getaway."

He got out, walked up to the glass storm door and knocked, then waited at the base of the two concrete stairs.

I wanted to hear what they said, so I leaned over and pressed the button on the driver's door to roll the window down.

The wooden front door opened, and a big, burly man with a bushy beard appeared behind the storm door glass. While the guy looked to be in his fifties or sixties, his broad chest, arms, and shoulders suggested he worked out regularly. "Whadaya want?" he barked through the door.

Noah held his gaze. "Mr. Pitcavage? I'm a friend of Howard Bergan's—"

The man crossed his arms over his barrel chest. "Howie ain't got no friends. Try again."

"Okay, I'm not a friend," Noah admitted amiably. "But Howard said he asked you to keep something for him, and he'd like for you to give it to me."

The man burst out laughing, then turned serious. "That's funny. Now get off my land."

He started to shut the wooden door, but Noah called out, "He said to tell you to fuck a duck."

The glass door burst open so quickly that I barely registered the movement before the man was down the steps, grabbing Noah's shirt in a clenched fist. Noah wasn't a small man at six foot two, but Stewie Pitcavage towered over him and outweighed him by at least fifty pounds of pure muscle. "Who the fuck are you?"

Crap. Not only were we not going to get the box, but Noah was about to get his face punched.

"Mr. Pitcavage, I'm Maddie Baker," I shouted as I scrambled out of the SUV and hurried around the hood. "Andrea Baker's daughter."

"Get back in the car, Maddie," Noah shouted, his eyes wide with panic.

I held my hands up as I moved closer. "I swear to you, Mr. Pitcavage, Noah's telling the truth. I met Detective Bergan yesterday while I was touring St. Vincent's for my aunt. He lives in the same hall as the available unit, and I helped him with his TV remote. He told me a few things that made me suspicious, so my boyfriend came with me today to talk to him again." I stopped about six feet away from him, my hands still in the air. "Howard was more lucid this afternoon. He told me that he'd destroyed my mother's file but gave you a few things related to her case. He said I could have them and told us to tell you to fuck a duck so you'd know he'd given us his blessing."

"That don't sound like Howie at all."

I took a step closer. "That's the code word he gave us, I swear."

He snorted. "Not that part. Telling you about the box, period. Why would he do that?"

I shrugged, lowering my hands to my sides. "Maybe I made him feel guilty for not solving her murder."

His eyes narrowed. "Not likely."

I glanced at Noah, who looked like he was about to shove himself out of Pitcavage's grip.

"Okay," I said, purposely sounding defeated. "Noah threatened to beat the shit out of Howard if he didn't tell us."

"And Howie didn't throw a punch?" Pitcavage asked with a short laugh.

"He's an old man who looks like he's skin and bones, not to mention he was sitting in a recliner. He looked like he couldn't get out of his chair without help, let alone throw a punch," I said. "But he told us that he gave some evidence to you, including a gold necklace with an eagle."

The amused look on Stewie Pitcavage's face disappeared. "Why would he give it up now?" he asked, his fist clenching tighter around Noah's shirt. "He's scared to death of the guy who threatened him."

"I guess he was more scared of Noah," I said.

Noah took a step back, jerking out of Pitcavage's grasp. "I can be persuasive when need be."

Pitcavage turned to face me. "I'm still not buying it."

"When was the last time you saw him?" I asked. "He looks pretty old and frail. A hell of a lot older than the last time I saw him sixteen years ago."

He'd been downright hateful the day I'd stopped by his office to request an update on the case. I was home for Christmas break my freshman year of college. He'd told me that he'd get in touch when he had something and not a moment before and to leave him alone. I never heard from him again.

"Aren't we all?" Pitcavage scoffed.

"Look," I said. "I don't know how you and Howard know each other, and frankly I don't give a shit. All I want is the box of evidence so I can find out who killed my mother."

"You don't want to be doin' that, little girl," he sneered. "The man who killed her is dangerous."

"I'm not a little girl," I shot back, "and for what it's worth, it's none of your concern what happens after you hand over the box. After that, it's on me."

He released a chuckle. "You're a spitfire, ain't ya?"

Noah sidled up next to me. "We just want the box, and then we'll leave you in peace."

Ignoring Noah, Pitcavage eyed me up and down with a gleam in his eyes. "Fine. It's your funeral. Wait here. It's gonna take a minute to retrieve." He went back inside the house, leaving us on the front stoop.

"What were you thinking coming out here like that?" Noah snapped under his breath.

"Cool it, Noah," I grunted. "I'm not the little girl Pitcavage thinks I am, and I'm the one who hopefully got results."

He grumbled under his breath, obviously not happy, but he couldn't argue with me either.

It took more than a minute. In fact, after about five minutes, I wondered if he was coming back at all and mumbled as much to Noah.

"He's coming back, and the longer he takes means he's less likely to show up with a shotgun and shoot us."

Sure enough, about thirty seconds later, Pitcavage opened the door holding a small brown cardboard shipping box with the word *white rabbit* written on the side. He marched down the steps and shoved it at me. "That's all Bergan gave me, but if you tell anyone I've been holding it all these years, I'll hunt you down and kill ya myself."

I grabbed the box, nearly dropping it when I felt how light it was. Was there anything in it? The slight rattle suggested the answer was yes, but it wasn't much.

Noah stood taller, and I knew he was about to say something in my defense, but I grabbed his arm and dragged him toward the car. "Thank you. I've already forgotten who you are."

He gave me a satisfied nod as I turned around and headed to the passenger side door. Noah backed up until he reached the side of the SUV and opened the door. He was inside when I got in, his hand on the gear shift to put the vehicle in reverse.

Pitcavage stood on the porch, watching us drive away, and I couldn't help wondering what could make a man his size so nervous about another man.

And here I was, rushing straight toward the boogeyman.

Chapter Nine

Maddie

I was eager to open the box and search the contents, but Noah convinced me it would be better to open it together. After he drove a few miles, he pulled onto the widened shoulder of the county road next to a historical marker.

"Let's open it," he said as he shifted the SUV into park.

I expected him to try to take the box from me, but he gave me an eager look, waiting. My heart swelled. I couldn't help thinking he'd been placating me by "letting" me start the interview with Howard Bergan. But the fact he was letting me open the box suggested he saw us as partners in this.

The packing tape keeping the box closed was brittle and yellow. I grabbed a loose end and pulled it off the top of the box. The flaps partially opened, and I pushed them the rest of the way down. Inside were several small clear evidence bags.

I started to reach in for them, but Noah said, "Wait," as he pulled out his phone and snapped a few photos of the contents. Then he turned on the phone's flashlight and shone it inside. "There might be spiders. Who knows where it was stored."

I nearly tossed the box off my lap, but he seemed satisfied after his examination. "It looks clear. Go ahead."

I pulled out the first evidence bag and held it up so Noah could see it. There were preprinted lines on the plastic. Numbers and letters were handwritten on them in black marker. But the bags themselves were translucent, the contents easily visible.

"A gold key," Noah said, tilting his head to get a better look. "Looks like a house key."

"Why would they keep a key as evidence?" I asked.

"She must have had it on her person or close to her at the crime scene. They would have kept it as potential evidence if they couldn't figure out what it opened. I know it's been a long time, but do you think it could have been a key to your house?"

"You just said they probably kept it because they couldn't figure out what lock it would open."

"True, but we're dealing with a lazy, incompetent, crooked detective and his cronies."

I pushed out a sigh. "Honestly, I'm not sure, and I don't know how we'd find out. We sold the house a few months after Mom died, and surely the new owners changed the locks."

"You'd be surprised. It's worth checking out." He took the bag and laid it on the console. "What's next?

I grabbed the next envelope. It was slightly bigger with similar markings. Inside was a torn piece of lined notebook paper with chunky handwriting.

MEET ME IN YOUR ROOM AT 8:30, AND I'LL TELL YOU EVERYTHING.

I turned it around to show Noah, my heart beating rapidly. I felt like I was going to throw up. "This was premeditated."

His lips pressed together as he read the note. "Not necessarily, but it's compelling. For what it's worth, I've always suspected as much, but this helps solidify my suspicions. I don't suppose you recognize the handwriting?"

I shook my head and handed it to Noah.

There was one last envelope. I pulled it out and saw a chunky gold chain with a bird pendant. The clasp was still attached, but the chain had broken. Dried blood covered some of the links.

My mother's blood.

I swallowed the bile rising in my throat.

Noah gently placed a hand on my arm. "Maddie, it's only going to get harder from here on out."

I couldn't look at him, my gaze was locked on the broken chain. "I know."

"You don't have to be involved in everything," he continued. "I can investigate on my own and keep you updated on what I find. I won't hide anything from you, I promise."

I was tempted to accept his offer. This was harder than I'd expected, although I wasn't sure why. Of course I couldn't investigate her death as a neutral observer. She was my *mother*, the person who'd held me when I was little, snuggled with me in bed, and orchestrated movie nights and dance parties. I had countless happy memories with her up until a few months before her murder.

I'd gone so long with nothing, and now I finally had evidence literally sitting on my lap. It was killing something in my soul, but as much as it hurt, I couldn't walk away. I owed it to my mother to be part of this investigation, and also to myself. After so many years on the see-saw of uncertainty, I needed closure. I had to know who killed her and why. And while I knew Noah was dedicated to solving her murder, no one could be more dedicated than me.

I lifted my gaze to his. "No, I'm not walking away from this."

He studied my face, then tipped his head in acknowledgment. "Okay, but if it's ever too much, or even just part of it is too much, don't hesitate to tell me you need to sit it out."

I didn't respond, and he added, "I won't hide things from you, Maddie. I know everyone who's been part of this investigation has kept things from you. I won't do that." Resolve filled his eyes. "I'm in this with you. But if this skinny man freaked out Bergan and Pitcavage, you should be afraid of him too."

"But not you?" I countered.

"I'm respectfully cautious," he said carefully. "I don't intend to rush into anything. We have these pieces, but we still don't know how they fit together."

He was right. We didn't have an obvious next step.

"Don't get discouraged," he said. "We'll figure it out." He glanced at the dashboard. "For now, I need to get you back to your car so you can get home."

My gaze followed his to the radio. It was close to six, and I hadn't told Mallory I'd made this field trip to Galena. I pulled out my phone and sent her a quick text telling her I was going to be late and would explain everything when I got home.

I put the first two bags back in the box as Noah pulled away from the shoulder, but I couldn't bring myself to let go of the bag with the necklace.

We drove in silence until we were almost to Cockamamie. I was mulling over what we'd discovered, trying to imagine how my mother's blood had gotten on the chain.

"I'm going to make some calls tomorrow morning," Noah finally said as we approached the Cockamamie city limits. "I'll see if the crime lab has anything from your mother's case."

"What about DNA?" I asked. "Surely there's some of the killer's DNA on the necklace."

"True, but there's no chain of custody, and we only have Bergan's statement saying it was found in your mother's hand. We both know he'll never admit to it. And even if he *did* admit it, it would never hold up in court. DNA could have been planted. And even if *that* could be overlooked—and it couldn't—I'd have to get the case reopened before I can send it off for analysis. This case is nineteen years old, and it would take months to get the DNA results back. That's if the state approves the expense. I think we're better off leaving it closed so we can find out as much as possible before I make a case for reopening it." He paused. "Are you okay with that?"

"Yeah, but what about one of those mail-in tests?" I asked. "You know, like 23andMe?"

"I doubt the killer's the kind of guy who'd use something like that, *but* it could help narrow the results down to his family. However, there are a couple of problems..." He ran a hand over his head. He looked exhausted in the dim lighting from the dashboard. "One, they use saliva, and we have blood. I'm not sure they'd run it. Second, they'd have to isolate his DNA from your mother's, and they'd have to get it off the chain. That's if his DNA is even on there. I suspect most of the blood is your mother's."

"Yeah," I said, swallowing bile and trying not to think about the fact I was holding an evidence bag with my mother's dried blood in it. "You're right."

As though reading my mind, he took the bag and tucked it into the box. "I meant it, Maddie. The killer's name may not be engraved on the necklace or signed on the note, but we'll find something. This isn't a dead end. We still have people to talk to. They might give us something that'll point us in the right direction."

"Okay."

He turned onto Main Street. "Can you get off work the rest of the week?"

"It's short notice. And I just took off three weeks with my shoulder," I said, sitting back in my seat and staring out the windshield. "It's Wednesday, right?" This week already felt like it had been nine days long.

In response to his nod, I said, "I work tomorrow and Friday, then I have Saturday off. But I have to work Sunday morning. I traded with Trista so she'd cover for me when I went to Nashville. I can possibly trade for Friday, but Sunday will be harder."

"Don't worry about tomorrow morning. There are plenty of things that I can't do with you." His eyes narrowed, probably because he could read my expression. "I'm not leaving you out. I plan on chatting with the coroner's office and the sheriff's department."

"I thought this was unofficial," I said. "I really don't want you to get into more trouble, Noah."

"Don't worry. I have a few friends who will look into things off the books. In the meantime, if you could make a list of teachers and some students who knew your mom, I can try to set up some interviews for us for tomorrow afternoon."

That made me feel less guilty about choosing work over finding my mother's murderer. "Most of the teachers Mom worked with are still at the school. They won't be able to talk with us until midafternoon anyway."

"See?" he said with a soft smile as he turned onto the side street next to Déjà Brew and pulled into the lot, parking next to my car. "There's no reason for you to take off in the morning anyway." He turned serious as he shifted his car into park. "I know you're worried about money, especially with Deidre's nursing home expenses looming over your head."

"I don't want you to think my mother's not a priority," I said, feeling sick.

"Maddie," he said emphatically, reaching over to cup my cheek and turning me to face him. "That's the last thing I'd think. The sad fact is your mother was murdered almost two decades ago. It won't matter if we spread out the investigation over a few weeks."

I knew weeks were nothing compared to the years I'd already waited, but I was getting impatient for answers. "On second thought, maybe I should take the time off anyway."

He was silent for a moment. "I'm not gonna tell you what to do. If it were my mother, I'd feel the exact same way. But I plan on spending tomorrow morning making phone calls to the crime lab and detectives in the sheriff's department. Other than listening in on those calls, there's nothing for you to do." He paused. "When I said I wouldn't hold anything back, I meant it. I swear."

Tears stung my eyes. I felt so close to finding answers, but I was still so very far from getting them. "Okay."

He leaned closer as though he were about to kiss me, and then seemed to realize he was still touching my cheek. He dropped his hand, looking chastised. "You're sure you're okay with this plan? I don't want you to feel pressured or think I'm going behind your back."

I read the sincerity in his eyes. "I trust you."

"Even though I've given you every reason to think otherwise, you mean a lot to me," he said, looking broken to admit it. "As you've likely suspected, things didn't go well with my father on my trip home over Christmas."

Was he finally opening up to me? "Can you tell me what happened?"

"I can't."

I nodded, but it was a bitter disappointment, because as long as there were secrets between us, this would never work.

"But I'm working through it." He drew in a breath and seemed to choose his words carefully. Grimacing, he added, "I'm kind of a moody asshole if you hadn't figured that out yet."

I released an exaggerated gasp. "*You?*"

He rolled his eyes. "I deserved that."

I gave him a mock glare. "You did." I shrugged. "Turns out I apparently have a thing for moody assholes."

A smile spread across his face. "I really don't deserve you or your patience, Maddie Baker."

"Yeah, I know," I said with a hint of a smile. "Just keep reminding yourself of that."

"I want to work things out with you, Maddie. There's nothing I want more than to be with you...if I'm not holding you back. I understand why you want to keep our relationship platonic while we work on this," he said. "I don't want you to think I'm going to pressure you into anything."

I nearly laughed. Noah had never pressured me into a relationship. If anything, it had probably been the other way around.

He looked serious. "I prefaced that before my next statement because I don't have a right to ask you what I'm about to ask you, but I'm going to ask anyway. I will completely understand if you say no."

"Okay," I said, anxiety bubbling in my stomach.

"I'd like for you to meet my mother," he said, then quickly added, "If you're up to it."

Did I want to meet his mother? That was next step material, and I felt like we were practically back at square one in our relationship. If it could be called a relationship. Then again, the fact that he wanted me to meet her meant something, and I couldn't deny that I wanted to meet the woman who'd raised him. "Yeah," I said softly. "I'd like to meet her."

His shoulders settled like he'd been tense waiting for my response. "Good, because she's already asked to meet you." He gave me a reassuring look. "I suspect she'll be here for a few days, so maybe we can arrange to have dinner tomorrow night." He hastily added, "If that works for you."

I was still trying to wrap my head around the fact that he wanted me to meet his mother. "I'll see if Mal can stay with Aunt Deidre. I'm sure you don't want to introduce your mother to the circus act that's currently my life. At least not yet. Let's give her a good impression first."

He started to say something then stopped. He let out a breath and said, "Maybe it would be better to meet in a neutral place, just the three of us. We can introduce her to your aunt next time."

I was pretty adept at reading between the lines. "So your mother will be bothered by my circus act life?"

"No, of course not," he said, but it sounded a little too rushed to be sincere. "When my mom's not worrying about me getting shot, she's pretty chill."

"Well, in her defense, I was pretty upset about you getting shot too." From all that he'd told me on the drive to Galena, it was obvious that he loved her and valued her opinion, and I knew her approval of me was important. "Does she know that we're taking a break?"

"No, and I'd rather not tell her, if you're open to that. It will raise too many questions neither of us are ready to answer."

"So we're supposed to pretend to be together?"

"No," he said, his voice tight. "We don't have to label it. I doubt she'll ask us to."

I frowned. This sounded like it could be a recipe for disaster, but my curiosity won out. "I think tomorrow night will work. I'm sure Mallory can stay with Aunt Deidre, and if she can't, Margarete can." It helped that Aunt Deidre's longtime next-door neighbor was often willing to pitch in when needed. I groaned as I remembered something. "But Mallory is going to Chattanooga to meet some of her old coworkers this weekend, so I might have to arrange for someone to stay with my aunt on Saturday. Her home health nurse has a friend who's already agreed to stay with her on Sunday while I work."

"Don't worry. We'll figure it out."

I almost leaned over to kiss him. Now that we'd opened that door, it was hard not to. But I'd been the one to set up the boundaries, and I needed to keep them in place, so instead I opened the door and started to get out.

"Maddie."

I glanced over my shoulder at him.

"I'll tell you about my dad. Soon, okay?"

A tight smile twisted my lips. I hoped he was right. Something told me our relationship depended on it.

Chapter Ten

Noah

On Thursday morning, the first order of business was to call the Wayfare County crime lab to see what they had on Andrea Baker's case. I should have checked into it last November after I'd learned the case file was missing, but I'd presumed Martin Schroeder was the perpetrator. I definitely should have called after Maddie told me about Schroeder's alibi, but I'd been caught up in other cases—and in Maddie. There was no good excuse, though, especially since it involved Maddie's mother.

Part of me worried that Bergan hadn't sent anything to the crime lab. Then where would we be?

I was about to find out. But first I had to leave the house and get out of my mother's earshot.

Mom still didn't know I was on administrative leave. She thought I was taking sick days because of the stitches in my arm, which barely bothered me. She'd driven me crazy the night before, wanting me to buy a closet system for the small bedroom closet so she could organize my clothing by colors. She'd suggested a day trip to the IKEA in Atlanta, which might as well be a day trip to hell, so I'd been grateful to tell her I had something to do for work and would be back by dinner.

"I thought you said you had the day off," she told me with pursed lips.

When I was eight, I'd broken a window in the neighbor's house, and somehow, my mother had magically known. Suddenly I felt like I was eight again.

"I did," I said, trying to squirm. "But this was important."

Her face softened. "They're all important, Noah. But so is family."

I felt properly chastised and almost told her it *was* for family, but Maddie wasn't family. Not yet. It surprised me that the thought of making a family with her felt good. Right, even.

When I'd gone to Memphis, I'd spent a lot of time with my niece and nephew, loving every minute with them. My sister was a good mother, and she'd come from the same family I had. My mother had been a good parent. For the first time, I'd not only acknowledged that I could be a better dad than my father had been, but actually believed it.

I wasn't ready to fully jump on the fatherhood train, but when I pictured a life with Maddie, I could see the hint of kids.

But first I needed to exorcise my father's voice from my head. As long as I gave him residence in my head, I'd never be good to anyone.

I understood why Maddie had friend zoned me, and I couldn't blame her. Truth be told, I was frustrated with myself, so she had to be that much more frustrated. Things had been going well before I'd left. We still hadn't slept together, although there had been a lot of kissing. We'd agreed we would wait until I came back. And instead of sweeping her off her feet into my bed, I'd told her I needed some space.

It had been hard not to reach out and touch her yesterday. When I'd dropped her off at her car, I'd practically glued my ass to my seat to keep from kissing her.

My own wants and desires could wait. I needed to prove to her that she could trust me, and helping her solve her mother's murder was a good first step.

I was working on an excuse to leave the house to make my calls when a knock landed on the front door.

My mother was sitting at the kitchen table making a menu of freezer meals. She peered around the doorway to watch as I answered it.

When I opened the door, Lance greeted me with a grim look.

"Hey, Noah, sorry to bother you on your time off, but I'd like to run some things by you on this auto parts case." He looked past me, and a huge smile spread across his face when he saw my mother. "Your mom's still here."

"She is," I said blankly, still standing in the doorway. "Which should have been obvious since her car's still parked in front of my house, *Detective* Forrester." He may have wanted to discuss the case with me, but he could have called. I knew why he was really here. He wanted to meet my mother. I had every intention of introducing him to her, but there was no sense in making it easy for him.

He gave me an amused look. "You gonna let me in?"

I hung onto the side of the door, trying to block his view of the interior. "I haven't decided yet."

"Noah," my mother called out. "Where are your manners?"

Chuckling, I stepped back and let Lance in. Based on the look on his face, you'd think he was five years old.

He'd been to my place once, but now he looked around the place with a gleam of appreciation. "I can see you've been busy, Mrs. Langley. This place doesn't look like a bachelor pad anymore."

"Please," I grunted. "It looked perfectly fine before."

"He's right, of course," my mother said, walking into the living room. "The place looked pretty good on the surface when I showed up Tuesday night, but it was totally disorganized. I spent most of yesterday getting things in order."

Lance grinned from ear to ear, shooting me a mischievous look.

"You must be Lance," my mother said. "I'm Laura Langley, as you figured out. Noah's mother. But please call me Laura." She gave me a look of reprimand for failing to have made the introductions.

"I would have introduced you," I said in self-defense. "But you two were having too much fun bashing my organizational skills."

Lance held out his hand to my mother. "Pleased to meet you, Laura. Sorry if we scared you on Tuesday, but in our defense, all we knew was that there was a lot of blood. The EMTs wouldn't tell us anything. We didn't even think of it until Maddie suggested you should know."

My mother's face lit up. "Maddie?"

Lance shot me a questioning look, then turned back to her. "I thought you knew about Maddie."

"Oh, I do," she said with a grin. "Noah's making arrangements for us to meet for dinner tonight, but other than that, he hasn't mentioned her once since I've gotten here. I was beginning to wonder if she even existed."

Lance laughed. "Oh, she exists all right."

I shot him a dark look.

Lance chuckled, turning his attention to my mother. "Is he as tight-lipped with you about his personal life as he is with me?"

"I suspect even more so."

"I need more coffee." I walked into the kitchen, refilled my mug, and then returned to the living room. Lance and my mother had settled on the sofa and were having a lively discussion about my moodiness.

"Would you two like some tea while you gossip about me?" I asked dryly as I sat in my recliner.

Lance laughed. "I was telling her that my mother had informally adopted you and makes sure you eat."

"Someone has to," my mother said. "In Memphis, after he broke up with Monica, he mostly ate takeout and frozen meals he heated up in the microwave."

Monica being the woman who I'd dated and lived with for years. We'd even been engaged until she realized I could never give her what she wanted.

Funny how Mom had changed her tune about the tavern since showing up on Tuesday night.

Lance nodded. "I'm pretty sure he did the same until my mother took pity on him."

"I'd like to meet your mother," my mom said.

"And she'd love to meet you," Lance said. "It will have to be at the tavern since she works most nights, but it's a nice place. You'd like it."

"How about tonight?" my mother suggested.

"Hold on there," I said, holding up a hand. "Mom, we're having dinner with Maddie tonight."

"Then we'll have it with Lance's mom too. Lance, would you like to join us?"

Lance beamed from ear to ear. "Love to." He made a face. "But unfortunately, I have other plans, so I'll have to take a raincheck."

What was happening? Why had she invited Lance? Why didn't my mother want to have dinner with just Maddie and me?

A smug smile lit up my mother's face. "I'm going to take you up on it. I have to confess, I'm intrigued by this mystery woman. Maddie."

The way she said Maddie's name put me on edge. I'd thought she'd genuinely wanted to meet her, but now I was second guessing her intentions. My mother wasn't devious, but I knew she didn't want me getting too involved with a woman from Cockamamie, especially one who had roots here. She'd been very straightforward about the fact that her goal was to get me back to Memphis.

Maybe I should reconsider this dinner.

"Maddie's been great for him," Lance said, sensing the shift. "She's really brought him out of his moody shell."

"How could I disapprove of a woman who could perform *that* miracle?" my mother asked, but she didn't look entirely on board.

"I'm sitting right here," I said in a droll tone.

Lance laughed, then he and my mother launched into more stories about me, from the way my palate had changed after stalking the coffee shop while I was pining (Lance's word) for Maddie, to how I'd sworn I wouldn't become a cop like my father then turned out to be a damn good one. (My mother's story, although Lance added the last part.)

After about ten minutes, I'd had enough.

"Lance," I grunted. "Didn't you come here for a reason other than swapping stories about me with my mother?"

He let out an exaggerated sigh. "He's right, I did." He glanced around. "Is there somewhere private we can go?"

He knew damn well there wasn't, but it was his not-so-subtle way of telling her we needed privacy.

"I think I've made a decent enough grocery list that I can head to the store while you two talk," she said, getting up and walking over to the coat tree next to the front door. She grabbed her coat and picked up her purse. "I'll get some bandages for your arm, Noah. You only have small bandages for your gunshot wound."

"It's two tiny holes," I protested, "and you don't have to do either of those things. Mom, I'm perfectly capable of getting my own food and bandages."

She gave me a dark look. "Your pantry says otherwise." Then she walked out the door.

"I like your mom," Lance said with a laugh.

"I'm sure you do," I said dryly as I watched her walk to her car through the windows. "She likes you too."

"Of course she does," Lance said. "All moms like me. I'm a likable guy."

"Humble too. Now tell me what's up."

He leaned forward, turning serious. "One of the guys on patrol caught a kid stealing a car last night. We've got him in holding."

"You haven't interviewed him yet?"

"Nope. We're letting him sweat a bit. I thought you might want to be part of it."

I nearly jumped up to head to the station, then thought better of it. "As much as I'd like to, I can't. The chief would kill me. Is Cuso going to conduct the interview?"

Lance swallowed. "No. He's busy on something else. Chief wants me to do it. Alone."

Now I understood why he was here. "You've got this, Lance."

"Do I?" He looked like he was about to be sick. "This is important. The department's been trying to pin something big on the Brawlers for years. If they're involved, this could be our big chance."

I snorted. "While I agree it's an opportunity, I highly doubt the department's tried to nail them in the past. I'd be surprised if Bergan hadn't been on their payroll. If so, he would have destroyed everything he had on them before entering St. Vincent's."

"All the more reason not to fuck this up. We can make up for past mistakes."

"You won't fuck it up," I assured him. "And you know I'm not one to blow smoke up your ass. You've been with me on multiple interviews over the past few months. You led questioning on the last few and were great at it. You know what to do, but if you want to tell me your strategy, I'll share my thoughts."

We spent the next five minutes discussing his plan of attack, and after I gave him a few minor suggestions, I said, "You're ready for this. When you're done, let me know what you find out."

"You still planning to contact the county crime lab?"

"Yeah. I planned on calling, but I think I'll pay them a visit in person instead."

"There's a good chance the department sent everything to the state lab."

"On this case?" I asked. "Not likely. Bergan tried to lock it down as best he could." A new thought hit me. "Why don't you take a look at the evidence we got from Bergan's contact and tell me what you think."

"Me?" he asked in surprise.

I was already getting out of my chair. "You might notice something I didn't."

Although I'd spent a good half hour examining all three items last night after my mother had gone to bed, I'd come up with nothing.

The box was on my dresser, and my house was so small it took me all of about five seconds to grab it and hand it to Lance.

"White rabbit?" he asked, reading the side.

"Yeah. I have no idea what it means. Could have already been on the box, but it looks like Bergan's handwriting." We'd looked at enough of his notes on the cases in the storage unit for both of us to know.

"Yeah, agreed," Lance said. "Mind if I get out my phone and jot down some notes?"

"Definitely not."

He pulled up his note-taking app and typed on it, then took a photo of the outside of the box.

"Was there anything related to *Alice in Wonderland* happening in town around them?" I asked. "Like a play, or maybe they were reading it in her class?"

Lance shook his head. "I couldn't tell you. I didn't pay much attention to the plays, and I wasn't in any of her classes. She taught sophomores."

"I can ask Maddie," I said. "Or some of her teacher friends. I'm going to try to set up some interviews for after Maddie gets off work. She sent me a list of people to reach out to."

"You're going to let her sit in on them?" he asked in surprise.

"I'm on leave," I said. "I'm not supposed to be investigating anything. I'm just going with Maddie."

Mischievousness washed over his face. "That sounds like a very un-Noah Langley-like thing to do. I approve."

I shook my head, then picked up the bag with the key, handing it to him. "It looks like a house key, but I doubt it went to her house."

"Did Bergan say why he held onto it?"

"No. I plan on asking her friends about it. Maybe one of them gave it to her to water their plants or watch their pets while they were on a trip."

"Yeah, maybe." But he sounded less than convinced. I didn't think it squared either, but I believed in chasing down every possibility.

Next I showed him the note.

"So we were right. She was set up," he said, taking the bag.

"Looks like it."

"Did Maddie recognize the handwriting?"

"No."

"It's like looking for a needle in a haystack. It would help if we could get DNA analysis done."

"Good luck getting *that* approved," I said. "We'll try some other leads first."

I handed it to him and pulled out the bag with the necklace.

"Shit," Lance said when he saw the bloody chain. "Maddie saw this?"

My stomach roiled. "Yeah."

"And that's the eagle Bergan mentioned?"

"Appears to be. He said Andrea was holding it when she was found. Does it look familiar?"

He took the bag and studied the pendent, then shook his head. "No."

I sighed. "It was a long shot that any of this would mean

anything to you. I'm really hoping we'll get more from the teachers Maddie's mother worked with."

"If I can help, let me know. This case is personal to me too."

I gave him a grim look. "I know. Thanks."

Lance stood. "Let's see if I can go crack this kid."

I laughed as I stood and clapped his shoulder. "You've got this."

I had no doubt that he did. It was *my* investigation I was worried about. This was a nearly two-decade-old cold case. People with information might have died or moved away. We were starting at practically square one, and unless the county and state crime lab came through, we had very little to go on. But I'd do anything to find the murderer. Maddie deserved for the killer to be brought to justice.

So did Andrea Baker.

Chapter Eleven

Maddie

Noah walked into Déjà Brew a few minutes before three, looking just as fine as he had the day before, maybe more so since he was smiling. It had been a long, exhausting day, and I'd second-guessed my decision to work. My mind kept circling around the things tucked into that box—the last pieces of my mother.

I'd just finished making a drink for a customer, so I started making Noah's usual Americano.

He sauntered over to the counter and gave me a long, appreciative look.

I cocked my head. "Does that look mean you're happy to see me? Or that you're excited to see I'm making your drink before you even ordered?"

"You, of course," he said, his eyes warm. "You still good for dinner tonight?"

Nerves twinged at the back of my neck. "Yeah. Mallory said she can stay in with Aunt Deidre."

"Do you mind if we eat at Lance's mother's tavern?"

My brow shot up. "No, but does that mean he's going to be joining us?"

"God, I hope not. He says he has plans. My mom wants to meet Matilda, so this way she figures she can meet both of you at once."

Did she feel like she needed a buffer?

"We don't have a definitive time," Noah continued. "I told her I was working on something and didn't know how late I would be, so I'll just text her when we figure it out."

"Okay." I looked over my shoulder toward the back. "As usual, I'm waiting for Trista to show up."

He rested a hand on the counter, looking more relaxed than I'd ever seen him. Was it because he wasn't working? "We're good on time. Our first interview is with Dawn Heaton."

I poured hot water into his cup, briefly lifting my gaze to meet his before returning to my task. Dawn had been my mother's closest friend at the school. "I already talked to her when you were investigating who killed Martin Schroeder."

"I know, but I think you should circle back to her. If I remember right, you were talking to her specifically about Schroeder," Noah said. "Maybe if you broaden the scope of the conversation, she'll have more information."

My head jerked up. "Wait. *Me?*"

"Since this is unofficial..."

I nodded, grateful that he was giving me an active role in this investigation. Somehow he knew I needed to feel like I was a part of this—like I was doing something that would make a difference. Plus, he'd be there to ensure I didn't screw anything up.

"Start with her personal life. The killer may not have had any connection to the school. Maybe they saw an opportunity and took it."

I inwardly cringed. I knew I had to harden my sensitivities to get through this. "Did you find out anything from the crime lab?"

A scowl darkened his eyes. "No. They had next to nothing. I went in person and talked to someone who worked for the lab when your mother was murdered. They remembered the case, but they say they weren't called in to handle the scene."

"What?" I practically shouted in disbelief, then checked around the room to make sure I hadn't disturbed anyone. I lowered my voice and leaned closer. "How can that be? Isn't that protocol?"

"You would think, but I've come to learn that the police department did pretty much whatever they damn well pleased before Chief Porter came on board a few years ago."

"So there's absolutely no evidence other than what we have?"

"Other than a few photos that were passed on to the lab tech, no." When Noah saw the defeat in my eyes, he said, "We might be down, but we're not out, Maddie. We still have a lot of options. And this way, Bergan and his ilk won't taint anything we learn."

Trista popped out of the back and leaned against the counter, appraising Noah with a focused gaze. "You becoming a regular?"

"He *has* been a regular," I said as I handed Noah his cup.

"I come for the coffee and my adorable girlfriend," Noah said. "Maddie, you ready to take off?"

I stared up at him in surprise. Girlfriend? It didn't seem like our "just friends" relationship status warranted it, but I had to admit I liked hearing him call me that.

Dawn was in her classroom when we arrived in the doorway a few minutes early. She sat at her desk in front of a stack of papers. She was so lost in her work I had to knock on the door frame to get her attention.

She glanced up with an anxious look and stood. "Maddie. Detective Langley. Come on in." She gestured to a table in the back of the room. "Let's sit back here."

We followed her to the small rectangular table. There was a

chair on one side and two on the other. Once we were all settled, she folded her hands on her lap, then gave me a disappointed look. "Detective Langley said you both would like to ask more questions about your mother. I have to say, I'm surprised. I thought the case was closed."

"It is," Noah said. "And call me Noah, please. I'm not here in an official capacity. Maddie has a lot of questions about her mother, and as Maddie's boyfriend, I'm here to offer moral support." He reached over and clasped my hand.

A shiver ran down my back at his touch. He declared us to be in a relationship again, but this time I suspected it helped sell the unofficial status of our investigation.

Dawn's face lit up. "Oh. That's surprising. You were the detective investigating Martin Schroeder's murder."

Noah shrugged. "Maddie's a special woman. I know we met under unusual circumstances, but..." He gave me a soft smile. "Sometimes you know when you have to get to know someone more, no matter how you met."

My stomach somersaulted, and I told myself this was still part of the act, but I knew that he was being sincere.

Dawn nodded, but she didn't necessarily look like she approved, which surprised me. It also hurt a tiny bit. It felt like her approval or lack thereof equaled my mother's.

"I appreciate you talking to us," I said, eager to change the subject. "I'll try not to keep you long."

"Don't be silly," Dawn said, smoothing a wrinkle out of her pants. "Of course you're curious about your mother. I'm surprised you haven't asked questions before now." She hesitated, then added, "Without a detective."

Noah dropped my hand. "I can leave if that makes you feel more comfortable."

Dawn hesitated. "No, you can stay. I'm sorry. It's just the last time either of you were in the school, it was because of Martin, and we were all so certain he'd killed Andrea that it dredged up a lot of unpleasant memories."

"I understand," Noah said, "but please just think of me as Maddie's boyfriend."

Her lips pressed into a tight line. "I'll try."

I flashed a look at Noah. He gave a slight nod of encouragement, and I turned back to face her. "Dawn, it occurred to me that I was a typical teenager who paid little attention to her mother's life. I'm now closer to the age she was when she died, and it's become obvious to me that she had a life outside of me that I know nothing about. Since you were her best friend, I hoped you could help fill in the gaps."

The tension in her shoulders eased. "Of course, but we could have met at my house for that." She shot a glance at Noah, then turned back to me. "And you could have arranged it yourself."

She was right, of course. No wonder she struggled to believe this was an unofficial investigation. But even if we were asking questions about the murder, why would it make her nervous? "Sorry about that," I said apologetically. "Noah has the week off and was trying to be helpful since I had to work today. He's here for emotional support."

"Hmm," she said, obviously still not entirely buying it, but she settled back in her chair. "What would you like to know?"

"When did you and Mom become friends? When she began teaching?"

She laughed. "Good heavens, no. We had known each other since we were practically in diapers. We went to church together, then school and college. We even got jobs together. I knew Andrea her entire life."

I stared at her, trying to wrap my head around what she'd just said. I'd had no idea they'd known each other that long. Then again,

I couldn't remember much about my mother's life outside of me. Was it because I'd been that self-centered as a kid, or had I blanked it out? But another thought occurred to me. "So you were already good friends with my mom when my father left." I knew next to nothing about my father other than what little my mother told me. It occurred to me that Dawn might be able to fill in some of those gaps too, even though I'd never been very curious about him. Mom had told me he'd left us when I was a tiny baby, and that had been enough to convince me I didn't want anything to do with him. Especially since he hadn't stepped forward or even gotten in touch with me after she was killed.

Dawn gave me a grim smile. "Tony was never meant to be domesticated, and deep down, Andrea knew it. They met in college. He was from money, and his family didn't like that she wasn't. In the beginning, he didn't care. Then again, neither one of them was thinking about forever. Andrea was a free spirit and didn't want to be painted in by convention. Tony was intrigued by her. She was different than the usual girls he dated, and her wildness fascinated him."

"Wildness?" I was even more shocked. "My mother was the last person I would describe as wild."

Dawn waved a hand in dismissal. "That's because you didn't know her when she was young. She changed after you were born. She took her role as your parent very seriously. Tony didn't, unfortunately. He only married your mother because his family insisted when they found out Andrea was pregnant, which is part of the reason the marriage didn't last long. I also think he was taken aback by how much she changed. His free-spirited, rebellious lover had been replaced by a mother." She gave an exaggerated shudder.

"They were married?" I asked in shock. "I didn't know that. I always thought she got pregnant, and Tony didn't want to be part of our lives."

She shrugged. "Truth was, he didn't want to be, but even assholes can be pressured into doing things they don't want to do. Only he couldn't be pressured for long. You were only a few months old when Tony took off, so your mother returned to Cockamamie."

I blinked hard. "I wasn't born here? She said we'd always lived here."

"She preferred to think of it that way. She lived with Tony in Nashville in a cute little house his parents bought for the three of you. But once Tony left, she came back home and pretended he'd never been part of your lives, like you were immaculately conceived."

"And she took back her maiden name?" Noah asked.

A mischievous grin lit up Dawn's face. "She never took his to begin with, and she insisted that Maddie have her last name on her birth certificate. His parents were furious."

"What about Tony?" Noah asked. "Did that piss him off too?"

"Honestly, if he cared, it was only because of his parents. By the time Maddie was born, I think Andrea could tell it wasn't going to last, and she didn't want her daughter to be like her in-laws, so she insisted on making you a Baker."

"She never talked about my father," I said in disbelief. It was like a whole new reality had been opened to me. "I knew his name, that they'd met in college, and that he didn't want to be part of our lives. That was it."

Dawn gave me an earnest look. "That's all she *wanted* you to know."

"What about Tony's parents?" Noah asked. "If they insisted on Tony marrying Andrea, did they try to be part of Maddie's life?"

"I don't know," Dawn said. "Andrea never mentioned any of them again."

"What about financial support?" Noah asked. "Either from Tony or his parents?"

She shrugged. “Andrea refused to talk about it. I know money was tight for her. She lived with Deidre and Albert when she came back, but their father died soon after, and Andrea bought a small house with the money she got from her father’s estate. She never made much as a teacher, but she never complained about not having enough money.”

“So it’s possible someone was giving her support,” Noah suggested.

“I suppose. But if she’d been getting any kind of child support, I think she would have told me.”

“Did she have boyfriends after Tony left?” Noah asked. “Any serious relationships?”

Dawn shifted in her seat. “No. She said she didn’t want to introduce a man as a father figure into Maddie’s life only to potentially lose him, so she never really dated much.”

“Really?” Noah countered, sounding incredulous. “From the photos I’ve seen, she was a beautiful woman. She surely dated from time to time, even if she hid it from Maddie.”

Dawn glanced out the window to the parking lot with a faraway expression. “No. She didn’t date.”

Noah turned to me with a pointed look, which I interpreted to mean he thought she was lying, and it was up to me whether or not I wanted to press it.

I didn’t have to consider it long. I was here for answers, regardless of whether I liked them.

“Dawn.” I said softly. “I know my mother wasn’t perfect. I’ve heard she didn’t have a single enemy in town.”

“Well, that’s not entirely true. She and that woman from the women’s club didn’t get along. She got Andrea kicked out of the club and took over as president. I think the police may have even looked at her as a suspect, but she was in New York City that weekend, watching a Broadway show.”

I gave Noah a quick glance.

"Other than the president of the women's club," I continued, "I had the impression the entire town loved her, but the truth is, I always thought she spent more time helping the community than she did with me."

Dawn's eyes widened in dismay.

"In fact, I told her so the night she was murdered. She was always running off to help some organization or person in need, and I felt neglected. That night, I asked her to stay. She said she couldn't, so I accused her of caring about everyone else but me. The joke was on me, though, because that's why she was supposedly at the school. Trying to help me."

That's why she'd asked for a meeting with Schroeder that night—not just because she'd heard the rumors about him, but because she was worried he might be molesting me.

Dawn looked uncomfortable. "Maddie. I had *no* idea..."

I steeled myself. I didn't want her sympathy. I wanted answers. "I know she was part of the women's club, but what else was she involved in? Maybe I'll understand if I knew what was so important to her that she left me so much."

Tears flooded Dawn's eyes. "I'm sorry. I don't remember."

"Please," I begged. "Anything would help."

"It's been too long," Dawn said, wiping tears from her cheeks. "I don't remember."

Noah reached over and placed a hand on my thigh but kept his gaze on Dawn. "That's okay," he assured her. "It's been twenty years. Of course you forgot some details." He gave her a smile. "Is there anything else you can remember for Maddie? Anything at all?"

Dawn was silent for a few seconds, then sniffed. "You were her life, Maddie. She loved you with everything in her being." Fresh tears slid down her face. "Even if you felt differently. I promise she loved you more than anything."

"Thank you." And I was grateful for what she'd told me, but I also knew she was lying. Dawn knew more about my mother than she was telling me. The question was, what was I going to do about it?

Chapter Twelve

Maddie

We left Dawn soon after that. Noah gave her his card on the way out, telling her to contact him if she ever thought of anything either of us might want to know.

We headed down the hall before I stopped, pressed my back to the wall, and closed my eyes, taking several deep breaths. I was close to crying, but I knew Noah had another interview set up. "We're meeting with Rebecca Hennessy next?"

Noah wrapped his arms around my back and pulled me to his chest, tucking my head under his chin. I told myself it was okay if he hugged me. Friends offered hugs when they were in pain. But I couldn't ignore the fact that he'd been declaring himself my boyfriend. With Dawn, I could see it as part of the ruse for him being with me while I asked questions. But he didn't need a reason with Trista.

I liked him claiming me, a little too much. It gave me hope that we really could make this work.

He held me for several seconds before saying, "I'm sorry if I talked too much. I said I would let you ask the questions, but I jumped in anyway."

"No," I said, my voice muffled as I pressed my cheek to his shirt. "I'm glad you asked. Thank you."

"That had to be hard. She told us some difficult things."

"I'm more upset by the things she refused to say."

He pulled back slightly, studying my face. "You caught it too."

"I'd have to have been on the other side of town to miss it. I just can't put my finger on what she was leaving out."

"I think your mom had a boyfriend she never told you about."

"I know that's what she implied, but I don't see how," I said, pulling out of his embrace. "There were never any men."

"Dawn said your mom didn't want to introduce men to you. It doesn't mean she wasn't meeting them somewhere else. Your mom was beautiful, and she was pretty young. Not only would she have attracted men's attention, but she probably wanted it too."

I shook my head. "No. Not my mom."

"Dawn said she had a wild streak before she had you. It's not an easy trait to smother." He paused and seemed to choose his words carefully. "What if she just didn't date anyone seriously enough to want to introduce them to you?"

I narrowed my eyes. "Are you calling my mother a slut, Noah Langley?"

He held up his hands in defense. "Far be it from me to judge someone's sex life or lack thereof. I'm saying that Dawn said she didn't want you to meet the men she dated. For all we know, she could have had many boyfriends or one-night stands." He paused again. "Remember how I told you the crime lab had photos of the scene? The tech showed them to me. Whoever killed your mother didn't do it in cold blood. It was vicious."

The hall spun slightly, and I reached out and grabbed fistfuls of Noah's shirt to stay upright. His arm returned behind my back, holding me with gentle pressure.

"Sorry. I should have phrased that differently."

I shook my head. "No. I want to hear the truth, even when it's hard." I drew in a breath. "So you think one of her many boyfriends could have killed her. I may not be a cop, but it sounds like you're talking about a crime of passion."

He nodded slightly. "She was raped, stabbed, *and* strangled. Whoever killed her was furious." He tugged me a little closer. "It could have been a spurned lover. I think that's one possibility we need to pursue."

"What about the president of the women's club?"

"It's worth looking into, but given the fact your mother was raped and the president was out of town, likely confirmed, it seems weak."

"And the other possibilities?"

"We need to look into Tony and his family."

"Why? I never met my father *or* his family. Aunt Deidre said the authorities contacted him after Mom was killed about taking custody of me, and he refused. What possible motivation would they have had to kill my mother?"

"You were close to finishing your sophomore year. College was on the horizon. Dawn said you were the most important thing in her life. What if she was trying to make sure financial constraints weren't holding you back from going to the school of your choice? She might have asked them for money and pissed them off."

"I doubt that's likely," I said. "I'd planned to go to Knoxville. That's where my mother went and apparently met Tony. It's a state school. I would have probably needed loans, but I could have done it."

"How did you afford it after she died?"

"The proceeds from the sale of our house and my aunt and uncle. But I got loans for my master's in library science."

He stared at the wall behind my head. "Let's go talk to Rebecca Hennessy and then the next teacher on the list."

"Okay."

Noah had arranged for us to meet Ms. Hennessy, a history

teacher, at her home at four-thirty and then Carolyn Dunhurst at five-thirty at Déjà Brew. Neither interview was eventful. Both teachers remembered my mother fondly and extolled her virtues as a teacher and as a person. Noah asked Ms. Hennessy about my mother's volunteer projects, but she couldn't remember anything about them other than she was always quick to volunteer to stay after school to give students extra help. Ms. Dunhurst said she remembered the women's club and that my mother was always willing to take part in teacher skits for assemblies. Neither woman could remember my mother having a boyfriend. Other than Martin Schroeder, neither one could think of anyone who'd even disliked her.

After Ms. Dunhurst walked out of the coffee shop, Noah and I sat in silence as we took in what we'd just heard: a whole lot of nothing.

"The only person who told us anything useful was Dawn," I said in frustration. "That was pointless."

"No, it wasn't," Noah said earnestly. "All three teachers said pretty much the same thing about her, so we know it's probably true. It's good to have a story corroborated by multiple sources." He rested his forearm on the table as he turned to face me. "Did you go to church when you were a kid?"

"Everyone who had the slightest bit of character went to church. You were definitely looked down on if you didn't."

"So, did you go to church?" he asked with a deadpan look, then grinned.

"You're the worst," I said with a laugh, and I felt dangerously close to kissing him. This was the Noah I loved, the carefree happy man who wasn't running from me.

I sat back because Noah *did* run, and while I'd promised to wait while he did, now that I'd experienced three weeks of it, I wasn't sure I could deal with it again. One night? Sure, I'd need a night away from time to time, but not lengthy breaks, and right now, he couldn't promise that he wouldn't run.

"So what now?" I asked.

He noticed my change in demeanor, and some of the sparkle left his eyes, almost making me regret my decision to pull back. Almost.

"I have nothing else scheduled for today other than the dinner with my mom." He glanced at his phone. "It's nearly six. We should figure out a time to meet her."

"I need to go home and change," I said. "I'm wearing jeans and a sweater that smells like coffee."

"I like that you smell like coffee. It's one of my favorite scents."

I laughed, letting some of my hesitation fade. "So now I know what reeled you in. It wasn't my charming personality or my looks. It was my aroma."

"Not true," he teased, leaning back in his seat, and looking like he was in no hurry to leave. "I was captivated by both, but I'm not complaining about your perfume either."

"Well, I doubt your mother will be so appreciative."

"I'm not so sure about that. She can appreciate a good cup of coffee and is not-so-secretly thrilled at my expanding coffee tastes which Lance attributed to you."

"Lance?" I asked with a laugh.

"He poured on the charm this morning." His smile faded slightly. "So about dinner...how does seven sound? That gives you time to change, check on your aunt, and get to the tavern."

"Sounds like a plan."

"Don't look so worried," Noah said. "My mother's going to love you."

"I'm not worried. I'm sure we'll get along just great."

I WALKED into Lucky's Tavern at 7:02, my stomach a ball of nerves. I hated being late, and I had no idea if Noah's mother would hold it against me. I may have told Noah I wasn't nervous, but that was a lie. I didn't know why, especially since the parents of my previous boyfriends had all loved me.

Noah and a middle-aged woman resembling him were sitting in a booth in the back. He'd been watching the door when I walked in, and a bright smile lit up his face. It was impossible not to smile back.

I slipped off my coat as I approached the booth and stopped next to the table. Noah had climbed out before I reached them, and he drew me in for a hug as his mother got out and stood behind him.

"You must be Maddie," she said with a smile, but I could see the reservation in her eyes. "I've heard wonderful things about you."

"I'm so thrilled to meet you, Mrs. Langley."

She chuckled and gave me a loose hug. "None of that Mrs. Langley nonsense. Call me Laura."

That had to be a good sign. "Okay, Laura."

She slid back into the seat, and I climbed in on the opposite side. Noah sat beside me, and he grabbed my hand under the table and squeezed it.

His mother's gaze was intense as she seemed to take me in. "I hear you're the person responsible for Officer Erickson calling me to say Noah had been shot."

"Mom!" Noah protested, sitting upright.

"It's okay," I said reassuringly to him, then turned back to face her. "You're his mother. You had a right to know." I grimaced. "Then again, we thought it was more serious at the time, so I apologize if we scared you. It wasn't until I practically forced myself into his ER room that I found out it was a minor injury, and I didn't think about having someone let you know he was okay. I didn't even know they'd actually called you."

She nodded, her face looking more relaxed. "I appreciate that you were making sure I was in the loop. Noah would never have let me know otherwise. Or at least until a few years from now, when I noticed the scars on his arm. So thank you." She nodded, a soft smile easing the tension in her body even more.

"You're welcome," I said, relief pouring through me. "I'm sure Noah didn't want to worry you. I know he feels terribly for everything you and your family went through after he was shot last year."

Crap. Wrong thing to say. The color drained from her face, and the tension was immediately back. "Yes." She sipped her water before setting the glass on the table, her hand shaking slightly. "It was extremely traumatic. We didn't think he was going to make it."

"I'm fine, Mom," Noah said with a sigh. "Then *and* now. Have you looked at the menu? Everything is good here."

Laura ignored him. "Tell me about yourself, Maddie. Noah tells me you're an Uber driver. That must be...different." I was sure she was trying to hide her disapproval, but she didn't quite make it.

"Mom," Noah interjected, sounding angry. "I told you she was a barista."

"That's okay," I said. "I'm actually both. And yes, it's different. I meet a lot of interesting people."

"Including that man you brought to his murder," she said disapprovingly.

Noah's face reddened. "Mom!"

"Which is also true," I said, giving Noah a pointed look before turning back to his mother. "I'm sure I'll be written up in the Uber monthly newsletter at some point since it has to be pretty rare. I don't foresee it ever happening again."

Her jaw dropped. "They have a monthly newsletter?"

I shifted in my seat. "Uh...no. That was my lame attempt at a joke." This was *not* going well. Could I walk out and come back in and start over?

"Matilda makes a great bangers and mash," Noah said in a rush. "Her mother was from Manchester, England, so she makes a lot of English food."

His mother ignored him. "Maddie, I hear your mother was murdered when you were a girl. That's quite tragic."

I swallowed, taken aback that she'd brought it up so bluntly. "Yes, it was. I was sixteen when it happened."

"Here in Cockamamie?"

"Yes."

"And it happened in her classroom? I heard she was a teacher."

I shot a glance at Noah, who looked just as confused as I felt.

"And then you were caught up in a young woman's murder last December," she continued. "A woman who was in a self-defense class you were leading?"

Noah stared at his mother like she'd grown three heads.

"Yes." I wasn't sure what she was working toward, but I doubted it was anything good. My mouth felt dry, and only two water glasses sat on the table.

"Your mother, your Uber passenger, then a woman in a self-defense class?" She twisted her lips to one side. "Death seems to follow you around."

"Mom," Noah protested in frustration. "Are you suggesting that Maddie instigated any of those situations?"

"Of course not, but I'm sure I'm not the only one to make such correlations. Especially since you were just shot a couple of days ago."

"What has gotten into you?" Noah spat out. "If you can't be nice, then Maddie and I are leaving."

"It's okay," I said because I *did* believe her statements and questions were coming from a place of motherly concern. "I can assure you, other than my mother's murder and the two incidents in November and December, I lead a pretty boring life. I used to be a middle school librarian." I reached over and picked up Noah's water glass. "Can't get much more boring than that."

I was pissed at myself for calling my librarian job boring. I'd loved my job, but I knew how most people saw it, and I was trying to convince Noah's mother that I wasn't dangerous to her son....which should have been amusing considering he was the police detective.

Matilda bustled over to the table, her cheeks red from the heat of the kitchen. "Laura Langley," she said as she approached. "I'm so pleased to meet you. I'm Matilda Forrester."

Laura got out of the booth again and gave the woman a warm hug. "I've heard a lot about you the past few days. I hear you're the person who's keeping my son from clogging his arteries with frozen and fast food."

Noah rolled his eyes. "You make it sound like I'm the kid from *Home Alone* eating a bunch of junk food."

His mother lifted her brow. "If the shoe fits..."

Matilda laughed and pointed a finger at him. "She's got you pegged." Turning back to face Laura, she said, "I hear you met my boy, Lance, this morning."

"I did," Laura said with bright eyes. "Lovely young man. So respectful. You raised him right."

"I could say the same to you," Matilda said, winking at Noah.

"Oh, for heaven's sake," he grumbled under his breath, taking the glass of water from me and taking several gulps.

"Well. I'm honored to meet you," Laura said, then gazed around the room. "And your tavern is lovely."

"Thanks. It wasn't always easy while raising all my kids. Still, it paid all those grocery and orthodontist bills after their rotten daddy took off."

"I'm so sorry," Laura said, sounding like she genuinely meant it. So it was just me she'd taken a kneejerk dislike to. Fantastic.

"Water under the bridge," Matilda said, shaking her head. "He's someone else's problem now, bless her heart." Matilda studied the table and frowned with displeasure. "That Janie's fallin' down on the job. There's only two water glasses and two sets of silverware."

"She was waiting until Maddie got here," Noah said. "And it looks like she's had her hands full." He motioned to a table with eight men in their late twenties and early thirties who were going out of their way to flirt with the pretty waitress, but a couple of them looked like they were being a little handsy.

A dour look pinched Matilda's face. "If you'll excuse me, I'm gonna have to put the fear of Matilda into a few men."

"Of course," Laura said.

Matilda waddled over and leaned over the table, pointing her finger in a few men's faces and lecturing them in a tone too low for us to hear. A few seconds later, their gaze landed on an elderly man on a barstool at the counter. Their attention shifted back to Matilda, all the men nodding with looks of terror on their faces.

Matilda came back, grinning from ear to ear. "We should be good now. Janie'll be over in a few minutes." She started to walk away.

"Wait," Noah called after her. "What did you tell them?"

Her brow rose. "I told 'em if they didn't treat my waitress with respect, I was gonna pull their balls out through their ears and, if they didn't believe me, they could look at Tim over on the stool." Chuckling, she headed back to the kitchen.

Noah burst out laughing, but I struggled to hold back my own laughter because Laura didn't seem amused. Tim was a regular who had moved to Tennessee after living in Alaska for forty years. He'd suffered frostbite on his ears and lost part of his earlobes. What he did still have was swollen and misshapen. Matilda's threat might have been cruel if George weren't constantly telling strangers horrific and not-so-horrific completely false explanations of what had happened.

I *loved* Matilda.

Janie came over with another water glass, apologizing profusely. Since Noah and I had both been there several times, we already knew what we wanted. Laura quickly glanced at the menu and ordered a chef's salad.

Once Janie walked away with our menus and order, Laura

returned her attention to me. "I hear you have an elderly aunt who's unwell."

So the interrogation had resumed.

Noah sighed, but I answered Laura's questions about Aunt Deidre for the next few minutes.

"I hear she might be moving into a nursing home," Laura said. "Would you still feel tied to Cockamamie?"

Laura's questions confirmed what I already suspected. I knew she wanted Noah to move back to Memphis. His feelings for a woman tied to this town only complicated things. It was little wonder she was acting hostile.

"My aunt will go into a care facility. It's just a matter of timing at this point. When that happens, there's a good chance she won't know me anymore. I'll have to sell her house to help pay for her care, so I'll be looking for somewhere to live. I'm just not sure where yet. My friend Mallory suggested Chattanooga, because it's only forty to forty-five minutes away, and I might be able to get a librarian job there."

Noah looked surprised but didn't say anything.

"They have excellent nursing homes in Memphis," Laura said. "I'd be happy to look into a few for you."

"Mom," Noah cut in. "I'm not going back to Memphis."

Her icy gaze landed on him. "Your family is there."

Noah squeezed my hand under the table. "My family is where I decide it is." He forced a smile. "Now, tell me about my favorite niece and nephew."

"You only have one niece and nephew," his mother said tightly.

"They're still my favorite. Did they ever build that giant Lego set they got for Christmas?"

The rest of dinner was so tense you could have bounced a quarter off the vibes our table had to be exuding. A couple of times, I was sure Noah was going to get up and end dinner, food unfinished, but I kept squeezing his hand and knee under the table. His mother was obviously threatened by me, which I strangely understood.

Was it wrong that it filled me with reassurance about Noah's feelings for me that she thought I could influence his decision?

By the time we finished, Laura was quiet for a few moments before pausing and offering me an apologetic look. "I'm sorry if I've come across as difficult."

"Come across?" Noah stated bluntly.

I offered her a weak smile. "It's very obvious you love your son, Mrs. Langley," I said, purposely using her formal name, "and it's equally obvious that you don't think I'm good enough for him."

Noah's mother started to protest, but I held up a hand to stop her.

"Mom, let her finish," Noah barked.

I took a moment to get myself together. "I really care about your son, Mrs. Langley, and while you find me lacking, he doesn't." I looked up at him with a grim smile, then turned back to her. "I can't promise you that I won't put Noah in danger, just like I can't promise I won't get hit by a bus tomorrow."

Janie crept toward the table and slipped the check onto it, her body bent forward. "You're lucky we don't have any buses in Cockamamie," she said softly, then cringed as though realizing she probably should have kept that to herself. She lowered her head to Noah's eye level and added, "You can pay at the counter when you're ready so I don't bother y'all again." Then she turned and hurried to customers two tables away.

"I think I've said all that needs to be said," I continued, "other than this: Noah is a good man, and I'm grateful to have him in my life. I will do everything in my power to make sure he doesn't get hurt—physically or emotionally—and that's all I can promise." I gave Noah a slight shove, and he moved out of the seat. Grabbing my coat and purse, I slid out. "I'll talk to you later."

I headed for the exit, ready to burst into tears, but he stopped me a few feet from the door.

"Maddie, I'm *so* sorry. I've *never* seen her behave this way. Let me walk you out," he pleaded, concern in his eyes.

"No, stay with your mother. I think she needs you right now."

"Are you kidding me? After the way she just treated you? She'll be lucky if I let her sleep in my house tonight."

I put a hand on his chest. "She's scared she's going to lose you to me. Just reassure her that it's not true."

I stretched up and kissed him lightly, then headed out into the cold night.

I needed a glass of wine, a hot bath, and a good cry.

Chapter Thirteen

Noah

I took a small amount of reassurance from the fact that Maddie had kissed me on the way out, but I couldn't help thinking it was partially habit. Months ago, I would have scoffed at the idea that kissing someone for only a few weeks could turn into a habit, but I felt exactly the same way. I'd had to force myself *not* to kiss her all afternoon and evening. I'd found myself touching her most of the night.

Now, after my mother's performance, there was a strong likelihood she'd never kiss me again.

I returned to the table, snatched the bill off the counter, and paid it at the bar. My mother was still in her seat when I went back to grab my coat.

"We're leaving."

She looked up at me with wide eyes. "I thought we could get a drink and discuss dinner."

Gritting my teeth, I said, "I think this is a discussion better suited for somewhere private."

She heaved out a breath. "Noah, if you'd just—"

"I'll be waiting in the car." I couldn't stand there one more moment and pretend, so I spun around and headed out the door.

The engine was running when my mother came out and climbed into her seat. I waited until she shut the door before I started in on her.

"What the hell was *that*?" I was so furious I had to spit the words out through my teeth. I pulled out of the parking space and turned onto the street.

"I was asking questions," she said primly. "I'm sorry if you disapproved."

"That wasn't asking questions. That was an *attack*." I was furious with my mother, but even more so at myself. I'd assured Maddie that my mother would love her, and she'd treated her like shit. I should have gotten her out of there as soon as my mother started in.

"She's a nice girl, Noah, but she's not right for you," my mother insisted. "After everything you've been through, you deserve better."

"Bull-fucking-shit," I spat, my anger rising. "You are *not* the judge of who is or isn't good enough for me. And even if you were, you'd have to be blind not to see how special Maddie is."

"She has so much *baggage*, Noah."

"*And I don't?*"

"That's different."

I shook my head in disbelief. "Are you kidding me right now?" I turned a corner and continued driving. "Maddie's like a ray of sunshine cutting through the fog I've been shrouded in. Her belief in me is more than I've ever felt from—"

"Don't you dare say I never believed in you!" she shouted.

"I was going to say *my father*."

That shut her up.

I took a deep breath and held it to try to settle down, then lowered my voice. Shouting wasn't going to get her to listen to me. "I like her, Mom. A lot. If anything, I'm not good enough for *her*."

"That's nonsense," she snorted.

"Just admit that you don't like her because you think I won't come back to Memphis if I'm seeing Maddie."

"You *won't* come back! I saw the way you were looking at her, Noah. You never once looked at Monica like that. And from what I can tell," she continued, "that woman is good and stuck here until her aunt dies, as morbid as that is. What happens when you have babies? When will I ever see them?"

"*Babies?*" I choked out. "I've already told you I don't want kids." I wasn't about to tell her that Maddie had me reconsidering that decision. Right now, I didn't feel she deserved to know.

"A woman like Maddie is going to want babies," my mother said. "She has maternal instinct written all over her." She paused. "Have you told her you claim you don't want children?"

"She knows," I said, a tightness building in my chest.

"And she's okay with that?" she asked in disbelief.

"We're still discussing it."

"Then you're wasting her time," my mother declared, pity heavy in her tone. "It seems to me she's been through enough without you misleading her."

"*Enough,* Mom. One minute, you're telling me she's not good enough for me and the next you accuse me of lying to her."

"Not lying. Giving her false hope."

I turned to her, staring in disbelief. "What the hell has happened to you? Where is the woman who raised me?"

Tears filled her eyes. "I've learned I have to fight for what I want."

"Did you learn this lesson from *Dad*? If so, you picked the wrong battle. I'm *never* going to give him what he wants."

Did she even know what he wanted?

Mom started to cry. "You're right. I wasn't myself tonight. I was positively awful to Maddie. She seems like a very lovely girl, but I still don't think she's right for you, Noah."

"And someone like Monica is?" I asked dryly.

"No, of course not. Monica treated you terribly."

"Maddie would *never* treat me that way. She doesn't have it in her."

"Then maybe you should be protecting her from *you*," she said, more subdued.

My heart stumbled for a beat. I stopped at a stop sign on my street and turned to look at her. She'd just voiced my worst fear. "What?"

"You took this job to run away from the memories you left behind in Memphis. Monica and your dog and that awful boy who shot you."

"Caleb. He had a name, Mom."

"It doesn't matter; what *does* matter is that you're running away, but you can't run forever. Eventually, you'll realize what you gave up and return home. What happens to poor Maddie then?"

I turned a corner, my hands gripping the wheel so tightly I expected it to snap into pieces. "I'm not going back to Memphis."

"You *have* to come back to Memphis," she insisted.

"I am a grown fucking man. I can do whatever I want." I shot her a scathing glare. "I don't need your permission *or* approval."

"Language, Noah!" she snapped tightly. "Treat me with respect!"

"How about you start treating me and my decision with respect, then I'll show you the same courtesy?"

I pulled into my driveway, but I was so furious I wasn't sure I could sleep in the same house as her.

"You have to come home, Noah," my mother pleaded. "Your father is dying."

If she'd thought I would be surprised by her bombshell, she was about to realize her mistake. "I know."

"You *know*? How? Did your sister tell you?"

"No." I swallowed the lump in my throat. "He told me at Christmas."

"What?" She lifted a hand to her hair. "*I* didn't even know at Christmas."

"Then maybe he's not the great husband you think he is," I said with a snide tone I instantly regretted.

Her face fell.

"Mom, I'm sorry. That was uncalled for."

She wiped a tear from her cheek. "Your father wants you to come home and make things right."

"I know."

"So why are you still here?" she demanded.

"I don't owe him a damn thing. If he were to apologize, then I would come home for short trips to see him before he dies, but he's dug his feet in the sand and refuses to accept any responsibility for the state of our relationship. In fact, the word pussy was used quite a few times during our Christmas chat, and I wasn't the one who used it."

"Noah, he's scared, and he's lashing out."

"Jesus, Mom. Like you are?" I shook my head. "I have no idea who that woman was at dinner tonight, but I didn't like her much."

"I just see you slipping away..."

I drew in a breath. "Acting like you did tonight will only push me farther away."

"But your father—"

I got out of the car and walked up to the door. My mother followed behind me, climbing the steps as I unlocked the deadbolt and pushed the door open.

I couldn't look at her, so I faced the street. "Go on inside. I'm not staying here tonight."

She gasped, then said in a strangled voice, "Noah..."

I dropped my gaze to hers. "I love you, Mom, but I can't handle this right now. We won't resolve this tonight, so before I go, let me state a few things so they are perfectly clear. *One,* I will live wherever I goddamn please. *Two,* I will love whoever I goddam want, and you will treat her with respect because, I swear to God, Mom, if you try that shit with Maddie again, it won't just be Dad who doesn't see me anymore."

Her eyes widened.

"*Three*, I will not discuss Dad or his terminal prognosis with you, and I will not let it guilt me into something I don't choose. He made his fucking bed, and now he can lie in it."

I left her on the porch, mouth hanging open in shock, and drove to Lance's apartment. When he opened the door, he took one look at me, and panic washed over his face.

"Jesus, you okay? I heard things got a little rough tonight."

I ran a hand over my head, feeling more raw than I had since Caleb had shot me. "Understatement, and no, I'm not okay. Do you have any beer?"

"Yeah, come on in."

I stayed in place. "One more question: Can I stay here tonight?"

He looked even more worried. "Yeah, of course. I'm always here for you, Noah."

Lance let me inside, grabbed two beers from the fridge, and led me to the living room. I plopped onto the sofa while he took a recliner.

"What the hell happened?" he asked without preamble, which was fair given how I'd shown up at his front door.

I took a long pull from my beer before I answered, "You already said you'd heard things didn't go well."

"Not in detail, and you're stalling. Spill."

So I explained everything that had happened, including telling off my mother. The only thing I left out was our discussion about my father. By the time I finished, I'd started on a second beer.

Lance listened without comment, then said, "You're an idiot if you let Maddie go."

"I know."

"You've left that woman hanging for nearly a month, Noah, and now this?"

My gut clenched, and I felt a cold sweat break out across my forehead. "I know it's bad."

"You've been different since you came back from your trip home. It's like you had a personality transplant."

"It's not that bad," I grumbled, taking another long pull from my beer.

"Trust me, it is. What are you going to do about your mother?"

"She obviously can't stay," I said with a sigh. "So I'll head home in the morning and tell her it's time for her to go back to Memphis."

He burst out laughing. "If I tried something like that with my mother, she'd kick my ass into next week."

I lifted a brow. "Well, Laura Langley is a completely different woman than Matilda Forrester."

"Thank God for that. There can only be one Matilda Forrester."

I held up my nearly empty beer bottle. "Amen."

We sat in silence for several long seconds before Lance broke the silence. "What are you going to do about Maddie?"

I almost told him he was out of line asking me that question, but I decided to be forthright. "Well, first I'm going to beg her forgiveness for putting her through that nightmare and pray to God that she forgives me."

"She will," he said confidently. "But what about after that?"

"I've already copped to being an asshole over the past few weeks. She's the one who wants to put our relationship on the back burner while we investigate her mother's murder. She may decide to keep it that way...except..."

He sat up straighter. "Except what?"

"She kissed me when she left."

Excitement filled his eyes. "She did?"

"Yeah..." I relived the moment in my head. "It was just a peck, but it was on the mouth. I offered to leave with her, but she told me to reassure my mom because she was scared. Then she kissed me and walked out of the tavern."

"She hasn't written you off yet."

"Maybe after she stews on it with Mallory, she'll realized she's a hell of a lot better off without me." I drew in a deep breath. "Can't say I'd blame her. She may not think I'm a good bet."

Lance seemed to ponder my statement as he sipped his beer. "There are no guarantees in this life, my friend. You, of all people, should know that. Take happiness when and where you can. And give Maddie happiness while you're getting it. Make sure she knows you're all in. No backpedaling. That's what she wants, Noah. A man who will be there for her, no matter what."

I mulled over his advice for a few moments. There was no denying I hadn't been that man, but I wanted to be. I just needed her to show her. "Thanks. That's actually good advice."

"Of course it is," he said with a shit-eating grin. "People underestimate me all the time."

"And still just as humble as this morning," I said with a grin.

"What are you talking about? I'm ten times more humble than I was this morning." Lance burst out laughing, then sobered. "So what's your plan?"

"I need to apologize for my mother—and for not handling that situation better." I glanced at the nearly empty second beer bottle. "But I'm in no shape to drive, and I doubt she wants to see me in person."

"There's this new-fangled thing called a cell phone," he said, his brows lifted playfully.

"You're a dick."

"But you love me anyway."

Rolling my eyes, I shook my head. "I don't know what to say to her. There's nothing I can say that will make what happened right."

"Then tell her that. Reiterate that you're sorry she had to go through it. Tell her you'll never let your mother treat her like that again. Tell her you love her."

I gave him a hard stare. "We're not at that stage. We're not even really dating right now." But I knew I did love her, I'd just smothered it with my fear.

"So tell her how much she means to you, you dick."

I ran a hand over my head. "Yeah, you're right."

"Of course I am," he said.

"Don't let it go to your head." Then I picked up the phone and pressed Maddie's number in my speed dial list.

Chapter Fourteen

Maddie

"I can't believe her!" Mallory said, staring at me in disbelief. "What the actual hell?"

We were sitting on my bed with two glasses and a bottle of wine. I finished off my first glass of rosé and poured myself another.

"She hates me, Mal."

"Then she's an idiot because everybody loves you."

"Martin Schroeder didn't like me. He was rude when I picked him up for his Uber ride."

"Martin Schroeder was a pedophile, so that's probably a good thing."

"I guess you're right." But I started to cry again anyway.

"And where the hell is Detective Americano?" she asked, picking up on Chrissy's nickname for Noah.

"I told you that he didn't condone it. He was horrified and upset on my behalf. He threatened to end dinner early, but I told him we should stay. And when I left after dinner, he wanted to walk me out, but I told him no." My throat tightened at the memory of the devastation on his face. "He was really upset, Mal. He stood up for me. This isn't his fault."

Mallory leaned back and crossed her arms, still holding her half-full wine glass. "That doesn't answer my question, now does it?"

I swiped a tear from my cheek. "He sent me a text profusely apologizing."

"A *text*?" She sat upright, sloshing wine on the sleeve of her sweater. "A fucking text?"

"He said he'll call when he calms down."

"When *he* calms down?"

"Quit repeating everything I say." I took a gulp of wine. "It's not helping."

She rolled to her side, set her wine glass on my nightstand, and pulled out her phone.

"What are you doing?" I asked in a panic.

She started tapping furiously on her phone. "I'm texting Noah's cohort."

"Why? He wasn't there."

"Because those two are like two peas in a pod," she said, looking up with an expression of reproach. "Not to mention Lance is nosy as hell. He'll know what's going on." She gestured to her phone. "And there it is. Noah's at Lance's apartment."

My brow shot up. "Where's his mom?"

"Hell if I know, but I doubt she's hanging out at Lance's."

I sat back against my pillows. "He left her at his house."

"Why isn't he *here*?" she demanded.

That was an excellent question and a scary one at that. Was he mulling over all the points his mother had made about me? Or was he staying away because I'd told him I wanted some time to myself? Knowing Noah, it was the latter. "I told him I couldn't deal with it right now. He's probably giving me space."

She started to say something, then stopped. "Well, what do you know? You found a guy who actually listens."

"Yeah," I said in defeat. "Too bad." I took another sip, starting to feel fuzzy-headed from the wine, but my thoughts were rampaging in my head.

"I'm going to lose him," I said softly, sorrow filling my heart. "I felt like we were on the cusp of something, you know? That it was finally going to work out. But he *loves* his mother. He'll care what she thinks."

"Then good riddance to him," she said in disgust. "You need a man who wants you so much that he would never consider letting you go, despite what *anyone* thinks, his mommy included."

"I don't want to talk about Laura Langley anymore," I said tightly. "Let me tell you what we found today." I rehashed our interview with Dawn.

"Your parents were *married*?"

"Yeah. Dawn said Mom probably gave me her last name because she already thought Tony would flake out on her."

She twisted the comforter between her finger and thumb, her forehead creased with concentration. "Yeah, maybe," she said. "But I also find it hard to believe your mom was wild. From everything you've said, she was like a PTA, minivan mom."

"That's what I don't get. But Dawn knew Mom since they were kids, so she would know." I paused and took another sip of wine. "Noah finds it hard to believe my mom never dated after Tony. He thinks she might have had secret boyfriends. Dawn seemed kind of evasive when she was talking about it, like she knew something and didn't want to say."

"Do you remember your mom having boyfriends?"

I shook my head. "No, but she was gone a lot with her volunteer work. Only, when we asked Dawn and the other two teachers, they couldn't remember her doing much volunteer work other than the women's club and helping students after school."

Mallory's mouth dropped open. "She was seeing her secret lover!"

"We don't know any such thing," I protested, but there wasn't much heat behind it. It suddenly didn't seem so far-fetched.

"Was she always volunteering?" Mallory asked. "Or was it more recently before she died?"

I gave it some thought. "I remember her volunteering at a soup kitchen when I was younger. I helped out. But we didn't do anything like that together when I was in middle and high school. I remember she was gone a lot at night when I was really little. I had babysitters, but she would wait until I was about to go to bed before she left."

"How old were you?"

I made a face. "Little. Like preschool? Kindergarten? I had a pretty early bedtime back then."

Mallory cocked her head. "Plenty early enough for her to hit some bars."

"In Cockamamie?" I scoffed. "It doesn't have much of a nightlife."

"But Chattanooga does," she countered.

I pressed my lips together and considered it. It was a short drive. She'd could have sidled up to a bar by nine. Still, it didn't fit with the cookie-making mother I'd known.

"Do you remember what time she'd get home?"

"Not really, but she was always home when I woke up the next day. I think I remember waking up once and finding my babysitter asleep on the sofa. I was crying and had a bad dream, and I couldn't find my mom. I think I started spending the nights she went out at Aunt Deidre's after that."

"We need to ask Deidre."

I shot her a look of disbelief. "Are you crazy? She can't remember who I am lately. How's she going to remember that?"

"You know her short-term memory is worse than her long-term. Besides, it won't hurt to ask."

"She's already in bed."

"Not now, stupid," she said with a laugh and poured more wine into my glass. "We're too busy getting shitfaced about Laura the..." She shrugged. "I was going for alliteration, but nothing comes to mind. We'll go with Laura the Bitch."

I cringed. "Don't call her that. She's Noah's mom, and even if she hates me, she still loves him. I think she sees me as a threat."

"Don't give a shit," Mallory said, filling up her own glass. "Nobody treats my bestie like that and gets away with it." Her eyes lit up. "Let's go TP Noah's house."

I snorted. "First of all, we're not middle schoolers. Second, that's not fair to Noah. And third, we're too tipsy to drive."

"We can take an Uber or call Sir Lancelot."

"Sir Lancelot?" That was a new nickname. "What happened between you two on New Year's Eve, anyway? You were so into each other, and then suddenly you didn't want anything to do with him."

She held her wine glass in salute. "None-ya."

"Come on, Mal. I tell you everything about Noah. You owe me."

She pursed her lips for a few seconds then said, "Let's just say we have a difference of opinion."

I narrowed my eyes. "What does that mean?"

She started to say something, then stopped and downed the rest of her wine. Giving her head a shake, she said, "He's end game, Mads."

I tilted my head. "What?"

"He's the real deal. Like forever."

"And he's not interested in you?" I asked in confusion because I hadn't gotten that impression at all.

"Oh, no. He's interested. He's made it very clear that he thinks we're end game too."

"So what's the problem?"

She leaned forward, her eyes wide. "I'm not ready for forever!"

I laughed and shook my head. "Oh, Mal. Sometimes you're your own worst enemy."

"He said he'd wait for me to change my mind, Mads! Who does that?"

I grinned. "A guy who knows what he wants and is patient enough to wait for it."

"He barely knows me!"

"You've known Noah the same amount of time but think *he's* the one," I countered.

She started to protest, then refilled her wine glass. "I'm scared. I've never felt what I feel with him. What if he—"

"Changes his mind?"

Her eyes turned glassy. "Hurts me."

"He probably will at some point," I said, reaching over and squeezing her hand. "It's inevitable, but I also know that Lance is the kind of guy who will make things right when he screws up."

She rubbed the bottom of her nose with the back of her hand. "Yeah, well, that's all hypothetical." Her back straightened and an evil smile lit up her face. "But it's a known fact that Noah's been an ass. If I ask Lance to take us to Noah's to TP his house, he'll do it."

"No TPing," I said, shaking my head with a grin. "With my luck, Laura would look out the window and see me. Then I'll be a vandal on top of being dangerous."

"She's ridiculous. That man was almost killed two days ago, and it didn't have a damn thing to do with you. He's got it covered all on his own."

My blood turned cold at the reminder of how close he'd come to getting seriously hurt or killed. She was right, of course. Still, it hurt that Laura Langley considered me a threat.

"Well. TPing isn't vandalism, if you ask me," Mallory continued, her words slightly slurred. "And if we were in Memphis, I'd TP Lying Laura's house in a heartbeat."

"Noah's dad would probably shoot you dead," I said. "So that's not a good idea either." I lifted my chin. "We'll take the high road."

She started to counter when my phone, which was lying in the middle of the bed, face up, started to ring. Noah's name appeared on the screen.

Mallory snatched it before I could reach it and answered, putting the call on speaker. "You've got a lot of explaining to do, asshole."

He hesitated for less than a second. "Mallory, I deserve that. I should have taken Maddie and left the moment my mother started in. I stayed because Maddie insisted, but I now realize she was trying to please my mother. I should have just left, and I hate that Maddie went through that for me." He paused. "Is she there? Can I apologize to her?"

"I'm here," I said, fresh tears stinging my eyes as I held Mallory's gaze.

"I'm so sorry," he said, his voice tight. "You have no idea how sorry I am."

I closed my eyes, fighting tears. "You didn't do anything wrong, Noah."

"I disagree with that."

I turned off the speaker phone and picked up the cell, sliding off the bed and going into the bathroom. I shut the door and pressed my back against it. "Noah, I don't blame you for any of it. *I* wanted to stay and try to change her mind about me."

"I dropped her off at my house and came over to Lance's. I'm spending the night here because I can't stomach the idea of sleeping in the same house as her."

"Noah," I breathed out. "She's your mom. Don't let me come between you two."

"This isn't about you, Maddie. I know it came across that way, and she's got a lot of apologizing to do to you, but this is about..."

"She wants you to come back to Memphis," I finished.

"Yeah, but it's more than that."

"Your dad."

He was quiet for several long seconds. "Yeah. And what happened over Christmas." He let out a ragged breath. "I can't control my family, but they are part of me. I'm sorry for that. I won't stand for them to treat you like shit, and next time something like this happens we'll leave. But they'll still be there, festering in the background."

An image of the impeccably dressed Laura Langley came to mind. "I wouldn't say your mother was festering," I teased half-heartedly.

"We'll agree to disagree," he said, and I was relieved to hear the smile in his voice.

"I don't hold your mother's behavior against you, Noah."

"Maddie, you're the best thing that's happened to me in a long, long time. Nothing's going to dissuade me from that."

My stomach felt like I'd just plunged down a hill in a roller coaster. "We're supposed to be just friends right now," I said breathlessly.

"And I will be that for you, if that's what you want," he said. "I'll take you any way I can get you." His voice lowered. "And for the record, I still have some major groveling to do for not preparing you for that ambush." He paused. "I shouldn't have let you walk out the door alone. I should have gone with you out of solidarity."

"I needed a moment or twenty to calm down," I said, "and honestly, I needed to do it without you." I paused. "I hope that doesn't hurt your feelings."

"No, I understand. I should have come over after I dropped my mother at my house, but I came to Lance's to decompress first, and now I've had three beers and can't drive. I'm sorry about that too."

"No apology needed. I just finished my second glass of wine." I smiled softly to myself. "You need your space, and I need mine."

"I miss you," he said, the words barely a whisper.

"You spent all day with me," I said with a laugh. "And tonight too."

"I mean like we were before I left for Christmas."

His statement caught me by surprise. I hesitated, scared I'd send him running again, but I was going to be honest. And if he went running, so be it. "I miss the way we were too. But we can't be together if you're going to only stick around for a few weeks, then disappear for nearly a month."

He was silent for several seconds, and his voice was husky when he spoke. "I'm not going anywhere, Maddie. I swear. I'm done running."

"Don't make any hasty decisions because you feel guilty about the way your mother treated me."

"I'm not, I swear. I've felt like this all day, but I know I've hurt you and I know I have to prove I'm worthy of your trust. I know I'm not there yet, Maddie, but I want another chance with you."

He was saying everything I wanted to hear, but I was still feeling cautious. "I don't know if I'm ready. Especially right now after what happened with your mom and the fact we're investigating my mom's murder... That's important to me, Noah. I'm finally getting answers." I paused. "I need more time."

"Then you have it," he said emphatically. "You're calling the shots right now. Just tell me what you need, and it's yours. I'm yours."

I hoped I could count on that.

Chapter Fifteen

Maddie

Mallory was up by the time I headed downstairs with Aunt Deidre in the morning. She usually took full advantage of her working-from-home uniform (sweats and a T-shirt) and the commute (thirty-seven seconds from the coffee pot—she'd timed it), which meant she typically got up about eight-forty, early enough to take care of some basic personal hygiene, grab a cup of coffee, and turn on her computer.

But this morning, she was up and sitting at the kitchen table at seven-thirty. Her brow rose as she took in my aunt, then turned to me. "Is it a good day?"

I knew what she was asking—was Aunt Deidre lucid? My aunt shuffled to the coffee pot as she scolded, "Every day is a good day if you're determined enough."

That was something I'd heard her say since I was a kid. I shrugged, meaning we could ask questions, but we might or might not get answers.

I'd been tempted to ask Aunt Deidre questions on my own as I helped her go to the restroom and get dressed. While she was confused about the season and had wanted to wear a pair of capris and a short-sleeved shirt so she could garden, she knew who I was and that I needed to go to work as soon as Linda arrived.

"Aunt Deidre," Mallory said as the older woman sat in front of her with her cup of coffee. "I wanted to ask you some questions about Maddie when she was little."

My aunt's brow furrowed. "Who?"

"Maddie," Mallory said, undeterred. "Andrea's daughter."

Aunt Deidre's face lit up. "Andrea? Is she coming over today?"

My heart constricted as I pulled a carton of eggs from the refrigerator. I should be used to her memory loss by now, but sometimes it shaved off a larger piece of my heart than usual.

"No," Mallory said. "Andrea can't come today, but she wants Maddie to stay with you. Is that okay?"

I gave Mallory a sharp look as I pulled an egg from the carton. I hated to confuse her this way, and Mallory knew it.

But Mallory ignored me, giving my aunt her full attention.

"Sweet little Maddie," Aunt Deidre said in a dreamy tone, then sharpened her gaze on Mallory. "Where's Andrea going?"

"I'm not sure," Mallory said. "Do you think she's going to see her boyfriend?"

I dropped an egg on the floor and started to tell Mallory to stop right now, but my aunt said, "Oh dear. She's seeing him again?"

My stomach dropped faster than the egg had. Why had I expected my mother to turn into the Virgin Mary after Tony left? Why did it feel like a betrayal that someone other than me had captured her heart?

"Who?" Mallory asked without missing a beat. "Do you mean Tony?"

"Tony?" my aunt scoffed. "She'd never sleep with Tony again. Not after she caught him cheating on her right after Maddie was born."

My father had cheated on my mom after I was born? I wasn't

sure why I found that surprising. He'd left and never wanted anything to do with either one of us.

"Then who?" Mallory asked.

Aunt Deidre's mouth shifted to the side. "What is his name?"

"That's okay," Mallory cajoled sweetly. She'd been around my aunt long enough now to know she sometimes got frustrated when she couldn't remember something. "Take your time. Do you know where Andrea and her boyfriend might be going?"

Deidre's eyes narrowed. "To that bar in Chattanooga. I thought she'd burned the wild out of her when Maddie was born, but when the girl was three, Andrea said she may be a mother, but she wasn't dead. Twenty-six was plenty young enough that she should still be out having fun. She said lots of women weren't tied down at her age, and she hadn't planned on motherhood. It was so hurtful, especially when she knew how badly I wanted a child of my own."

"I'm sorry," Mallory said, reaching over and putting her hand on my aunt's.

My heart hurt for my aunt and her pain, but it also hurt to think my mother might have said such a thing. Did my mother resent having me? Was it true or part of her dementia?

"Andrea takes off every weekend to those bars in Chattanooga," Aunt Deidre continued. "I love having sweet little Maddie here. Andrea used to leave her with us for the whole weekend, and I'd get to do everything I'd love to do with my own child. But Albert says we're encouraging bad behavior, so he put his foot down and said we can't watch her anymore. It breaks my heart. I love that little girl so much."

Mallory patted her hand. "She loves you too. Very much."

Aunt Deidre sniffed. "Andrea started hiring a babysitter, but then Maddie had a nightmare, and when she couldn't find her mother in the house, she went outside to look for her while that babysitter slept on the couch. Andrea came home and went to check on Maddie, and she wasn't in her bed. The police were called, and they found the poor dear at the next-door neighbor's house, huddled up on the back porch holding her stuffed rabbit."

I stared at her in shock. While I was sure the memories of waking up and not finding my mother were from the same incident, I had no memory of wandering out of the house.

Aunt Deidre tutted. "Andrea didn't leave her again for years. Not until she started seeing *him* again."

"And what is his name?" Mallory asked.

Aunt Deidre rubbed her temples, looking distraught. "His name is right there, but I can't seem to recall it."

"That's okay," Mallory assured her. "You don't need to remember, but do you remember how old Maddie was when Andrea started seeing him again?"

"She was in middle school. Maybe twelve or thirteen. He blew back into town and swept Andrea right off her feet. He said he loved her and wanted to be with her."

"Why did she keep it a secret from Maddie?"

She pressed her temples harder. "I can't seem to remember that either." Her leg started twitching, and she pounded the heel of her hand against her temple. "Why can't I remember?"

"That's enough," I said to Mallory and walked over to my aunt, squatting beside her. "Hey, Deidre. How would you like your eggs today? Scrambled or fried?"

Her hand dropped to the table, and her mouth twisted into a sour expression. "I want French toast."

Mallory glanced up at the rooster clock. It was 7:40. "Maddie doesn't have time to—"

"Maddie? What's Maddie doin' cooking in the kitchen?" my aunt demanded. "She's too little to be unsupervised."

"She won't be," Mallory reassured her. "I'm going to be in the kitchen with her."

"Good morning," Linda called out from the front door. "It's a beautiful sunny day!"

Mallory shot me a look. "You need to go to work."

I knew that, but I also knew I'd never be able to focus. Not after what I'd just heard.

"Linda?" I called out. "Can you take Deidre into the living room while my friend and I make breakfast?"

"Of course!" Linda entered the kitchen and greeted Aunt Deidre. I began cracking eggs into a bowl as she helped my aunt out of her seat and through the dining room.

"What are you doing?" Mallory whispered. "You're not going to make her French toast, are you? You don't have time, and I wouldn't know how. I'd either burn it or serve her raw, soggy bread."

"No. I'll make her some eggs, and she'll probably forget about the French toast by the time Linda serves it to her."

"Do you think she was telling the truth?" Mallory asked, her brow furrowed.

"I don't know. I know she gets stories mixed up, but it does correlate to some of my memories, so I think there's at least some truth to it."

"What good does it do you if she can't remember his name?"

"I happen to know both next-door neighbors are still living next to our old house," I said, scrambling the eggs with a fork. "I'll just pay them a visit. They'll be happy to see me."

"Yeah," she said, leaning against the counter. "That's a good idea."

"The only problem is I can't leave Petra and Chrissy short-handed, and I don't want to wait until I get off at three. That would give me less than two hours before I have to be back before Linda's shift is over." I leveled my gaze. "Are you still planning on going to Chattanooga with your friends?"

She gave me an apologetic look. "Yeah."

"Then I definitely need to be back before five. That doesn't give me enough time to do anything."

"Why don't you see if that Trista chick will cover for you?"

Mallory suggested. "She's always showing up late and making you stay past your shift."

I poured the eggs into a hot skillet. "She's really not a morning person, but she was saying she wished she had Friday nights off. She might be willing to trade with me."

"Tonight just so happens to be Friday night," Mallory said with an exaggerated grin, which quickly turned into a frown. "But that means you'd have to work tonight. Margarete might be able to stay with her."

"No, it's my responsibility. I'll stay with her," I said with plenty of guilt. This felt a lot like what my mother had done with me—pawning me off onto her sister and babysitters, which wasn't fair, but I was feeling ungrounded. I'd seen my mother as a homebody with a low-key job she loved and a normal life, and it turned out that she'd likely had a second life that had been completely invisible to me.

Mallory had already pulled out her phone and was tapping on the screen. Her face screwed up with concentration.

Anxiety stretched my nerves like a rubber band. I'd seen that look before, and it often meant she was doing something I wouldn't like. "What are you doing?"

"Texting Detective Americano." She looked up from her screen with a look of triumph. "He says he'll babysit Aunt Deidre so you can work tonight."

"What? I can't ask him to do that. His mother is in town."

"He said that won't be a problem." She held up her phone and showed me his response to her asking if he could watch my aunt so I could work tonight.

> Yes. My mother won't be here so it's not an issue.

"Did he kick his mother out?" I asked, feeling panicked.

"I know as much as you do, Maddie. Now call Larissa and ask her to switch."

"Trista."

She shrugged. "Whatever. Call her."

I hated calling Trista this early when I knew she wasn't a morning person. Still, she'd mentioned more than once that she wanted to go to a concert in Chattanooga tonight. She had passive-aggressively tried to get someone to trade with her, and last I'd heard, no one had taken the bait. Texting would be preferable, but I doubted she was up. I wasn't even sure a phone call would wake her.

I grabbed my phone out of my pocket and called, steeling myself for what was likely to start out as an unpleasant conversation.

She answered after several rings, sounding half-asleep but also pissed. "What the hell? This better be an emergency."

"I don't think offering to work for you tonight is an emergency, but time is definitely an issue."

"Wait," she said, sounding more agreeable. "You're offering to work for me tonight?"

"I'm offering to trade you for tonight."

"Okay." She sounded less excited. "When?"

"Today."

It took her two seconds to respond. "Are you out of your mind?" She ranted for a half minute about how unfair this was and couldn't I trade her for another day?—but by the time we hung up, we'd agreed that she'd show up at nine-thirty and work until three, and I'd cover her five-to-nine shift.

"I've got to go," I said to Mallory, shoving the skillet with the cooked eggs to the other side of the stove. "Trista's coming in at nine-thirty, and I'm working her shift tonight. Which means I need to work the first part of my shift, and I'm going to be late."

"I'll take care of Aunt Deidre's breakfast. You go find out who your mom was sleeping with."

I shot her a dark look and raced out the door.

Chapter Sixteen

Noah

I drank two cups of coffee by eight, preparing myself to head over to my house to face my mother. Just as I was about to head out the door, Maddie called.

While I was happy to see her name on my phone, I was also worried. What if she'd slept on everything and decided she was done with me?

"Hey," I said softly, unsure of what to say other than I'm sorry, but the more I said it, the cheaper it felt.

"What are you doing this morning?" she asked breathlessly as though in a hurry.

"I don't know yet. Do you need help with your aunt this morning too?"

I heard her car door ding, followed by the sound of her door closing. "No, something else. Mallory and I put some things together last night, and we caught Deidre in a semi-with-it state this morning." She paused and told me that her aunt remembered about Andrea leaving Maddie with her and then a sitter, ending with the story of how she'd wandered out of the house one night, looking for her mother.

"There might be a police report," I said. "I can look into it."

"Last I checked, both neighbors are still living in the houses next door," Maddie said. "I want to talk to them and see what they remember."

"Good idea. Do you want to do that when you get off this afternoon?"

"Actually, that's why I asked what you were doing this morning. I traded with Trista for her shift tonight. She's going to cover me at nine-thirty, and I'm going to work her five to nine tonight."

"Which is why Mallory asked me to stay with Deidre," I said.

"Yeah," she said, sounding apologetic, "but I understand if you only said yes because you felt pressured. It's a big ask."

I felt like an asshole. She shouldn't consider this a big ask. It should be part of being her boyfriend, but then again, I'd walked away from her for weeks. I hadn't given her reason to think otherwise. "I want to be part of your life, Maddie, and your aunt is part of it. I don't have plans, and I'd be honored to help."

"Thank you," she said, her voice tight. "You have no idea how much I appreciate it."

If I was really committing to this, I realized there was another way I could show her. "Why don't you come over to my house after you get off work, and then we can head to the neighbors' together?"

"To your house?"

"Yeah. You haven't seen it, and my mother's organized the hell out of it. Might as well see it before it returns to normal, which isn't all that bad, by the way."

She hesitated. "I'm not sure that's a good idea."

I knew what was giving her pause, and it made me sick to my stomach. "My mother won't be there, Maddie. She'll be on her way back to Memphis."

"Noah, don't kick her out on my behalf."

"I have plenty of reasons to send her home. But if you're worried, text me when you get off, and I'll tell you if the coast is clear."

"Okay." But she didn't seem convinced. "I've got to go. I'll see you when I get off."

I rinsed out my coffee cup and then headed back to my place. Lance had left early to follow up on some leads with the car theft case. The kid he'd interrogated had talked but hadn't given any big player names, just his associates who got the orders. Lance planned to bring them in for questioning today, and I felt like a proud father.

My mother's car was parked in front of my house, and I found her sitting at my kitchen table. She was sipping a cup of coffee while writing something on a notepad. While she was dressed, she wasn't wearing makeup, and her hair was uncharacteristically pulled back into a short, low ponytail. She looked up in surprise when she saw me.

"Noah."

"We need to talk," I said, resting my hand on the back of a chair and holding her gaze.

Her mouth twisted, and tears filled her eyes. "I'm sorry."

"I'm sorry too," I said, feeling my resolve start to soften, but I also knew my mother. If I gave an inch, she'd take a mile. "While I appreciate you coming to make sure I'm okay, you know that I'm fine. I think Dad needs you more."

Her mouth dropped open. "You're kicking me out?"

"You can only rearrange my kitchen so many times, and I can assure you the alphabetical organization won't last longer than a couple of days after you leave."

"I was going to make you more freezer meals. You know the hardware store on Main Street has a small upright freezer on sale. I can fill that up with—"

"No," I said firmly. "I'm a grown man, perfectly capable of feeding myself. I don't need my mother to take care of me."

The look on her face suggested I'd shot her through the heart with an arrow.

I pulled out the chair across from her and sat. "Mom, I love you, but you won't change my mind about *anything*. If you keep trying, you're only going to push me away."

She sniffed and grabbed a tissue from a box she must have placed on the table, then dabbed her eyes. "I can't bear the thought of anything happening to you, Noah, I can't go through all of that again."

"I know," I said, softening my tone. "I thought this town would be a lot safer than it's turned out to be, but I love my job, and I love this town."

"And you love the girl," she finished flatly.

"She's a grown woman," I corrected. "Not a girl, and yeah, I think I do love her." Deep down I knew it. It just scared the hell out of me. Especially since we still had some issues to work through.

"So you won't be moving back to Memphis?" she asked, her voice breaking.

"No."

"But I miss you," she said, openly crying now. "And your sister and her kids miss you. We used to see you practically every week, and now we barely see you at all."

"I'm sorry about that, and maybe after things die down here, I'll make an effort to come home more often."

She glanced down at the tissue in her hand, tearing a hole with her thumb. "No, you won't." She lifted her gaze. "Not while your father's still alive."

I swallowed the lump in my throat. "You're right, probably not."

"I just wish that you and your dad—"

"This is real life, Mom," I said, my voice breaking. "Not a fairy-tale. Sometimes there isn't a happily-ever-after. Sometimes things don't happen like you want them. Dad's made up his mind about me, and we both know I will never live up to his standards. You know, I'm a hell of a lot happier now that I've stopped trying."

Her face crumpled. "I'm sorry."

"So am I," I said, tears burning my eyes. "But I'm glad I moved here. I'm making a difference. I've made friends and found an amazing woman who seems to put up with all my fears and insecurities and believes in me more than I believe in myself. I'm sure as hell not going to throw that away."

"Nor should you," she said quietly. "That's a rare gift."

"You owe Maddie an apology."

"I know."

"Like a massive one."

Her mouth lifted into a small smile. "I know."

"But maybe not right now. She's at work, and you're going home."

A hopeful look filled her eyes. "I can wait until she gets off—"

"No. Send her a letter on one of those engraved note cards you like so much. I know Leah got you a new box full for Christmas. Surely, you haven't used them all yet."

She smiled, but this time it seemed more genuine. "I have a few left."

"I'll get you her address."

She drew in a breath and turned serious. "You never would have done this for Monica."

"That's because she wasn't the one," I said, pushing my chair back. "And Maddie is." And I had a lot to make up for after all the crap I'd put her through. "Do you need me to help you pack?"

She laughed. "You know, kicking me out will be a great story for years to come."

I cocked a brow. "And so will your behavior at dinner last night."

She grimaced. "Maybe we'll keep this whole visit to ourselves."

"Good choice."

Chapter Seventeen

Maddie

Much to my irritation, Trista didn't show up until close to ten. As soon as she walked in from the back, I took off my apron and clocked out.

Although I'd never been to Noah's house, I knew where to go. I'd gotten his address for Margarete so she could send him a Christmas card, and I'd plugged it into my phone.

His police-issued sedan was in the driveway, and his Cherokee was parked behind it. I didn't see another car parked in front of the house, so it looked like his mother really was gone.

I hadn't texted because I'd decided I wouldn't hide from her.

Noah opened the front door before I climbed the steps to his porch. "You didn't text," he said, and I could see the worry in his eyes. "It's past ten."

"Trista was late, and I decided it didn't matter," I said, walking up toward him. "Your mother will just have to get used to me."

He nodded with determination. "I'm good with that."

I climbed the steps and stood in front of him. "You invited me to your house."

"It's about time, don't you think?" His expression was serious, and I saw that this invitation meant something to him. It wasn't a casual *come over and pick me up*. He was inviting me into a new part of his life.

I gave him a coy look. "How about you give me a quick tour?"

The dark cloud hanging over him faded, and a grin spread across his face. The happiness radiating from him made my heart skip a beat. "It's not very big, so it won't take long."

He reached out his hand toward me and gave me a questioning look. Was I ready to hold his hand? It seemed like a stupid thing to consider, but it was a line, even if it was a very narrow one. If I took his hand, I was telling him that I was ready to move this past being friends.

Was I ready for that?

He'd told me that I could set the pace, so I kept my hands by my sides.

He didn't look insulted; instead, he gestured for me to enter. I stepped inside and took in his uber-neat living room.

"My mother is a neat freak," he said, rubbing the back of his neck. "She even washed her coffee cup before she left this morning."

I nearly apologized for being the reason she'd left early, but I bit my tongue.

He took me into his kitchen and I glanced around the room, my mind wandering to the rooms he hadn't shown me.

"And your room?" I asked, my voice husky even though I hadn't meant for it to sound that way. We still hadn't slept together. We'd been saving that for when he came back from Memphis, but obviously that didn't work out. There was no doubt I still wanted him, and I had to admit, there was something seductive about seeing his room. Thinking of us in his bed.

How much time did I need before I was ready to shift our relationship? What was I looking for? Time? Proof? Was I stupid if I decided to just go for it? He'd sent his mother home because of the way she'd treated me. That had to mean something, not to mention he'd declared he wasn't running. Should I take him at his word?

One thing I'd learned in the past few months was that life changed in an instant and there was no guarantee we'd get a tomorrow.

His eyes hooded as his gaze landed on my lips. "We should probably head out to go talk to your old neighbors."

I looked up into his face and I saw an honorable man who was scared, only he didn't look as scared as he had before. He looked sure. Determined.

"What happens if you go home and need space again?" I asked, my heart pounding in my chest.

"That won't happen again, Maddie," he said, certainty covering his face. "For one thing, I won't be seeing my father again, and for another, I'm done giving him control over me. There's no making the man happy, and I refuse to try."

I gasped. "He wanted you to break up with me?" I knew his mother didn't approve of me, but his father too?

He shook his head, frustration filling his eyes. "No. While he knew I had someone here, he doesn't know anything *about* you. It wasn't you. It was me. What he convinced me about myself. But he's wrong. I just had to get him out of my head. I'm sorry I hurt you during the process."

"And is he out of your head?"

He hesitated. "No. I suspect he'll always be there, whispering that I'm worthless. That I fail everyone. But now I know he's a liar."

I reached out and took his hand and squeezed. "You're not worthless. You are so very far from it, but I can't take you running away like that again, Noah. I can handle one night, but not weeks."

"I know, and I swear, I won't do that to you again."

Holding his gaze, I squeezed his hand once more. "If you run again, I won't be there when you come back. You need to know that before we start this again."

He swallowed. "That's only fair."

I took a step closer to him, inches between us. "We don't have appointments with my old neighbors, which means we can go whenever we want. Do you want to show me your bedroom?"

His eyes were stormy with conflict. "I'm going to need you to tell me what you want, Maddie. Otherwise, I'm going to presume we're still in the friend zone."

"I'm scared," I admitted in a whisper. "I'm terrified you're going to hurt me again."

"I know," he said, sorrow filling his words. "You have no idea how sorry I am, but I'm here, and I'm not leaving again. The only way I'll leave you is if you tell me to go."

I pulled my hand away from his, and disappointment filled his eyes, but then he looked startled when I rested my hands on his chest. The muscles under his shirt were firm under my palms. "I don't want to be just friends with you."

"Then what do you want, Maddie?" his asked, his voice husky.

I swallowed, holding his gaze. "I want *you*, Noah. As more than friends."

His free hand lifted to my cheek, and he brushed his thumb along my cheekbone, staring into my eyes before he lowered his face to mine. His lips were soft, the pressure gentle as though he was giving me a chance to back out.

Need flooded my veins and my mouth parted as I slipped a hand up to his neck, pulling him closer.

Wrapping a hand around my back, he pulled me flush to his chest as his kiss turned hungry.

I kissed him back, just as hungry, needing so much more.

He pulled back, gathering my hands in one of his. "I want you, more than you could possibly know," he said breathlessly, "but when I sleep with you, Maddie, I want it to be special. Not something we fit in before we meet your old neighbors."

His words sent a thrill through my blood, making me want him even more. But I liked that he wanted to wait. "I want that too."

He kissed me again, making it clear that his postponement of our first time wasn't due to a lack of interest. Then he lifted his head and grinned. "You're making it hard for me to stick to my honorable intentions."

I took a step backward, resisting the urge to convince him to stay. "Then let's get started. I have to be back at work at five."

"And we should probably get to your house by four-thirty. You can show me your aunt's bedtime routine, and it'll help her get comfortable with me being there."

"I really appreciate you doing this, Noah."

He reached for my hand. "Maddie, like I said, I want to help you in every way I can."

He locked up his house, and we decided to take my car. If we were pressed for time, I could just take him to my house to go over everything, and I'd bring him home after I got off work.

I headed toward my old neighborhood, which was only a half mile away. I parked in front of the house I'd shared with my mother from when I was a toddler to my teenage years, and the familiar melancholy of everything I'd lost swept over me. The house was still the same pale tan with black shutters, and while the bushes out front were bigger, they were neatly trimmed. The place looked nearly identical to the one in my head, but it wasn't my home anymore. Now, it was just a house. Still, the memories kept flooding me—planting flowers along the sidewalk from the driveway to the house, playing in my turtle sandbox in the back yard, learning how to ride my bike in the street I'd just driven down—and I fought tears.

What would our lives have been like now if she were still alive? Would I have come back to Cockamamie after college? Would I have gotten married and had kids? I had a hard time imagining my mom as a grandmother, but that was probably because she'd only been thirty-eight at the time of her death. I had no doubt she would have been an incredible one.

"You okay?" Noah asked softly, taking my hand.

I started to tell him I was fine, but I didn't want any lies between us anymore. Even small ones. "No, but I will be. I just had a rush of memories hit me."

He squeezed my hand. "I'm sorry."

Pressing my lips together, I lifted a shoulder in dismissal. "I can't change the past. I can only remember it with fondness and carry on."

"It's okay to be sad about what you lost. You're allowed, Maddie."

I looked up at him, his face blurry through my tears. "So are you."

Surprise lit up his eyes, and he leaned forward and gently kissed me. "You're right."

"Is that why you pulled away after Christmas? Were you sad?"

A torrent of emotions rolled over his face. Finally, he said, "Yeah. Sad. Mad. Uncertain." He gave me a grim smile.

"I know you think you don't deserve me, but maybe I don't think I can give you everything you need either," I said. "Like your mother and your family. You deserve to be with someone they approve of, and that's obviously not me."

"As hard as it is to believe, my mother's bad behavior isn't because she dislikes you. It's because she's scared of losing me. It doesn't make it right, but I do believe she'll come around. Not that any of it is fair to you." He tilted his head and studied my face.

I took a moment to respond, choosing my words carefully. "No man will be able to give me everything I want. None of my ex-boyfriends were ever as considerate of me and my feelings as you are. That's more important than you know, Noah." I gave him a sly grin. "Even if you've been a shithead recently."

A sheepish grin lifted his mouth. "I deserve that. But you still want kids, Maddie, and I'm not sure about that. My mom pointed out that it's not fair for me to continue this if I'll only hurt you in the end."

I sat back in my seat and stared at the stop sign at the end of the street. "Sitting here in front of my old house, I realize I had a lot of dreams when I was a kid. Marriage. Kids of my own. But those plans all included my mother. And the cold, hard truth is that my path has changed."

"You can still have a family, Maddie."

"With an asshole like Steve?" I turned back to him. "If I have to decide between potentially not having kids and being with a man who's respectful of my feelings, or having kids but being stuck with a self-centered jerk, I think I'm going to choose the former." I gave him a soft smile. "I choose you, Noah."

He shook his head. "Why does that make me feel like a first-class asshole?"

I laughed as a tear slid down my cheek. "Then you got the wrong message."

"I promise you, I'm done running, Maddie," he said, reaching over to wipe my tear away. "It's okay if you need me to reassure you ten times a day that I'm not. We had something great before I left, and I blew it all to hell. But I'm. Not. Running." He grinned. "It's already feeling impossible to run from you."

"Thank you for reassuring me."

"It's the least I can do." Noah gave me a soft kiss then glanced over his shoulder at my old house. "Is it very different than when you lived here?"

"No, but it *feels* different. The house seemed to exude love." I cringed. "That sounds stupid."

"Not at all. I feel that way about your aunt's house," he said without embarrassment. "There's so much love in her house that a person feels it when they walk up to it." Then he released my hand. "Let's go talk to some neighbors."

Chapter Eighteen

Maddie

We got out, and I led him to the home on the left, Mr. and Mrs. Lebowski's house. When I was little, the elementary school was dismissed late enough that my mother was usually home by the time I got back. But when I graduated to middle school, I got home earlier than her. Mom often stayed after school to help her students, so on those afternoons I'd go over to visit Mrs. Lebowski, who always seemed to have warm cookies or banana bread. I remembered her fondly, and I knew she'd cared deeply for me and my mother. She'd been devastated by my mother's murder and had sobbed inconsolably when I'd officially moved in with my aunt and uncle.

Noah and I walked up to the front of the small house. Concrete steps led up to a small square porch. I knocked on the glass storm door, then waited at the bottom of the steps, Noah standing behind me.

A few seconds later, an older woman opened the steel front door and peered through the glass at us. For a moment, she looked confused, then her jaw dropped, and she pushed the storm door open in a rush of warm, sweet-scented air. "*Maddie?*"

My heart burst with warmth and affection. "You remember me?"

"I could never forget you, sweet Madelyn. You look just like your mother." She beckoned me inside the house. "Come in. Come in. And bring your handsome man."

I glanced back at Noah, then followed Mrs. Lebowski inside.

The living room was just as I remembered it—a blue-and-white-checkered sofa and love seat, and white coffee and end tables. They'd been out of style back when I'd known her, and they were downright vintage now, but they didn't look old or tattered. Nostalgia washed through me, stealing my breath. I'd spent hours in this room watching TV and putting together jigsaw puzzles.

Mrs. Lebowski approached me, reaching up to take my face between her hands. "As I live and breathe...I can't believe you're here. I never thought I'd see you again."

I felt guilty for never coming back to visit. Not even once. But the first few years after my mother's death, it had been too painful to drive by our old house, let alone spend time in the house next door. And later...well, it had felt easier to pretend I'd put it all behind me.

"I'm sorry," I said, placing my hands over hers. "I should have come."

She'd been in her fifties when my mother was murdered, which meant she was now in her seventies. Years of gardening and being outdoors had left her face heavily wrinkled. However, her eyes were lively and shone with merriment and a tinge of sorrow.

"Don't you dare say you're sorry," she said with a scowl, then dropped her hands to her sides. "I would have come to see you, but Albert and Deidre thought it might be too painful."

I'd had no idea she'd asked. My jaw dropped. "What? Why?"

"Something about being reminded of that night. I was the one who sat with you after the police came. Deidre and Albert were spending the night in Atlanta, and we had to get ahold of them to come home. It took hours."

I stared at her, slightly shaking my head. "I don't remember any of that."

"I'm not surprised," she said with a sympathetic smile. "You were understandably in shock. You were so catatonic that I almost took you to the ER."

Noah placed a hand on my shoulder.

Mrs. Lebowski's gaze lifted to him, and she cringed. "Oh, dear. Where are my manners? Introduce me to your young man."

I started to introduce them, but Noah stuck out his hand. "Mrs. Lebowski, I'm Maddie's boyfriend, Noah Langley. Pleased to meet you."

The older woman shook his hand, beaming up at him. "You really are a handsome devil, aren't you?"

"So I've been told," he said with a wink.

She turned to me with a broad grin. "Oh, I like him."

I took his hand and squeezed. "I like him too."

"Are you here for a chat?" she asked. "I'm in the middle of making cookies for a church bake sale. I have some cooling and a batch in the oven." A mischievous grin spread across her face. "Do you still have a sweet tooth?"

"Of course," I said with a laugh. "Who do you think nurtured it?"

She laughed and headed into the kitchen, leaving me and Noah to follow.

The kitchen was also nearly unchanged; only the range and refrigerator looked newer, but she still had the same country blue cabinets and white laminate counters.

The aroma of freshly baked chocolate chip cookies was stronger in here.

"Have a seat at the bar," she said as she grabbed an oven mitt. "I need to get a tray out of the oven."

Noah and I sat on the backless stools in front of the peninsula—something else that brought back memories.

"I remember staying with you after school some days," I said. "You were always so kind to me."

"Kind?" she scoffed as she pulled a cookie sheet out of the oven. "It had nothing to do with being kind. You were such a sweet girl, and Bill and I never had our own children." She set the tray on the stove and turned to face me. "I loved every minute of the time you spent over here. We loved you."

Now I felt even more guilty that I'd never come back to see her.

Her brow lifted, obviously reading my mind. "Don't you dare feel guilty about a thing. Bill and I only wanted you to be happy and healthy. And if leaving us behind helped your healing, we accepted that."

Had it helped? I wasn't so sure.

She opened a cabinet and pulled out a small plate, loaded it with four cookies and set it in front of me and Noah. "Do you prefer coffee, milk, or water, Noah?"

"Coffee if you still have some."

"Coffee is the elixir of life," she said. "I drink it all day long, much to my doctor's chagrin, although I tell him I've made it seventy-eight years drinking six to eight cups a day, and I don't see any point in stopping now."

"I like your motto," Noah said with a laugh.

"I'll take coffee too," I said, picking up a cookie. "I've outgrown milk."

"I suppose you have," she said, beaming with happiness. She pulled two coffee cups out of the cabinet and filled them.

Once she set the cups in front of us, along with creamer, she refilled her mug and leaned against the counter. "Now, tell me what brings you by today."

I set my half-eaten cookie back on the plate. "I want to ask you some questions about my childhood and my mother."

Her lips pressed into a thin line, and she nodded. "I always wondered if you'd have questions."

I leaned my forearms on the counter. "Do you remember my mother ever having a boyfriend?"

She let out a nervous laugh. "You jumped right in, didn't you?"

I shrugged.

She pushed away from the counter and started scooping cookies off the sheet and onto the wire rack. "Yes, I do. Your mother had multiple men in her life over the years."

Multiple? But I kept my voice even to hide my surprise when I said, "I don't remember any of them."

"She never brought them home. She discussed it with me a few times, saying she'd never let you get attached to another man, only for him to walk away from you. She said one man had already done that, and she wouldn't let it happen again."

"My father?"

She nodded.

"I heard she went to bars on the weekends when I was little."

She hesitated. "Sometimes. Other times, it was parties, I think."

"In Chattanooga?" I asked.

"When you were little, she'd go there or sometimes Atlanta if she wanted to get away for the weekend. She said the nightlife in Cockamamie was lacking."

I wasn't surprised she'd left Cockamamie for an active nightlife, especially since she was a schoolteacher and had a reputation to maintain, but I didn't ever remember her going to Atlanta.

"It still is," I said with a wry smile.

"True, but it was even duller back then." She grinned. "Or so I'm told."

"Did you know my mother when she was younger? Before she went to college?"

"No, we went to different churches. I didn't know her until she moved in next door. You weren't quite two. Andrea was a sweet thing. Always cheerful. So full of life. I loved her instantly."

"Everyone loved her," I said softly.

"She loved *you,*" Mrs. Lebowski said. "Fiercely. She wanted you to have a loving, independent home like her parents had given her, but your aunt would have preferred if you'd both stayed at Cabbage Rose House with her and Albert."

"*What?* I didn't know that."

"Deidre gave up eventually, but she and Albert couldn't have children either, and I think she thought of you as partially hers. You and Andrea spent a lot of time with them, but your mother felt it was important for you two to have your own place."

"Yesterday, Noah and I talked to Dawn Heaton, Mom's best friend for her entire life, and she said that Mom had a wild streak when she was younger."

Her brow creased. "Dawn wasn't her best friend when you were little."

I stared at her in shock. "What?"

"Who was her best friend?" Noah asked, speaking up for the first time since I'd started asking my questions.

"Annamarie." She grimaced. "I'm struggling to remember her last name."

"Annamarie?" I asked. "I don't remember Mom having a friend with that name."

"That's because you were little when she used to hang around. Her name was too hard for you to pronounce, so you called her Maymay."

That name pinged a memory, and I remembered a dark-haired woman laughing with my mother. "Long dark hair? Sort of curly?" I asked, narrowing my eyes as I struggled to remember.

"Yes. About the same age as your mother. She was a teacher at the high school too."

Noah got out his phone and started tapping on the screen.

Mrs. Lebowski gave him a strange look, then turned back to me. "She was over at your house quite often because your mom hated that you were in daycare all day. Other than her Saturday night outings, she stayed home, and Annamarie would come over and hang out with her. They spent a lot of time together for several years. But then Annamarie got a boyfriend and stopped coming over as much, and I think your mother got lonely." She gave me a sad look. "You were about four, and while you were quite a chatty thing, it wasn't enough. Andrea vowed not to bring men home to you, but I think she was still lonely for adult company. For a man, really. She was a beautiful girl. She told me she used to date lots of boys in high school and college."

"Did she ever mention that she was married to my father?"

She looked shocked. "What? No. She led me to believe you were born out of wedlock, not that Bill or I cared. We loved you both."

"Dawn said they were briefly married."

She seemed to give it some consideration. "I never saw your father, not once. She told me about him a few times. She said he was a rich asshole—excuse my French—and he wanted nothing to do with either of you. She said you were both better off for it."

I glanced at Noah, and he gave me a serious look, then typed something else onto his phone.

"So my mom started going to bars in Chattanooga when I was four?" I asked.

"She went a few times when you were younger, but after Annamarie met her man, well...I think Andrea started getting stir-crazy. Her entire life consisted of school and home, and while she loved you, she needed..." Her voice trailed off.

"More," I finished.

"It's important you know that she loved you," Mrs. Lebowski said insistently.

"I know," I said. "But she was more than just a mother. She needed her own life outside of work and me." She'd told Deidre she needed to party. I'm sure tea parties with a four-year-old didn't feel the same as dancing with drinks and handsome men.

"Yes, exactly." She started dropping cookie batter onto the now-cooled baking sheet. "It was once or twice a month at first, and Deidre and Albert would watch you, but then it was every weekend, often from Friday night until Sunday late. They told her they wouldn't watch you anymore. It hurt your mother terribly, but she found a teenager to stay with you. The girl was sixteen or seventeen and lived a few houses down. She was a responsible girl, but she practically got paid to watch TV. Andrea would wait until you were in bed before she left, but she often came home in the wee hours of the morning. We're talking three or four a.m. This went on for months until..."

"Until I left the house in the middle of the night," I finished.

"You remember?" she asked in surprise.

"Bits and pieces. Aunt Deidre filled me in on a little of it this morning. She said I had a bad dream and went looking for my mom. My mom came home and found me on a neighbor's back porch."

"It was ours," she said sheepishly. "We had no idea you were there. Apparently, you'd knocked, but you were so little, it wasn't very loud, and we didn't hear. Bill and I felt positively terrible for months afterward. To this day, I think about it sometimes. It was cool that night. You were only in your nightgown, and you couldn't get back inside your house. You might have gotten hypothermia. If only we'd heard..."

"You didn't do anything wrong," I assured her. "Some people are hard sleepers and don't wake up for anything."

"If *we* felt guilty, your mother was positively drowning in it. It didn't help that the police had been called, and half the town knew. People treated her like she was wearing a scarlet letter for a while."

"It wasn't her fault," I said.

"No, but people judged her for not being here. They judged that poor teenager too. But it was three in the morning, and she was asleep on the sofa. She was doing what she'd been paid to do. Andrea hadn't expected her to stay awake all night."

"And that was the end of my mother's nightlife?"

"Yes," Mrs. Lebowski said. "She was terrified when she found you missing. She swore she'd never put you in danger again. And she didn't." She paused. "She waited until you were older to go out again."

"That's what I've heard, but I don't remember her going out. If she left me, it was for volunteering activities."

"She didn't go to Chattanooga, but right before she died, she started spending time at a local bar."

"Chevy's?" I scoffed. "That place is full of old men talking about the good ol' days while downing beers. Unless it was different back then."

"Oh, no. I'm pretty sure it was exactly the same back then. But that's not where she went."

"But there are no other bars in town," I said. "At least not now."

"There weren't any back then either, but this place was just outside of town."

Horror swept through me. "What? No."

"Are you saying Maddie's mother used to frequent Cock of the Walk?" Noah asked, sounding equally shocked. "I've heard it opened about ten years ago. The timing doesn't fit."

"Not that one, but there was another bar most God-fearing Christians steered clear of. Mad Hatter's. It was rough and full of hoodlums. When it shut down, I heard the patrons all headed over to Cock of the Walk when it opened shortly thereafter. I know Andrea went to Mad Hatter's from time to time. She told me so. I told her she was crazy, but she assured me that her boyfriend would keep her safe. She was more worried about her reputation."

Aunt Deidre said she had a boyfriend when I was older, but I'd wanted to attribute it to her dementia. But something else stuck out at me. Mad Hatter's. The word *white rabbit* had been written on the side of the box. Was it a coincidence? I didn't see how. But Bergan or someone else must have written it, not my mother. Which meant he knew more than he'd told us. Or had known more, before time had lost it to him.

"Was the relationship casual?" Noah asked. If he'd noted the connection, he'd ignored it and stayed on topic.

"Oh, no. She was very much in love," she said.

In love? My mother had been in love with a man—a man who frequented a rough bar—and she'd never told me? I shook my head. "I can't believe this. I don't remember her having a boyfriend."

"She never introduced you to him," she continued, "but he was at your house quite often. He came when you were gone or after you were in bed."

There had been a man in my house? Sleeping with my mother?

I pushed back the bar stool, the wooden legs scraping the vinyl floor. "I need some air."

I rushed out the front door and began to pace in the front yard. Noah followed but stood to the side and let me pace for a half minute before he said, "I know this was a shock."

I stopped in my tracks, giving him my attention. "You know how rough Cock of the Walk is. And if this Mad Hatter's place was just like it? You know what kind of people hang out there."

"I know."

"Not only did she go there, but she brought a man from that place back to our house, time and time again." The betrayal was so thick I was choking on it.

"I know," he repeated. "But I find it hard to believe your mother would have brought a dangerous man into your home. She stopped going out because you wandered away in the middle of the night. Your safety was important to her."

I shook my head, tears flowing down my cheeks. "I thought I knew her, but I never really knew her at all."

Noah approached me slowly and rested his hands on my shoulders. "We think we know our parents, but I'm not sure we ever really do, especially when we're kids. And besides, few people are truly good or evil. Your mom was an amazing woman, but she had needs that you couldn't fulfill. That wasn't a fault of yours *or* hers. Dawn said she was wild. Maybe that bar and her boyfriend fed her wildness."

"It was a dangerous place."

"Maybe it wasn't for her. They must have accepted her, especially if one of the members was her boyfriend."

"Members?"

"Cock of the Walk is a motorcycle club, Maddie. If all the patrons of Mad Hatter's moved to Cock of the Walk, it stands to reason it was one too."

"Did you catch the connection with white rabbit on the box and that my mother went to Mad Hatter's?"

He nodded, looking grim. "I did."

I pushed past my horror and latched onto something my aunt had mentioned. "Aunt Deidre said Mom's boyfriend came back." I stared up at him. "What do you think that means?"

"I don't know, but we'll see if Mrs. Lebowski remembers more about him." Worry filled his eyes. "I know this is all coming as a shock. Are you okay with hearing more?"

"I need to know the truth, Noah," I said, my voice hardening.

"I know, but I told you that if parts were too hard to handle, I could step in, ask the questions, and fill you in later."

"I want to know all of it. No matter how hard it is."

He nodded, dropped his hands, and reached for mine, lacing our fingers. "You're not doing this alone. We're in it together."

I smiled through my tears, surprised by how much I needed him by my side. I'd lived on my own since Mom's death. Sure, I'd had boyfriends, and Mallory was a great best friend, but I'd still felt unanchored. For the first time since Mom had died, I didn't feel like I had to do it all alone.

Chapter Nineteen

Maddie

I went back inside to find a contrite Mrs. Lebowski popping the cookie sheet back in the oven.

"I'm so sorry," she said. "I never should have told you *any* of that."

"No," I said, standing next to the peninsula. "I need to know anything and everything you remember about my mother."

"But why hear the things that make you uncomfortable?" she asked, closing the oven door and turning to face me. "You should remember the good and leave the rest in the past."

"I'm trying to find out who killed her," I said more bluntly than I'd intended. "And you've already given me more information than anyone else has. Please, I need to know everything."

Horror filled her eyes and her face paled. "Oh, Maddie. No. It's too dangerous."

"I wasn't totally forthcoming when I introduced myself," Noah said. He'd been standing behind me, but he stepped up next to me now. "I'm not just Maddie's boyfriend. I'm also a detective in the Cockamamie Police Force. This isn't an official investigation, but I'm supporting Maddie as she talks to people from her past. I'm hoping to get enough information to reopen the case."

Anger darted from her eyes, and for a moment I didn't recognize the mild-mannered woman who had been a surrogate grandmother to me years ago. "Where the hell were you years ago when I tried to get you all to listen to me? I told all y'all I had information to help solve her murder, and none of you would give me the time of day. That Detective Burger told me I was a crazy old lady, and I needed to leave the detective work to the professionals," she spat in disgust.

Noah leaned forward. "Mrs. Lebowski, with all due respect, I was in college when Andrea was killed. After I graduated, I became a police officer and then a detective in Memphis before I moved to Cockamamie last summer. I'm here to clean up the shitshow Bergan and his cronies created, and solving Andrea Baker's murder is one of the things I want to work on. I know you probably don't trust me, but Maddie does. I'm trying to help her get closure, and I'm certain you have valuable information that can help us."

Her eyes turned glassy. "She was brutally murdered, and I wouldn't be surprised if it had something to do with *him*. What if they find out Maddie's looking into it and kill her too?"

"What in the world was my mother mixed up in?" I asked, feeling light-headed.

"Not what. *Who*. I'm sure it had something to do with Gordy."

"Gordy?" Noah asked, barely containing his excitement. "That was Andrea's boyfriend's name?"

"Yes, but I don't know a last name. I don't even know what he did for a job. He drove a motorcycle, and I know he hung out at that bar."

"He was a biker?" Noah asked for confirmation.

She nodded.

"I don't remember him at all," I said, still baffled by the whole thing.

"Like I said earlier, your mother was careful. The first time, when you were little, he'd come over late at night. He wasn't around for several long years. When he turned back up when you were in about sixth or seventh grade, he usually came over when you were sleeping at a friend's house or staying with your aunt and uncle. Only on rare occasions would he come over when you were home, but it was always late at night, and he rarely stayed for long. He usually left early in the morning."

"You were paying attention?" Noah asked without a hint of criticism.

"It's not like I was spying," she said in disgust. "Like I said, he drove a motorcycle, and it was loud. My husband called it a hog."

"A Harley-Davidson," Noah said. "Was she still seeing him right before she died?"

"He was at her house the night before. It was the only time he spent the entire night when Maddie was home, although he was gone around the time the sun rose. But I *do* know they had an argument before he left. They were in the front yard—not shouting but talking loudly for five-thirty in the morning."

"Did you hear what they were arguing about?"

"No." She shook her head, looking sad. "I was about to cook Bill breakfast and was going out to get the paper. I stayed at the door so as not to disturb them but went out as he pulled away. Andrea saw me when she turned to go back in the house, and the look in her eyes was fierce."

"Like she was pissed?" Noah asked. "Like she'd kicked him out or sent him away?"

"Maybe?" She shook her head again. "I don't recall, and neither of us said anything. She just went inside and got ready for work, I guess."

Noah glanced at me to ensure I was okay before he pressed on. "And you're sure you don't remember his last name or what he did for a living?"

"No. Andrea was very secretive about him, but I did know his name was Gordy. She did love him, I'm sure of that."

"But she didn't intend to introduce him to Maddie," Noah said.

She shook her head. "No. She said maybe when Maddie was grown and off to college, but not before."

"Why?" I asked. "If she was in love with him, why not tell me?"

Mrs. Lebowski held my gaze. "Because he was a thug, Maddie. She knew he wasn't respectable, so she had to protect you."

Her words sunk in my gut like a rock.

My mother had dated a criminal.

"Do you know if Gordy wore a necklace?" Noah asked. "And if it had a pendant?"

Mrs. Lebowski frowned, looking deep in thought before she said, "I think he *did* wear a gold chain from time to time, lots of men did back then, but honestly, I never got close enough to see if it had a pendant."

Noah nodded. "Is there anything else you can remember? Anything that might help me find her killer?"

She shook her head, looking dazed. "No."

Noah reached into his back pocket, pulled out his wallet, then retrieved his business card and set it on the counter. He grabbed a pen from the counter and wrote something on the back before handing it to her.

"This is my business card, but I also wrote Maddie's number on the back. If you think of anything, anything at all that you think might help, please feel free to reach out to either one of us."

"I'm sorry I upset you," she said to me, looking close to tears.

"No. I *want* to know these things," I said, walking around the counter and pulling her into a hug. She felt smaller than my memories of hugging her. "I'm sorry I stayed away, but I want to keep in touch. I'm living in Cockamamie for the foreseeable future. So I'll be around. If you're willing, that is."

She looked up at me with tear-filled eyes. "I'd like that."

We started to leave, but Noah turned back. "One more thing, Mrs. Lebowski. Did you happen to give Andrea a key to your house?"

She frowned as though trying to remember. "No. Bill didn't like handing out keys like candy, he said. No one had keys to our house except for us."

"What about the neighbor on the other side of Andrea and Maddie's house?"

"Oh, no," she said with a short laugh. "Rita never would have given her a key either."

Noah nodded. "Do you know if the people who bought Andrea and Maddie's house changed the locks after they moved in?"

She laughed. "Oh, good heavens no. Even though Andrea didn't have one of our keys, she still gave us one of hers because we watched Maddie and all. In any case, I go over and water the new neighbors' plants when they're gone. All these years, I still use the same key."

Noah's eyes lit up. "Is it easy for you to get to? Could I see it?"

She shot him a reproving look. "You're not goin' in their house, are you?"

"No, I just want to compare it to a key Maddie found."

Relief swept over her face. "Oh, thank goodness. Let me get it." She walked over to a drawer in her kitchen and pulled out a key while Noah pulled a folded evidence bag out of his pocket.

Mrs. Lebowski gave him an odd look as he unfolded the bag, then took the silver key from her and placed it side by side with the gold key in the bag.

He shook his head and looked up at me. "They don't match."

Which meant it was one more mystery for us to keep poking at, one more mystery that might go unsolved.

"Thank you," Noah said, returning it to the older woman. "That was very helpful."

Mrs. Lebowski looked worried, probably because the word "evidence" was on the bag, clear as day, but she kept her concerns to herself as we walked out the door.

We went outside, and when we reached the sidewalk, Noah asked, "Do you want to go to the other neighbor's house?"

I shook my head. "No, Mom was much closer to Mrs. Lebowski. I doubt they know anything she doesn't."

"If you change your mind, we can always come back." He held out his hand. "Let me drive. You've had a shock, and you need to be able to sort through it all."

I didn't argue; I pulled the keys out of my jacket pocket and handed them to him.

He turned on the car once we were inside but didn't pull away from the curb. "I texted Lance to ask him to look into a few things she mentioned. One, her friend Annemarie. If she worked at the high school, we should be able to get her last name fairly easily. Two, it's a long shot, but I'm having him search for arrests for men named Gordy anywhere from thirty to eighteen years ago."

I nodded, still nearly frozen in shock.

"And lastly, this morning I asked him to look for the police report for when you were found on Mrs. Lebowski's porch. He hasn't sent it yet, so I reminded him to pull it up."

"Yeah," I said, my voice barely audible. "Good idea."

"It will probably take him a bit to get back to me, but we can look into Annemarie ourselves. We can either go to the high school and ask for the records or go to the library and look up the yearbooks." He paused. "We could ask Dawn, but she's in school, so she likely won't see our message until it lets out for the day."

"Library," I said. "They'll want to know why we're asking at the school, and I don't want to explain it."

"Good point."

"What about Bergan?" I asked, turning to face him. "Should we go see him again? He must have known about the connection to Mad Hatter's if he wrote 'white rabbit' on the box."

Noah's lips pursed as he considered it for a moment. "Let's look at some different angles before we question him again. If we find more things he kept from us, we can use it to our advantage to try to coerce him to talk."

"Yeah." I nodded, still numb. "Okay."

He hesitated, then said, "I know you're feeling unmoored right now, but she's still the mom you knew. She just had layers you didn't know about."

"Yeah, I know. It just feels weird." I searched for the right words. "Like I remember a lie."

"Not a lie, Maddie. Just part of her life. The part she kept to herself." His jaw flexed. "Parents always keep things from their children, and it sounds like she did it to protect you, not because she wanted power over you."

"It still feels like a lie."

He didn't respond. Instead, he drove to the library, and we both sat in silence. I was thinking about my mother, reexamining my memories in light of this new information, looking for any clues I might have missed. Sure, I'd been living in my own world of teen angst, but I still couldn't believe I'd missed the signs that my mother was in love. And involved with a thug, as Mrs. Lebowski had called him. Had he been mixed up in the Brawlers? Had their group even existed back then?

I glanced over at Noah, who seemed lost in his own thoughts. He caught my gaze and gave me a soft smile as he reached over and placed a hand on my leg.

While I'd been prepared to do this on my own if necessary, I was glad he was with me, keeping me anchored. I wanted to do the same for him if he'd let me.

He parked outside the library, and we went in. Noah asked the librarian at the counter for the location of the high school yearbooks, and we headed in the direction she pointed.

We searched for the year my mother was killed and looked through the staff, but we didn't find an Anne, Annemarie, or a Marie in any of the photos.

Noah grabbed another yearbook from ten years earlier and flipped pages until he found the staff photos.

"Found her," he said softly, then held the book toward me.

I instantly recognized Annemarie Bonay's warm, smiling face. "That's her," I said, pointing to the image, surprised at the broken fragments of memories that popped up in my head. "I remember her coming to our house. She was fun, always laughing."

"Let's look at the yearbook from two years earlier and see if she has the same name. This could be her maiden or married name."

"We don't know that she got married," I pointed out. "Only that she had a boyfriend."

"True, but it will be easier to find her if we know her most recent name."

I frowned. "Don't you have databases to find that stuff out?"

"We do, but I'm on leave, and I can't very well go looking people up."

"Which is why you're having Lance do it."

"True, but he's working his own cases, so we're doing what we can without his help."

We searched more yearbooks and discovered she used to be Annemarie Pope and later became Annemarie Bonay. As we continued searching chronologically through the years, we found her up until about five years before my mother's death. She wasn't in any yearbooks after.

"Time for some internet sleuthing," Noah said after he'd taken photos of the yearbook pages. "We could go to my house, but we might as well take advantage of the Cockamamie library computers."

We each sat at a screen and started looking up Annemarie—Noah doing an internet search while I looked for her on Facebook and Instagram. We both found hits within five minutes.

"She's on Facebook," I said. "And she's living up in Galena. She's married to Mel Bonay, and they have two kids—teenage boys."

Noah lifted a brow. "That fits with what I found on the internet. She got married when you were seven, so a couple of years after, she and your mother stopped hanging out. Her husband has been arrested for several DUIs and a petty larceny, by the way. The last arrest, his third DUI, was three years ago."

"They *do* live in Galena," I said as though it explained his history with the law.

"True." He looked at his screen. "Since Lance is tied up, I'm going to ask Neil to look up any other priors either of them might have." He leaned over to take in my screen. "Does her profile happen to say where she works?"

"She's a proud stay-at-home mom," I said with a sly grin. "And she posted ten minutes ago she was spending the afternoon reading in front of her fireplace until her kids come home from school."

"We could grab some lunch and head back up to Galena to see if she's open to talking about your mom."

I glanced at my phone. It was barely after noon. We had time to talk to her and perhaps chase a lead that she might give us before I took Noah to my house and then went back to work. "Let's do it."

Chapter Twenty

Maddie

Noah called in an order to the diner downtown, and we picked up our sandwiches and ate while we drove to Galena. We were five miles out of town when Lance called Noah back. He answered the call on speaker.

"Whatcha got for me, Lance?"

"Sorry. I've been busy with interrogations, so I don't have much."

"Anything you've got would be helpful."

"I found the police report for when Maddie wandered to the neighbors' as a kid. No charges were filed, and it was deemed an accident. I've sent you a copy of the report in an email."

"Perfect. Thanks."

"Neil dug into Melvin Bonay's record. As you found out, he has three DUIs and a petty larceny charge. He stole some tools from a neighbor, and the neighbor pressed charges. He was fined and received six months' probation. With the DUIs, he did six months in the county jail on the last stint and lost his license. He's had other arrests, but those didn't stick."

"What were the arrests?"

"Drunk and disorderlies. A few assault charges, mostly due to bar fights, but one of his neighbors pressed charges. There was another charge related to his wife, but that was over a decade ago."

"Domestic?" Noah asked.

"Yeah, they were both drunk, and it reads like he threw something at her but didn't mean to hit her. In fact, he claimed he was so drunk he figured his aim would be shit. He was surprised when the trophy hit her in the forehead."

"Trophy?" Noah asked incredulously.

"His. For a rec softball league."

Noah tapped the steering wheel, looking lost in thought. "So we're dealing with a habitual mean drunk."

"Possibly, although the assaults were a decade ago, so maybe he cleaned up some? His last DUI was five years ago."

"Let's hope he did for his wife's sake," Noah said.

"Speaking of his wife," Lance said. "We looked up Annemarie Pope and Annemarie Bonay and didn't come up with anything other than a few speeding tickets." Lance paused. "You think either of these folks have anything to do with Andrea Baker's murder?"

"Too soon to tell," Noah said. "Annemarie was best friends with Andrea when Maddie was younger. We're hoping to get more information about Andrea's personal life from her."

"So you're going to go talk to them?" Lance asked. "The guy's last known residence is in Galena. It has a reputation for a reason."

"Yeah, we gathered they lived in Galena from Annemarie's Facebook account. Can you send me the actual address?"

"Sure thing." Then he added, "I know I don't have to tell you to be careful, but be careful."

"Will do." Noah pressed his lips together. "I don't suppose anyone's had a chance to search for a Gordy?"

"Not yet. Neil's had his hands full, and like I said, I was busy with the interrogations."

"Get anything useful?"

"No one's ratted on Joe Kipsey yet, if that's what you're wondering. They're naming names, but only the low-level guys doing the thefts. Still haven't gotten to the higher levels."

"No mentions of taking the cars to George's Garage?" Noah asked.

"Nope, and from what we can tell, no cars have showed up there. But I'm working on 'em. One guy just turned eighteen, so I'm trying to put the fear of God in him to get him to turn in anyone above him."

"Good work," Noah said with a glint of pride in his eyes. "Keep me updated."

"You too. I'll send that address now."

Noah hung up, and his phone vibrated and he handed it to me. "Can you plug the address into the maps app?"

I took his phone and studied him. "Should we be worried about our safety visiting Annemarie?"

"Honestly, I don't know," he sighed. "But Annemarie and your mother were close enough that your mom brought her around you. I doubt your mom would have let her into your life if she didn't trust her. I mean, look at how she kept men away from you."

"Yeah." But I still felt uneasy.

I set up the navigation, then hesitated before returning his phone. "Do you mind if I look at the police report?"

Noah's brow shot up. "Of when you were little? Of course not. Take a look."

I opened his email folder and found Lance's email at the top. The report was short, with no blame placed on my mother, but it made it clear that a sixteen-year-old had been sleeping in the living room while my mother was bar hopping in Chattanooga. It didn't tell me anything I hadn't already known, but everything had been hearsay up until now. Seeing the police report made it real.

"We're getting close to the Bonay residence," Noah said, breaking into my thoughts. "How are you doing?"

"Okay."

"Really?"

I started to repeat my answer, then stopped. "I'm shaken, but I'm determined to pursue this to the end."

"Even if you keep finding out things you don't like?"

I twisted in the seat to face him. "Like you said, no one is purely good or bad. We're all shades of gray. Who am I to judge if my mother had more gray than I realized?"

"But it still hurts," he said.

"Yeah. It hurts, but my mother was more than a mother and a schoolteacher. She was human with wants and dreams, just like everyone else. I just didn't happen to know what they were." I sat back in the seat and drew in a breath. "I think that's what really hurts—that there was so much I didn't know about her."

"It's like I said earlier. We all have secrets, and parents especially want to hide them from their kids." He looked like it was tearing him in two to say so, and I remembered what he'd said earlier about my mother having the right motivations.

"What's your secret, Noah?" I asked, biting my lower lip in anticipation of his refusal to tell me.

He took a moment, then said, "My father is dying. Stage four prostate cancer. Supposedly, he only has six to twelve months to live." He cringed. "Well, I guess five to eleven now."

I gasped. "Oh, Noah. I'm so sorry."

"I've tried pretending it's a non-issue because of how messed up my feelings about him are. I've washed my hands of him, so what do I care?"

"He's still your father."

"I know, but I've let him hurt me too many times to count. I'm not letting him hurt me again."

"But you're hurting anyway," I pointed out.

"Yeah." The defeat in his voice broke my heart.

He slowed down as he turned into a rundown-looking neighborhood. "But I'm not giving him what he wants. I'm not moving back to Memphis and groveling at his feet. I'm living my own life, and I'm not letting him or my mother tell me how to live it."

"That's why your mom was so upset to meet me. She wants you home ASAP, and I'm standing in the way of that."

"No." He shook his head in frustration. "She wants me back regardless, but yeah, she feels like there's a ticking clock now."

"I'm sorry," I said, touching his arm. "I wish you'd told me."

He ran a hand over his head. "You're right. I should have, but he made me swear not to tell anyone, and it felt like telling you was just one more piece of proof that I wasn't an honorable man. He gave me an ultimatum—come home or he'd disinherit me"

"Noah! That's terrible."

"Just more of his mind games, but I never gave it a moment of consideration. I don't want his money. Not one penny. I'm my own man, and this is just helping me prove that."

"And that's part of the reason your mother wants you to move home?"

"Honestly, I'm not sure she even knows about that part." He was quiet for a moment. "I thought I could shove it into the background and ignore it, but all I really did was shut everything down. Including you." He gave me an awkward smile. "Sorry."

"Noah, we'll never work if you hide things like that from me."

"But you have your own shit to juggle without adding mine to the pile."

"That's what relationships are for." I grinned through teary eyes. "Sharing each other's shit."

He let out a strangled laugh. "I haven't read anything worded quite like that in any of the relationship books I've been reading."

My jaw dropped. "You've been reading relationship books?"

He turned to me, his eyes shining brightly. "In case you haven't figured it out by now, I'm Type A, and I hate when things aren't perfect. I don't want to fuck this up, Maddie. It's part of the reason

I've been staying away. I wanted to make sure I was doing things the right way, but all I've done is screwed them up more."

I frowned. "What did your therapist say about your dad's diagnosis?"

"I haven't told my therapist."

"*Noah.*"

He pulled up to the curb in front of an older-looking ranch house with bare landscaping. "I will. I promise. First, we'll find your mother's murderer, then we'll have our happily ever after."

His words took me by surprise. "You see us having a happily ever after?"

"I hope so." He gave me a hopeful look. "If I don't keep screwing things up."

"Just be honest and stop keeping secrets, then we'll work everything else out as it comes. You don't have to be perfect, Noah, no one is."

"I hope it's that easy."

I lifted a brow. "Why don't you try it, and we'll find out if it is?"

He laughed. "Touché." He turned serious. "You ready for this?"

"As ready as I'll ever be."

"I want you to take the lead on the questions, just like with Mrs. Lebowski."

Nodding, I held his gaze. "Okay. Thanks for doing this with me. I can't tell you how much it means to me."

"I wouldn't let you do it alone." He took my hand and squeezed it. "Now let's see what we can find out."

We got out and walked up to the house. A rusted minivan with a faded red paint job was parked in the driveway. It had to be a decade old. The house had a worn look too, but it didn't seem ominous. It looked lived in and loved.

I knocked on the front door, my stomach performing cartwheels while we waited.

About ten seconds later, a dark-haired woman opened the front door a few inches and peered out. "Whatever you two are sellin', I don't want it."

She started to close the door, but I called, "Annemarie? I'm not selling anything. It's Maddie. Maddie Baker."

The door stopped, and after a second, she pushed it open. "Maddie Baker?" she asked incredulously.

I nodded. "I wasn't sure you'd remember me." I released a tight laugh, my emotions getting the better of me. "I don't look like I did when you knew me."

She laughed too, tears filling her eyes. "You're all grown up."

"You look like I remember," I said truthfully. "Just a bit older." And more than a few pounds heavier.

"Over twenty years older. The last time I saw you, you were six years old." She shook her head. "What are you doin' here? How'd you find me?"

"You know small towns. Everyone knows everyone else's business," I fudged. "And I decided it was time to find out more about my mom as a person, you know? I only knew her as my mom, but it hit me recently that she was only six years older than me when she died. I want to know more about her, and I remembered you were best friends when I was little." I cringed. "I know I should have called first, but it's my first day off in ages, and my boyfriend Noah"—I gestured toward him—"and I were in Galena anyway, so we decided to take a chance and see if you were home."

"Oh my goodness! I can't believe you're here," she exclaimed. "Come in! Come in! Little Maddie Baker, all grown up."

I walked into the house with Noah following behind. The living room was filled with older furniture, but it was neat, clean, and homey. A fire blazed in the fireplace, and a soft throw was draped on the sofa along with an open book, the pages flat on a sofa cushion.

"Can I get either of you anything to drink?" she asked, staring at me like she was seeing a ghost.

"No, we're good," I assured her. "I hope we're not disturbing you."

"I was just reading." She gestured to a love seat opposite the sofa as she picked up her book, placed a bookmark inside before she closed it, then set it on the table next to her. "Sorry if I'm staring," she said as she took a seat on the sofa and Noah and I sat next to each other on the love seat. "It's just that you look almost exactly like your mother."

"I've been hearing that a lot since I've started talking to people who knew her," I said with a smile, resting my hand on the armrest.

"I hope that doesn't freak you out, especially how she ended up...dying." She cringed.

"Actually, it gives me comfort. Like some part of her is here with me."

"I get that," she said, settling back on the sofa and crossing her legs. "Who have you talked to?"

"Dawn Heaton," I said. "And also my neighbor."

"The middle-aged couple or the crotchety younger couple?"

I didn't remember the younger couple being crotchety, but I was little back when Annemarie knew them. "Mrs. Lebowski."

Annemarie nodded her approval. "Good choice. I've always liked her."

"I was closer to her. I stayed with her and her husband after school once I started middle school. She seemed like the logical choice."

"I can see her watching you," Annemarie said fondly. "She was a special lady, and I suppose you were probably getting home before your mom. She usually stayed after school to help kids. At least she did when I taught there. She loved it so much I didn't see her stopping. Especially if she knew you were being watched by someone who would love you like her own."

"It's funny how, as a kid," I said, attempting to steer the conversation to what I wanted to know, "you see your parent a certain way.

You don't think of them having a life outside of you or their job." I shrugged. "I mean, I knew Mom did volunteer work, but I didn't realize she used to be so heavy into the nightlife."

Her lips drew back. "Yeah, she did go through a wild phase."

"You knew her from teaching at the high school, right?" I asked.

"We started at the same time, both first-year teachers at the high school. I was from here—Galena—and she was from Cockamamie, but we'd never met until we were setting up our classrooms. She had a baby and then a toddler, and she spent all her time with you, but then she hit a point where she needed some me time. We'd been having some chill girls' nights at your house so she could put you to bed, but then she suggested a girls' weekend in Chattanooga. We had a lot of fun, so we started going there on Saturday nights. Your mom?" She shook her head with a faraway look. "She loved it. Probably too much."

"Why too much?" I asked.

"At first, we went once or twice a month, but she got to know people at a bar we frequented and wanted to go every weekend. It got to be too much for me. I like to party—or at least I used to when I was younger—but the noise and the crowds? I met Mel around that time at a softball game and started hanging out with him. He preferred the local bars, so I stopped going with her, not that it stopped her. She started going alone."

"You weren't worried about her?" I asked.

A strange look filled her eyes. "No, she had friends there to look out for her."

There was something she wasn't telling me, but I'd circle back to it later. She might shut down the conversation if I pursued it now. "I know Aunt Deidre and Uncle Albert watched me for a while, but then she started getting a babysitter. Were you still going out with her then?"

She squirmed in her seat. "Surely you want to talk about more pleasant things. The three of us did a lot together when you were little. Like, we went to the Chattanooga aquarium. Dollywood. We even drove to Nashville one weekend."

Part of me *did* crave those stories, but I felt like we were on the precipice of getting more information, and I couldn't turn back now. If I did, I might never get answers. "I would love to hear about those things, but before we move on...do you know if my mom had a boyfriend when she was going to Chattanooga back then?"

Her smile fell. "You know about Gordy."

My mother had met Gordy in Chattanooga? "Not a whole lot," I admitted. "I know they were seeing each other when she died."

"She was seein' Gordy again?" She shook her head with a look of disappointment. "She had a thing for bad boys, and Gordy fit the bill. Who knows how it would have ended if he hadn't gone to jail?" She grimaced. "What am I sayin'? Sounds like she got back together with him."

Gordy had been incarcerated? I tried to hide my shock.

Annemarie's brow lifted. "If I'm honest, I'm surprised she brought him around you. When you were little, she had a hard line she wouldn't cross—no men in the house. Men never met you. Seems like she would have kept a convicted felon away from you."

Who even was Andrea Baker?

I didn't want Annemarie to know my heart was being ripped apart, though, because then she might stop talking. So I took a note from Noah's playbook and shoved my feelings down.

"I never met Gordy," I admitted. "I didn't even know he existed until Mrs. Lebowski told me about him this morning."

Her mouth dropped open. "Your mother never introduced him to you?"

I shook my head. "Mrs. Lebowski said he only came over when I was sleeping at a friend's house or with my aunt and uncle."

She tutted, then reached over for a Diet Coke can on the table. "Andrea always was a mix of contradictions."

"How so?" I asked.

"You know, like sleeping with a drug dealer while portraying the squeaky-clean English teacher-slash-single mother. I think that's why she volunteered so much at that one soup kitchen. To atone for her sins."

My head felt fuzzy, but I forced myself to ask, "Gordy was a drug dealer?"

"Not hardcore," she said, then took a drink from the can. "The first time we met him, he offered us ecstasy. Everyone took it back then, so we didn't think a thing about it. But if I heard about either of my two boys taking drugs like that from a stranger now..." She shuddered. "We were stupid. Especially Andrea. She had a kid at home. You would have been an orphan if she'd died from an OD."

I cringed, and she looked horrified.

"Oh, God, Maddie. I'm so sorry! What a thoughtless thing to say."

"It's okay," I said, part of my heart turning cold. "It's true."

"Look," Annemarie said, leaning forward, resting the can on her knee. "Your mother wasn't perfect, but who is? She just went through a wild phase for a little while, got it out of her system, and returned to her mild-mannered teacher persona."

I nodded, then added, "Yeah."

"It's not like she was addicted or anything. She never did anything like coke or meth. Just pot and the occasional Molly. But she *never* took drugs around you. Not even pot. She only drank, and not very much at that. She said she needed to be able to drive if anything happened to you."

My throat felt tight, and I tried to swallow. I knew I should respond, but I couldn't process what to say.

Noah rested his hand over mine. "You said that Andrea met Gordy in a bar in Chattanooga. Was he from there?"

"Yeah, that's part of the reason she started going every weekend. To see him. But he got arrested shortly after she stopped going to Chattanooga."

"She stopped because I wandered out of the house, right?" I asked.

"Yeah, and then Gordy was arrested a couple of weeks later. He called your mom to bail him out of jail, but his bond was pretty high, and she would have had to put up her house. It killed her to refuse—she loved him—but she said she couldn't risk your home, Maddie."

"Was Gordy pissed?" Noah asked.

"Oh, God, was he! But he went to prison, and I never heard anything more about him. Then again, I was seeing Mel, and Andrea and I stopped hanging out as much. She didn't mention Gordy after his arrest, and I didn't ask. We mostly lost touch after I quit teaching and became a mom." She made a face. "The pay is crap, and it didn't make sense to pay most of it to daycare."

"How did Andrea afford it?" Noah asked.

Annemarie's face pinched. "That's an excellent question. I know Deidre watched Maddie a few days a week when she was little, but the rest of the time she was in daycare." She shook her head. "To be honest, I'm not sure how she afforded it. Even with Deidre's help."

Had Tony or his parents been paying child support after all?

"Did she have any other boyfriends?" Noah asked.

A frown creased her forehead. "Why are you both so interested in her boyfriends?"

"I got an email from a man claiming to be her ex-boyfriend," I lied. "He wanted some photos of her, but I didn't believe she had any boyfriends, which got me wondering about my mom's life." I made a face. "And so here we are."

Annemarie hesitated. "The only real boyfriend she had was Gordy. Before and after him, there were other men, but they never meant anything to her. Most were one-night stands."

I nodded again.

"So I wouldn't be giving that man any photos unless his name is

Gordy Smith," she continued. "He's the only one she ever cared about."

"Gordy Smith?" Noah asked. "That's his name?"

"That's what Andrea said, although I confess, it sounded like a fake name to me."

"What did the newspaper call him when he got arrested?" I asked.

She shrugged. "Is it bad I never looked? It happened in Chattanooga, and no one around here knew she was involved with him, so no one else was talking about it. I only heard from Andrea that he'd been convicted, and it was barely in passing at that. I told her she'd dodged a bullet with that one, she agreed, and that was that." She paused. "I truly can't believe she started seeing him again. When did she start?"

"A few years before her death."

"Was she still seeing him when she died?"

"Mrs. Lebowski said the only time he ever stayed over at our house while I was there was the night before she was killed."

"Oh, Andy," Annemarie said with a sigh as she looked up at the ceiling. "What were you *doin'*?"

"Do you think Gordy was capable of murdering Andrea?" Noah asked.

Annemarie gasped. "Maybe? I never knew him to be violent, but you never know about a person. Not to mention, he'd done time. It changes a man." The look on her face suggested she knew firsthand.

"Her murder was never solved," I said, jumping in. "The more I hear about her past, the more I wonder if it wasn't some random person who killed her like the cops suggested, but someone she knew."

"Last I heard, they thought it was Martin Schroeder," she said. "He was always a major creep. I could see her rejecting him and him killing her because he was pissed."

Little did she know that my mother wasn't his type. She'd been about twenty-five years too old.

"They say it wasn't him," I said. I didn't give her the details of how I knew. "It must have been someone else."

She pursed her lips for several long seconds. "Everyone loved her. I don't know who could have killed her."

Noah looked lost in thought, then said, "Gordy might have lived in Chattanooga before his arrest, but from the sounds of it, he was at Andrea's a lot. I wonder if he moved to Cockamamie after he got out of prison."

Annemarie looked clueless. "I'm sorry. I don't know. We fell out of touch, like I said, and even if we hadn't, she knew I disapproved of him. I doubt she would have told me anything."

"Do you happen to have any photos of Gordy?" Noah asked.

She frowned and shook her head. "No. We didn't take any photos when we were out. It's not like nowadays when everyone's snapping photos with their phones."

"Do you know if Gordy wore a necklace?" Noah asked.

Her nose scrunched as she considered it. "Honestly, I don't remember. It's been too long, and I didn't pay that much attention."

Noah leaned forward. "When you and Andrea hung out, did you ever go to a bar called the Mad Hatter's?"

Her eyes widened. "Why are you askin' about that place?" she asked, her face pale.

"I heard you guys went there," I said.

She shook her head. "I don't know what you heard, but that ain't true."

"So you two didn't go there before going to Chattanooga?" Noah asked.

"Look," she said, then licked her lips. "That place was bad news. You know why it shut down, don't ya?" She took another drink from her forgotten Diet Coke before setting it down on the table. "It got shut down because the owner was murdered."

"When?" Noah asked, his body tense.

"I don't know," she said, looking nervous suddenly. "But it doesn't matter because we didn't go there. Besides, he was murdered long after Andy and I stopped hangin' out."

We were silent for several seconds, the air so full of tension I could feel it when I sucked in a breath. I was worried she'd kick us out, so I quickly thought of a question to change the subject. "I know Mom was best friends with Dawn when she died. Were the three of you friends back then? You all worked at the high school together."

She released a nervous laugh. "Andy knew Dawn from growing up together, but they weren't all that close when you were little. I think Dawn judged her for bein' a single mom."

"So Mom wouldn't have shared information about her partying and her boyfriend?"

Annemarie shook her head, still looking spooked. "I doubt Andy would have told Dawn anything about Gordy, even after he got out. *Especially* after he got out. Dawn's pretty conservative, so there's no way she would have approved of Andy seein' him. In fact, she's uptight enough that she might have turned Andy in to the administration. There's no way they would have approved of her having a relationship with a convicted drug dealer."

I glanced at Noah. It looked like we needed to have another chat with Dawn.

A cell phone on the end table began to ring, and Annemarie jumped to grab it. "That's my mother-in-law. If I don't answer, she'll call Mel at work, and he'll come check on me. And once I answer, I'll be stuck for an hour."

I stood. "I've taken enough of your time. Thank you for everything."

"We didn't get a chance to talk about the good stuff yet," she said, looking genuinely sad. "I even have photos to show you."

"Maybe we can meet sometime for a chat," I said. "We'll schedule it instead of me rudely stopping by."

She engulfed me in a hug. "I'm so glad you did. Little Maddie Baker. I've thought about you, girl. I'm so glad you're happy." She released me and winked. "And got a good-lookin' man too."

I laughed. "Watch what you say. It'll go to his head."

"Already has," Noah teased.

The phone stopped ringing, and a panicked look covered Annemarie's face. "Crap."

"Quick," I said, heading for the door. "Go call her back."

"Will do. Bye, Maddie!"

While I was sad I hadn't had the chance to hear the good stories or see her photos, I'd gotten what I came for: more information, but it was obvious Annemarie was holding back.

What hadn't she told us?

Chapter Twenty-One

Maddie

"Annemarie knows something she's not saying," Noah said once we were in the car, and he was pulling away. He'd slid behind the wheel again, and it had never occurred to me to stop him.

"She got spooked when we brought up the Mad Hatter's. She claims they never went there, but I don't believe her. I need to do some investigating into the place. Especially if the owner was killed."

"Do you think the owner's death has anything to do with my mom?" I asked.

"Bergan claimed other people died around the same time as your mom, so it bears checking out." He grimaced. "Honestly, I meant to already check, but the dinner last night and my mom…I'm sorry, Maddie. I let you down."

"Let me down?" I shook my head. "Not a chance, so let that thought go right now."

He glanced over at me. "That was a lot to take in. How are you doing?"

"You mean after discovering my mother was in love with a drug dealer? Peachy."

Noah hesitated, seeming to choose his next words carefully. "I'm not condoning her dating a felon, and I can't believe I'm saying this, but there are multiple kinds of drug dealers. The kind who run empires and don't give a shit if they kill people, and the kind who take drugs and sell them to get a discount. Both are breaking the law, obviously, but there *is* a difference."

I didn't say anything, too mired in my anger and grief.

"And even though he was convicted," Noah continued when I didn't respond, "it doesn't mean he was a drug user or pusher when he got out. He could have given it up. He could have gotten his life straightened out. Lots of drug users do."

"Do you think he killed my mother?" I asked, turning to face him.

He considered it for several seconds. "My gut says no, mostly because of the note. If he had access to her at her house and possibly his if he lived in the area, why would he kill her at the school? Why not do it at his house or yours? Or somewhere else?"

"To throw the police off?"

"Maybe," Noah said. "But why would she meet with him at the school if she knew the relationship could get her fired?"

"Dawn said she thought Mom was going to meet Martin Schroeder. What if Gordy disguised his writing, and Mom believed the note was from Schroeder?"

"Yeah, it's possible. If we can find Gordy's family and friends, we can ask them if he wore an eagle pendant. We can't forget he and your mother were seen arguing that morning. She was murdered in a crime of passion. The person who killed her was pissed."

I resisted the urge to flinch. "Do you think Smith is really his last name?" I asked. "I've got to say, it sounds fake."

"You think he lied to your mom, or your mom lied to Annemarie?"

"I don't know," I said. "But it seems off."

"I'll look into it while you're working tonight," he said. "But my gut tells me it wasn't him."

"But who?"

"I don't know," he admitted, sounding like he hated to admit it.

"So we know she partied and took drugs and dated a drug dealer—*twice*—but we're no closer to finding out who killed her."

"Every piece of information we find is useful."

"I can't look into anything tomorrow," I said, frustrated. "Not with Mallory going to Chattanooga with her old coworkers this weekend."

"I never expected to solve the case in a couple of days, Maddie."

He was right, of course, but sitting on it didn't feel right now that we were getting information.

He reached over and took my hand. "We have time to stop by the high school and re-question Dawn if you want."

"Yeah, let's do it."

We pulled into the high school parking lot about five minutes after school let out. Noah fought the traffic of students leaving the parking lot, but when he pulled into a space in front of the school, he shifted his head, squinting. "Hey, isn't that Dawn hustling to her car?"

I looked in the direction he was staring and saw her walking fast across the parking lot, dodging between cars pulling out of parking spaces. "Um. Yeah."

"Let's go," he said, already opening his car door. I quickly followed, and we half-jogged to catch up as she opened her car door.

"Dawn," I called out, somewhat breathless. It was apparent I hadn't done any cardio in a while. "Wait up."

She paused, glancing around to see who'd called her. She looked like she was about to get back in her car when she saw Noah and me.

"I'm in a hurry," she said when we caught up to her. "I have a dentist appointment, and I'm going to be late."

"That's okay," I said. "This will only take a moment."

It was clear she didn't want to stick around, but thankfully, she hung her forearm over the top of her car door. "Okay. Make it quick."

"Thank you," I said, gratefully. "You don't remember my mom having a boyfriend at all?"

Irritation flashed in her eyes. "I already told you I didn't."

"What about a man named Gordy?"

Her eyes widened slightly. "Gordy?" she repeated.

From the way she said it, it was obvious she knew about him.

I pressed on. "Yes. My old neighbor says Mom was involved with him for several years before she was murdered."

She stared at me like I'd asked her if she'd stuffed the crown jewels in her purse, then gave me an exasperated look. "Maddie, do you remember a man named Gordy hanging around? Of course not. You weren't a small child. You would have known if your mother had a boyfriend."

"Mrs. Lebowski says he came over when I was staying at a friend's house or with my aunt and uncle."

She shook her head. "Sounds like this Mrs. Lebowski is suffering from dementia," she said with a laugh. "You and I would have known if she'd had a boyfriend."

"Did you know she had a boyfriend when I was little?" Then, I couldn't help adding with a slightly snide tone, "You were best friends, after all."

Her face fell. "You've been talking to Annemarie."

"Yes."

She turned to look at the snarl of cars still trying to escape the parking lot. "Annemarie likes to poison things."

"What does that mean?" Noah asked.

She turned to look at him. "It means she likes to be the center of attention. Andrea hated leaving Maddie in the evenings and weekends after she'd been in daycare all week, and Annemarie had no problem with hanging out at your house all the time. She liked that Andrea was a captive audience. She probably would have loved to keep things status quo, but then Andrea met someone in Chattanooga, and Annemarie didn't like it. So she latched onto Mel and didn't let go." She bobbed her head forward. "She found someone else to worship her."

"Worship?" Noah asked.

Rolling her eyes, she amended, "Okay, maybe not worship. More like being captivated by her." She shifted her weight. "Look, Annemarie can be a lot of fun, and Andrea needed that. But the moment she wasn't the sole focus of Andrea's fun, she moved on."

"What do you know about the man Andrea met in Chattanooga?" Noah asked.

Her mouth pinched. "That was a very long time ago, and years before she was murdered. It seems pointless to dredge it up."

"Humor me," I said. "I want to know everything."

She paused. "Look, all that happened ages before her murder, and she outgrew it. She realized she wasn't eighteen anymore, and she had a little girl to think about. She stuck to the straight and narrow after that."

"What are you talking about?" I asked in confusion.

Dawn shifted her weight and looked uncomfortable as she said, "Her boyfriend was arrested and used as a key witness in a big drug dealer case. He served some time, and she realized she'd put you in danger. She stopped going out after that, or at least she kept it closer to home with girls' nights out at friend's houses and the like."

"Do you happen to remember his name?" Noah asked.

Her face scrunched up like she was concentrating. Finally, she said, "Not really. His nickname was Gordy, like you said, but I'm pretty sure his first name was Gordon."

"Think hard," Noah said. "We really need that last name."

Pursing her lips, she shook her head. "I think it was Somato. Gordon Somato."

"He was from Chattanooga?" Noah asked.

"He lived there when Andrea met him, but I think his family is from Atlanta."

"Do you know what happened to him after he got out of prison?" Noah asked.

"As far as I know, he's still in there."

Her gaze landed on the traffic, and she stepped back. "I really need to go."

"One more thing," Noah said with urgency in his voice. "Do you know if Andrea frequented the Mad Hatter's when Maddie was a teenager?"

Dawn stared at him for a moment blankly, then burst out laughing. "That's hilarious."

"It's a serious question," I said.

"And my answer is no," she said, her laughter dying down. "That was a notoriously rough place. She would have been eaten alive there." She started to get in the car. "Now I really have to go."

"Sorry to keep you," I said absently. "Thank you."

She nodded and shut the door. Noah and I stepped away from her car so she could pull out of the space.

"At least we have a full name now," Noah said. "It gives me a place to start looking."

"He wasn't just a drug dealer. He was a witness against a drug kingpin," I said in a stupor. "This just keeps getting worse."

"Come on," he said, taking my hand. "We can discuss it on the way to the car."

We started walking. "We need to find someone else who knew my mother and isn't afraid to tell me the truth."

"It would be interesting to talk to someone who didn't like her."

I stopped walking and turned to face him. "I know exactly who we need to talk to."

His brow lifted. "The woman from the women's club?"

"Everly Barton and my mother were in the women's club together, and she's vindictive as hell. I can easily see her gathering information to use against my mother."

His forehead creased. "Why does that name sound familiar?"

"Because she's the current president of the club. She was the one who kept getting your name wrong during our self-defense demonstration in November."

His eyes shot wide, and then a grin spread across his face. "This sounds interesting. Let's go have a chat with Everly."

Chapter Twenty-Two

Maddie

"Do you know if Everly has a job?" Noah asked as we got into the car.

"If I had to guess, the answer would be a big fat no. Her husband is an attorney, and she prides herself on running her little world."

"So she might not be home?" he asked.

"Who knows? I don't keep up with the happenings of the women's club, not after Aunt Deidre's dementia worsened, but I might know someone who does. Want me to call her?"

"Go for it. I'll ask Neil if he can dig up anything on Gordon Somato. If he testified against a large drug dealer, we should be able to find something." He reached for his phone and started typing.

When I'd gone to the women's club meeting with Deidre in November, I'd met a woman who had told me she wanted to help with my aunt. I hadn't taken her up on it, but now I realized I'd been foolish not to. Aunt Deidre had lost Uncle Albert, and other than her neighbor Margarete, she was surrounded by unfamiliar faces–Linda, her home care worker, and Mallory. She probably would have fared better if I'd invited her friends to drop by for visits.

But dwelling on that now wouldn't help anything, so I searched my phone for Connie Smelton, the woman I'd met at the fateful women's meeting. She was a receptionist at a realtor's office, which probably put her in the path of lots of people.

She'd likely be at work, so I pulled up the number for the office and called it, hoping Connie was there today.

"Bob Parker Realty," a friendly woman said when she answered. "Connie speaking. How can I help you?"

"Connie?" I said tentatively. It suddenly occurred to me that she might not remember me. "It's Maddie Baker. Deidre's niece."

"Oh, Maddie!" she cried out gleefully. "I'm so glad you called. How's Deidre doing?"

I switched to speaker phone so Noah could hear. He was still parked in the school parking lot, waiting for an address. "Honestly, she's slipping faster than I hoped, but that's not why I'm calling. I wanted to ask you about Everly Barton."

"Oh," she said in disgust. "You must have heard what she did."

I turned to look at Noah as I said, "What did she do?"

"You didn't hear about her kicking Deidre out of the women's club?"

"*What?* No!" I exclaimed in indignation. "Why?"

"Oh, it was on account of the demonstration you did with that hot detective."

"Noah?" I asked before I could stop myself. "What about it?"

If she caught my familiarity with Noah, she didn't comment. "She said you were vulgar and disrupted the meeting, and she single-handedly kicked Deidre out of the group. It was totally against the rules. She's supposed to run it by the membership committee, but she didn't. Almost everyone is upset. Even the members who usually fall in line."

Anger simmered under my skin. How dare Everly treat my aunt that way?

"Does she realize how ill Deidre is?" I demanded. "If she found out in one of her clear moments, it would *kill* her."

"Everly doesn't care. She's just plain evil."

No one was just plain evil, but then I thought about Martin Schroeder and amended the thought to very *few* people were plain evil.

"Believe it or not," I said, forcing myself to remain calm, "that's not why I'm asking about her. I had no idea she'd kicked Aunt Deidre out."

"Well...the woman's on *my* poop list, so if you want any dirt on her, I'll tell you what I know."

Noah sat up straighter.

"This probably seems random," I said, "but I've been talking to people who knew my mom. I knew her just as my mother, and I'm trying to better understand who she was as a person."

"Oh, that's sweet, Maddie. I can tell you anything you want to know about her, but what does that have to do with Everly?"

"Well, while talking to people, it's come to my attention that Everly didn't care for my mother very much. I wondered if it had something to do with my mom being president of the women's club for a while."

"Your mother was an amazing woman," she said. "So good for the group. The best leader we'd had in ages, and in all honesty, no one who's come after her has been as dedicated and altruistic. The bylaws state that a president can only be in office for two three-year terms, but Everly always manages to put a puppet in the presidency during the years she's biding her time, waiting to be the official president again. But members still talk about how wonderful your mother was and I think it drives Everly bat poop crazy."

"She was an amazing woman," I agreed, only my already complicated feelings about my mother had grown even more complicated.

"It was such a shame when she stepped down," Connie said

with a sigh. "There were all sorts of rumors swirling about. And, of course, many of them centered on Everly since she took over."

"Everly replaced my mom?"

"In the middle of the term too," she said with a tut. "It was just so sudden. I'll never forget it. Your mother was running the meeting just like usual, but when she got to new business, she said she was stepping down due to personal reasons and forfeiting to the president-elect, Everly Barton."

I glanced at Noah, who was looking up from his phone at me. "Do you know what those personal reasons were?" I asked.

"No. Rumors were flying, of course. People halfway joked that Everly, who had wanted to be president desperately, had found something on her and blackmailed her to quit."

"Do you think that's true?" I asked, my blood running cold.

"Of course not. What in the world could Everly have found on Andrea? She was the sweetest woman you'd ever meet."

The look in Noah's eyes said he knew what Everly probably had on her. We were in agreement there. "How soon before my mother's murder did she step down?"

"About three months before."

Now, I was convinced Everly knew.

"So what were the rumors?" I asked.

"Oh, stupid stuff. Like Andrea was teaching subversive material in her English classes, and Everly was trying to get the board of education to fire her. And then there was one about her giving you favoritism."

"I wasn't even in her class," I protested.

"It was all nonsense," Connie said. "There was no basis for any of the rumors, but like I said, it was all so sudden, and Andrea's explanation was so vague, and well...nature abhors a vacuum. People had to come up with a reason for her sudden departure. No one ever believed any of it, mind you."

"No other rumors?" I asked carefully. "Anything so outrageous no one believed it?"

She hesitated. "Well...there was one."

"Yes?"

"One person claimed she had a secret lover who had a shady past. Everyone laughed at that."

"Who was saying that?" I asked.

"It was all so long ago," Connie said soothingly. "Let it be water under the bridge, Maddie." She obviously didn't want to tell me.

"I'm not going to attack her or anything," I said. "I just want to talk to her."

"That's really not a good idea."

I could let this go and hope Everly would tell us what we needed to know, but knowing Everly, she'd refuse to tell us anything. Or she'd give us just enough to tease us but nothing we could use. If the woman Connie was referring to knew something, then she was a better source. But I'd have to sully my mother's shiny reputation to get her to share it.

"Connie, if I tell you something in confidence, do you promise not to tell anyone?" I asked, already regretting this course of action, but I couldn't bring myself to stop now. We were getting closer. I could feel it. "I think my mother *did* have a secret lover."

The silence on the other side was ominous.

I continued. "I'm trying to find out who he was."

"I don't believe it," she said, incredulous. "Andrea never dated anyone. Like ever. We used to tease her about it, but she claimed she didn't need a man in her life."

"I know," I said. "I didn't even know about him, but that's not surprising since she told numerous people she wouldn't bring a man into *my* life. I suspect she kept this man quiet to keep from hurting me."

Which was funny since keeping him a secret had ultimately hurt me too.

"You promise you won't be too hard on her?" Connie asked. "The poor soul only told one other person, who told everyone else."

"Who did she tell?"

"Debbie Townsend, but she died about five years ago. Cancer got her. Debbie loved to gossip, God rest her soul. But this woman was new to the group and didn't know Debbie was a blabbermouth. She felt *terrible* about it. Especially after Andrea died."

"So who told Debbie?" I asked, trying to hide my impatience. I wished she'd just spit out the name already.

"Gina." She hesitated. "Gina Moore."

I racked my memory to see if I remembered her name but came up with nothing. "Did she work at the high school?"

"No. She was a bookkeeper. Rumor had it she'd worked at the Mad Hatter's before taking the bookkeeper job in town, but no one ever had any proof. When I met her at her first club meeting, she was working for an accountant downtown. In fact, she was engaged to him. I can't remember her maiden name. In any case, she didn't last long. She wasn't high class enough for the likes of Everly, so she either quit or Everly ran her off about a year after she joined. Which was such a shame because your mother had invited her."

"Do you know if she's still married to her husband?"

"Oh, yes. And they still work together too. They're one of those rare couples who seem to fall more and more in love the longer they're together."

I didn't need to ask her who Gina's husband was. Moore Accounting and Bookkeeping was downtown, a block from Déjà Brew. I'd seen Arthur Moore in the coffee shop. I'd probably seen his wife before without realizing she had any connection to me.

"Thank you, Connie. I really appreciate you telling me."

"If you want to know more about your mother, how about we meet for lunch soon? There's more to her than this awful Everly business."

"Thanks," I said, tears burning my eyes. "I'd like that."

I hung up and shifted in my seat to face Noah. "We have time to stop by Moore Accounting and talk to Gina before we head to my house."

"Sounds like a plan."

The traffic had cleared out, so he pulled out of the parking space and headed toward the exit. "Neil already got back to me about Gordon Somato." He shot me a glance. "There's nothing."

"But Dawn seemed so sure."

"Neil used multiple possible spellings. While I'm watching your aunt tonight, I'll do an internet search for articles about his arrest and see if I can come up with anything that way."

"Okay." I gave myself a few seconds to let the information sink in. "Do you think Dawn lied?"

"I'm not sure what purpose there'd be to lying, but I'm not ruling it out."

"None of this makes any sense."

"Let's go talk to Gina and see if we can get more information. If your mother invited her to the women's club, then she must have known her. And it's possible she might be able to give us a different name for Gordy."

"Yeah," I said absently.

"Hey," he said, reaching over and threading his fingers through mine. "We're going to get to the bottom of this. I promise."

That's what I'd thought I wanted, but now I was worried what we'd find at the bottom.

Chapter Twenty-Three

Maddie

It was almost four on a Friday afternoon, so I was worried the accounting office might be closed by the time Noah found parking in front of the building, but the lights were still on and an open sign hung in the window.

"I'm not sure what to say to her," I said as he turned off the car. "I've never met her before, and she's at work. This could be awkward."

"Just approach her like you have everyone else," he said. "And if you feel like you're not getting anywhere, I can pull out my badge."

My eyes widened. "You're not supposed to be working."

"We're getting close, Maddie. I can feel it," he said in frustration. "The shitty part about all of this is that we've easily followed a breadcrumb trail nearly twenty years old. If Bergan had actually worked this case, I suspect he could have made an arrest within the week."

"Still, I don't want you to get into trouble."

"We'll deal with whatever happens as it comes."

We headed inside. The office was warm and bright, not cold and sterile like other accounting offices I'd visited. Then again, the last time I'd been in an accounting office, it had been with my ex-boyfriend Steve, whose accountant had been dirt cheap.

The receptionist greeted us with a smile. "How can I help you?"

I approached her desk and said warmly, "Hi. I'm Maddie Baker, and I was hoping to speak to Gina. Is she available?"

The receptionist—Susan, based on her nameplate—looked wary. "I don't see that you have an appointment with her. What is this in regard to?"

I tried to amp up the friendliness. "She knew my mother, and I'd like to ask her a few questions about her." Even as I said it, I knew how strange it sounded.

Her smile wavered. "Since this is a personal matter and not a professional one, you can leave your name and number, and she'll get back to you as soon as she's available."

I shot Noah a questioning glance, unsure what to do next. Honestly, I couldn't fault Susan for guarding her boss.

Noah gave me a grim smile, then stepped in front of me, holding his badge out. "I'm Detective Langley with the Cockamamie PD. We need to speak to Ms. Moore as expediently as possible."

Fear filled Susan's eyes. "What's this about?"

"As Ms. Baker mentioned, it's regarding her mother."

"Who's your mother?" Susan asked me, wide-eyed.

I figured it wouldn't hurt to tell her. "Andrea Baker. Gina knew her about twenty years ago."

"Then why does she need to talk to you now?" Susan asked in confusion.

"Is Ms. Moore available?" Noah asked. "Is she here?"

Susan's gaze shifted to him, and she hesitated before she said, "She's gone for the day."

"You're sure about that?" Noah asked in his deep, authoritative cop voice.

She swallowed, then nodded. "Yes."

"Do you know if she went home?"

"I think she's running errands. It's Friday and all," she said, her eyes shifting even more as her fingers twitched. "And I have no idea where she went."

Noah pulled out a business card and placed it on her desk with a tap. "Be sure to let her know that we need to talk to her sooner rather than later."

Susan glanced at the card but didn't touch it. "You're that police officer they talked about in the paper, aren't you?"

Noah flinched, but it was barely noticeable. "The detective who has focused on making Cockamamie safer? That's me."

"I know the paper's trying to stir up trouble, but you're doin' a good thing." She picked up the card and looked at it with a wary expression. "You *are* makin' this place safer, and I'm not the only one who thinks so."

Noah swallowed, surprise in his eyes. "Thank you."

"But I still don't know where Gina is."

"We thank you for your time," I said as Noah turned to walk out, leaving me to follow.

Once we were out on the sidewalk, he turned to me grimly. "She's lying."

"About Gina? Yeah, I figured, but not about how she felt about the editorial."

His jaw set. "The editorial's not important."

"*Of course* it's important. You care what the people in this town think, and there's nothing wrong with that, Noah. And from what I've seen, everyone seems to be on your side."

He gave me a grim look. "Working on your mother's case is what we need to focus on."

"Just admit that you care what people think and I'll let it drop."

He drew in a breath then pushed it out. "Okay, I care. I shouldn't, but I do. Now you promised to let it drop, so let's get back to Gina. I'd bet ten bucks she's in an office in the back." He turned to face Susan through the window. She was still sitting at her desk, watching us on the sidewalk. "She's going to head straight back there as soon as we walk away."

I wanted to push him more on how he felt about the editorial, but I'd promised to let it go. I would...for now. "I don't suppose we can do anything about that?"

"Not a damn thing," Noah said. "Our only recourse is to find Gina out in the open somewhere. We could stake out the parking lot behind the building, but for all we know, her car's on the street."

I put my hands on my hips, my frustration simmering. "Now what?"

"We could run by Everly's place. I had Neil look up her address, but we don't know if she'll talk, and if she does, how long it'll take. It's already after four. We need to get to your house so you can show me what I need to do to take care of your aunt before you head to work."

I ran a hand over my head. "I'd call in sick, but that would leave Petra in a bind, not to mention Linda leaves at five anyway. Someone needs to be at the house with Aunt Deidre."

"It's okay," he said, placing a hand on my arm. "We'll talk to Gina. Maybe not today, but we will."

"Yeah. What about Bergan? We could try to talk to him again."

"I still think we should wait and try to talk to Gina first. The more we know, the better to make him squirm and talk."

"Yeah," I said, feeling unsettled.

"I know you're disappointed."

I glanced up. "I don't know if disappointed is the right word. More like frustrated that we keep hitting walls."

He reached out and cupped my cheek. "We'll tear through them, I promise. Now, let's go see your aunt."

We had enough time to stop by Noah's place to pick up his car and head to my house. Aunt Deidre was sitting in the living room with Linda, working on a kids' jigsaw puzzle at the coffee table when we walked in.

Her nose wrinkled when she saw us, and I could tell she recognized one or both of us, but who we were was just out of reach.

I hung my coat on the hooks in the entryway and walked toward her, sitting on the sofa next to her.

"Hey, Aunt Deidre," I said tentatively. After everything I'd found out about my mother today, I needed her to be the rock she'd always been for me.

"Maddie," she said, tears filling her eyes.

I threw my arms around her and hugged her tight, fighting tears of my own.

"There, there, Maddie," she soothed, running her hand over my hair. "Everything's going to be all right."

A small sob escaped me, because I knew nothing would be all right. I trusted that Noah and I would find my mother's killer, but I could never ask my aunt about all of the things I'd discovered. I'd always be aware that I'd only known half of her, not the whole woman she'd been. And Aunt Deidre's condition would only get worse and worse.

She hugged me tight, then leaned back and wiped the tears from my cheeks. "It's going to be okay, Maddie."

I offered her a shaky smile. "I love you, Aunt Deidre."

"And I love you too." She glanced up at Noah. "Now introduce me to your young man."

So she wasn't totally there, which wasn't surprising, but she'd given me what I needed, and I cherished it. For all I knew, it could be the last time she'd be able to give me comfort.

"This is my boyfriend, Noah," I said, gesturing to him. "He's going to stay with you tonight while I work."

"The library's open tonight?"

Noah shot me a sympathetic look as I said, "Something like that."

She leaned into me and half-whispered, "He's cute."

"I know," I said with a laugh. "I think I'll keep him."

Her cheeks flushed. "I'm not sure I should be left alone with such a handsome man without a chaperone."

Noah laughed. "I promise to be on my best behavior."

Her eyebrows waggled as her cheeks flushed. "Maybe I don't want you to be."

I burst out laughing. "Aunt Deidre!"

"You don't have anything to worry about," she said, fanning her face. "I'll always be loyal to Albert."

I got up and took Noah upstairs to show him Aunt Deidre's bedtime routine, but Linda said she'd finish the instructions so I could get going. She also promised to make sure they had something to eat.

Mallory was on a work call when I poked my head in her room, and she mouthed to me *I love you* and *have a great weekend with Americano,* then waggled her eyebrows.

It suddenly occurred to me that Noah could potentially spend the night.

I didn't have time to dwell on the possibility as I hurried to the coffee shop and clocked in a few minutes early. I was working with Troy, a high school kid who had recently started at Déjà Brew, and he made me feel positively ancient.

Friday nights could be hit or miss with busyness, and this Friday was a bust. Troy kept whining about missing the high school basketball game, and since Petra was gone and I was the one with the keys, I told him to leave at seven-thirty. There was a chance I'd get a rush of customers before we closed at nine, but I was used to working with a crowd. I could handle it.

I had enough customers over the next hour to keep me from being bored, including a group of fourteen-year-old girls who were giggly and sweet. They were having a sleepover, apparently, and a parent would be picking them up from the coffee shop right before closing. I chatted with them while I made their drinks, and they settled in at a table by the windows, discussing their crushes with a seriousness that made me smile.

At eight-thirty, they were the only customers in the room—until a man walked through the entrance. He hung back, sticking close to the door, and studied me with an intensity that made the hair on the back of my neck stand on end. He was under six feet with a stocky build. His black leather jacket and jeans were worn. He looked to be in his mid to late forties, and he had an air about him that suggested he didn't take shit and had no trouble starting it. He had dark brown hair, dark eyes, and a dangerous look.

"Welcome to Déjà Brew," I called out, hoping to either send him on his way or draw him away from the girls, who had stopped chatting to watch him.

He approached the counter, and I tried to keep my anxiety under control. The guy looked even more dangerous up close.

He stopped in front of me, and I could see the deep crow's feet around his eyes and the tattoos at the base of his neck, which were faded and looked like he'd had them a while. "I want a coffee," he grunted. He was jumpy, and his eyes kept darting behind me.

Sweet Jesus. Was he here to rob us?

I nearly asked him what kind of coffee, but he seemed like a black coffee kind of guy, coffee grounds included just to make him look tougher. I poured some into a medium size cup, finishing off the pot. After putting on a lid, I placed it on the counter before him.

"On the house," I said, hoping my smile didn't look as forced as it felt. "It's the last of the pot, so I can't guarantee it's as good as usual."

He'd made no move to reach for his wallet—or a weapon—so I wasn't sure he'd planned to pay anyway. He picked it up, his gaze still on me. "You usually work nights?"

My smile froze as I tried to figure out how to answer. I decided to go with the truth. "Not usually."

He gave a short nod and continued to stare at me for a moment. My gaze dropped to his neck. I figured I might as well get an inventory of his ink in case I needed to give a police report for what he was possibly about to do. And then I noticed them—wings in the mix of lines and color. "Nice tats," I said, hoping it didn't sound as lame to him as it did to me. "What is it?"

His brow rose slightly, and he smirked as he pulled down the collar of his T-shirt, showing me an eagle sitting on a branch, wings spread out.

Could it be a coincidence?

Noah had told me before that he didn't believe in them.

"Why an eagle?" I asked. "I'm always curious why people get permanently inked with designs. Tattoos are personal. That must have some special meaning for you."

I was crazy if I thought he was about to tell me why he'd marked himself with an eagle identical to the pendent my mother had ripped off her attacker. But I *felt* crazy.

Had *this man* murdered my mother?

His eyes were dark and cold as he released the collar of his shirt and grunted, "Personal reasons." Then he spun around and walked out the door.

The girls watched him leave, then turned to face me, terror on their faces. Suddenly, they all started talking at once.

"He was scary!"

"I thought he was going to rob you, Miss Maddie!"

"He looked like a serial killer!"

I glanced at my phone on the counter and saw it was eight-forty. I considered closing early, but the girls' ride wouldn't be here for twenty more minutes. I couldn't kick them out, so I settled for walking over to the door and turning the deadbolt, locking us inside and any potential threats out.

They watched my every move, a couple of them with fear in their eyes, while the others seemed more curious.

"Might as well be safe," I said, trying to sound reassuring. "If someone shows up, I can let them in. Or tell them we're closed."

They nodded their approval and started to talk all at once again as I headed behind the counter and picked up my phone to call Noah.

"Hey," he answered cheerfully. "I'm surprised to hear from you already. Did you close early?"

"I considered it." Then I told him what had just happened.

"I don't like it," he said, his voice tight. "But it could be nothing."

"He had an eagle, Noah!" I whisper-shouted, turning my back to the girls. "Just like the pendent."

"I know," he said, "but I suspect a large portion of men with multiple tattoos have some form of an eagle. Still, that doesn't mean I'm not worried. We shook a few limbs today, and it's possible we scared out someone from your mother's past."

"And they came to check me out?"

"Yeah." The word was short and deep. After a moment's pause, he said, "Don't leave the building until I tell you it's safe."

"What does that mean? What are you going to do?"

"I'm going to have someone come to the back door when you get off and walk you to your car. I'd do it myself, but obviously I can't leave your aunt."

"Maybe I'm overreacting," I said, feeling embarrassed.

"Maybe you are," he agreed, "but your instincts tell you that you're not, and you have to listen to your instincts. When will you be leaving? I'm guessing not right at nine."

"Maybe ten minutes after? I need to clean the machines. I locked the front door, which means I'm in control of who comes in."

"Good. Smart." I heard the pride in his voice. "I'll have someone out back by nine just in case you finish early. That way you're not sitting in there alone. But don't leave until I tell you they're there." He paused, and when he spoke next, emotion filled his voice. "I wish I could come get you myself."

"I'm fine. He left. He didn't do anything. He just looked scary."

He started to say something, then cleared his throat. "I think I should stay with you tonight."

My heart fluttered. "I think you should too," I said huskily. "But not because I got scared. I want you to stay for other reasons." I glanced back at the girls to make sure they hadn't overheard me, but their heads were all bent together as they rehashed what had just happened.

"Are you sure?" Noah asked, his voice deep. The timbre sent a thrill through my veins.

"Very."

"I'd like that." He paused. "Have you eaten dinner?"

"I had a muffin earlier and a chai tea an hour ago."

"I'll have something waiting for you when you get home."

I grinned. "That sounds kind of dirty, Noah."

He laughed. "Read into it what you will."

It felt weird and slightly wrong to feel so happy while all this awful stuff was going on, but if I'd learned nothing else over the last few months it was to take happiness where I could find it.

I hung up and started preparing to close the shop, but I kept shooting glances to the door.

The girls' ride showed up a few minutes before nine. I unlocked the door after they confirmed the woman at the door was one of their mothers.

I locked the door behind them after making sure they were all loaded into the minivan. I was nearly done closing when I checked my phone and saw that Noah had texted me his friend Neil's number and said he was waiting out back.

I texted Neil that I was about to come out, and when I opened the back door he was standing a few feet from the door, wearing jeans. His hands were stuffed in the pockets of a bomber jacket.

"You're not on duty?" I asked in surprise.

"No ma'am...er, I mean miss, but I wasn't doin' anything, and Noah's tied up."

I handed him a to-go cup. "Then I'm *really* glad I made you this latte before I cleaned the espresso machine. It's decaf, so it won't keep you up."

A smile lit up his face as he took the cup. "Thanks!"

He walked me over to my car, the only other vehicle in the lot besides his. Once I was inside, he got in his truck and followed me out of the lot.

I wasn't sure if I was imagining things, but I could have sworn there was a motorcycle in the lot across the street from the coffee shop, parked in the shadows. Only when I turned back to look again, it was gone.

Probably my imagination playing tricks on me.

Chapter Twenty-Four

Maddie

Neil followed me all the way home, and when I pulled into the driveaway, Noah was standing in the open front door. He waved to Neil as he stopped in front of the house.

I got out and walked to the porch. When I started to climb the steps, Neil pulled away. I glanced over my shoulder to watch his departing car and then turned back to Noah. "While I appreciated the escort, having him follow me home seemed like overkill."

He reached for me and took my hand. "We don't know why that guy was there or if he was involved with your mother's murder, so I'm being careful with something that's precious to me."

"My car?" I teased, but my heart still fluttered. I knew Noah cared about me. A lot. But he had never called me precious before. Then other parts of me tingled as I remembered he was spending the night.

He laughed. "Exactly. Come in." He tugged me through the doorway, shutting it behind us before helping me take off my coat. "I have dinner ready for you in the kitchen."

"You cooked?" I asked. "Or did Linda stay and make something?"

"Deidre and I cooked together. And it's edible. Come see for yourself."

He grabbed my hand and pulled me into the kitchen. A plate with spaghetti and a salad sat on the table, along with a bottle of wine and a couple of lit candles.

The thought he'd put into this filled me with an overwhelming sense of love. Noah might not be there yet, but I knew he'd get there if I gave him enough time.

"This is lovely, Noah. Thank you."

He grinned as he led me to the table and pulled out my chair. "Don't get *too* excited. You haven't tasted it yet, but your aunt loved it, so..."

I sat down and laughed. "My aunt has been into weird food combinations lately, *so*..." I mimicked.

Chuckling, he sat across from me and unscrewed the cap of the wine. "It's been a long, stressful day. I thought you might need a drink."

"Yes, that sounds great."

He poured some into a glass and handed it to me.

I took a long sip. "Thank you."

After he poured himself a glass, he sat back in his seat, watching me with an anxious look as I started eating. "You won't hurt my feelings if you don't like it."

"It's really good," I said through a mouthful of pasta. I was hungrier than I'd realized.

His eyes sparkled. "No need to sound so surprised."

"You yourself have admitted you don't cook much."

"True, but like I said, your aunt helped."

Oh yeah. He was here because he'd spent the last four and half hours with my aunt, and things had been hit or miss with her lately. "How did it go tonight?"

"It went great, actually. She helped me cook dinner and we made brownies—from scratch even. Then we cleaned up the kitchen and we worked on a puzzle. After that, she showed me photos of you when you were a little girl."

"What?" I asked before I shoveled another forkful of noodles into my mouth. Spaghetti wasn't exactly "date" food, but this was Noah. I was less concerned about impressing him than convincing him to risk his heart.

His brow rose. "Which part has you so surprised?"

I shook my head, then swallowed. "All of it, I guess."

"Well, she kept forgetting who I was, and when she showed me the photos, she said they were pictures of Andrea, but it was obviously you." He grinned. "You were a cute little girl."

"Obviously," I teased as I took another bite, then after a moment, I asked, "Did you have time to do any searching?"

His smile faded. "I did, but not as much as I would have liked. Do you want me to tell you about it now, or wait until you've finished your dinner?"

"As much as I'm enjoying this time with you, tell me now. I'm tired and I'm really looking forward to going to bed."

His eyes smoldered. "Do you have any idea how hard it is to concentrate when you say things like that?"

I laughed and took a sip of my wine. "I'm tired. Maybe I just want to go to sleep."

He turned serious. "Whatever you want to do, Maddie. It's all about you tonight."

To my aggravation, tears filled my eyes.

"What did I do wrong?" he asked with a panicked look.

"Nothing. You're doing everything absolutely right." I reached across the table and placed my hand on his. "I can't remember the last time anyone's taken care of me like this. I guess I'm not used to it."

"Then I'm an asshole for not doing it sooner."

"No, you're doing it at your own pace." I twisted my mouth to the side. "I think all of this means even more after today." I drew in a breath and sat back in my chair. "Sorry. I didn't mean to make things weird."

"You didn't, Maddie. We promised to be open and honest. I want you to know how much you mean to me, and I've done a piss-poor job of it. But I'll do better."

I set my fork down and pushed the plate away, eager to get to bed. "I'm done."

Worry covered his face as he took in the half-empty plate. "Are you sure?"

"You gave me enough to feed two lumberjacks." I lifted my brow. "But I do remember something was said about brownies."

"You stay here, and I'll get them." He stood, picked up my plate, and took it to the sink. "Did I mention they were made from scratch?"

A grin spread across my face. "I believe you did."

He grabbed a square glass pan from the counter and put in the center of the table, then refilled my wine glass. The brownies were already cut into squares, and several were missing. I picked up one and took a nibble before I exclaimed, "Oh God. This is *really* good."

A smug look lit up his eyes. "Told you."

"Okay, this means you're in charge of all brownie-making in the future."

"I can live with that. Especially since your aunt shared her recipe with me."

I took a sip of my wine. "I'm impressed. She doesn't share that with just anyone, you know."

"In the interest of full transparency, she shared it with me because she said that I have, and I quote, 'a great ass.'"

I cringed even though I was amused. "The Aunt Deidre I knew growing up would be horrified to know she'd said such a thing."

"Well, it is a great ass," he teased.

I took another bite of the brownie and tried hard to keep from moaning. Aunt Deidre's recipe had some secret ingredients that made them especially good, but they were even better tonight because she'd shared her recipe with Noah. She was pretty stingy with it. She may have given it to him because she appreciated his butt, but it still felt like she'd given him her blessing.

I was getting sappy. I needed to focus on something else. Like my mother's murder. "Tell me what you found."

"Like I said, not much." He took a sip of his wine, then helped himself to a brownie. "Lance and Neil were off tonight, so I had to do some amateur sleuthing. Since Aunt Deidre was more like herself than usual, I asked her about your mother's funeral."

My mouth dropped open. "Her funeral? You mean if anyone suspicious was there?"

"That too." He paused. "But I was more interested in whether your father showed up."

The blood in my head rushed to my feet, leaving me light-headed. "Did he?"

Sympathy filled his face.

I knew he had to wonder why I asked. Why I didn't know if he was there or not. "I only saw photos of him when he was in college with Mom," I said with a grimace. "And I was out of it, so I wouldn't..."

"Maddie, you don't have to explain. You never really met him. The answer is no. He didn't come. She said she called him to let him know about her death. He said he was in Amsterdam working on a business deal, and he couldn't get away." He hesitated again. "That's when he told her that he didn't want custody of you. That Deidre and Albert could take you in."

I nodded, surprised that it felt like a scab had been ripped from my heart. I didn't know the man. It would have been more surprising if he *had* wanted me. But it still hurt to hear the words.

"I plan to get proof that he was really there, but my gut says he had nothing to do with your mother's death."

I nodded again. "I agree. He had no reason to kill her."

He reached over and squeezed my hand. "But I did find something useful. There was a trial of a drug dealer in Chattanooga about a year after your mother stopped going there, but there weren't many details in the press. I did get the name of the drug kingpin—presuming it's the right trial. Scott Reed. The article I found said there was a key witness who testified at his trial, but it gave no name and no other information about him."

"Do you think it was Gordy?"

"Possibly. I need to do more digging. I want a name and if it's Gordy, if he went to prison."

I nodded. "Anything else?"

"The owner of the Mad Hatter's, Billy Hauser, was murdered the week after your mother's death."

My brow lifted. "That seems suspicious. Especially since Bergan claims the deaths that happened around the same time as my mother's murder helped convince him to back off the case. Maybe he wasn't lying."

"Agreed. I didn't see any other deaths, but tomorrow, I plan on finding out more about the bar, the owner, and the patrons. I'm going to check with some of the people I know at the sheriff's department to see what they can tell me about the place. It was outside of the city limits, so they'll have more information."

Picking up the brownie pan, I got up and returned it to the kitchen counter, where I covered it up with some tinfoil. "Okay. That's good."

"I'm sorry it's not more."

My heart burst. I went back to him and ran my fingers through his hair, lightly rubbing his scalp as I gazed down at him. A lump filled my throat, but I forced out, "Noah, it's more than I've had since her death. *Thank you.*"

He snagged my arm and pulled me to him, and I sat sideways on his lap. A wave of longing washed through me, stealing my breath. I wanted this man, and we'd wasted too much time getting to this place. I wasn't wasting another second.

Picking up a strand of my hair, he played with the end, then looked up into my eyes with a sorrowful expression. "I want to make this right for you, Maddie."

"Shhh..." I said, placing my fingertip on his lips. "No more talking about my mother tonight. For the rest of the evening, it's just you and me."

He kissed my fingertip, then pulled my lips to his and kissed me slowly and leisurely, as though we had all night.

Anticipation rippled through me as it occurred to me that for the first time since we'd been together, we really did.

I cupped the side of his face, brushing my fingertips along his stubble, loving the feel of him. He tasted of the brownie and the wine. My hunger for him grew.

"Let's go to bed," I murmured against his lips.

He pulled back slightly, cradling the back of my head. "We can just go to bed and sleep, Maddie. It wouldn't be the first time." Something deeper than longing filled his eyes. "And it won't be the last."

It was true that we'd slept in the same bed without anything sexual happening between us. After masked men had broken into my house and tried to kidnap me, Noah had spent the night here and slept in my bed with me. But that had been in the very beginning, when we were attracted to each other but nowhere close to letting each other in.

"Noah, the only thing I want right now is you," I whispered with a soft smile. Then I grinned. "Well, you and my glass of wine."

"I was hoping you'd say that."

"That I'd want my glass of wine?"

Laughing, he picked up my wine glass and handed it to me. "I'm counting on you wanting me more than the wine, but as long as I'm on the list, I can live with it." He blew out the candles, then scooped his arm under my knees and stood.

I held the wine glass out to keep from spilling it. "Noah, what are you doing?"

"What I should have done when I came home after Christmas. Making you mine."

He carried me up the stairs and I balanced my glass to keep the wine from sloshing over the edge. Just when I thought he'd topped the romance department tonight, he went and did something like this.

Steve had told me early in our relationship that men who carried their women to bed were trying too hard. I should have told him that he wasn't trying hard enough. But comparing Steve to Noah was like comparing a turd to a diamond.

He stopped outside my cracked bedroom door, then pushed it open with his shoulder. One of my bedside lamps was on, filling the room with a warm glow, but I gasped when I saw he'd placed multiple candles around the room. They weren't lit, but I knew he'd put some work into setting this up.

"Oh, Noah," I exclaimed as tears filled my eyes.

He turned to look at me, still cradling me in his arms. "Don't cry, Maddie. This is supposed to show you how much you mean to me."

"It does. All of this does. That's why I'm crying. I feel like I've been waiting my whole life for you."

He kissed me again, but this time with a sense of urgency and possession. When he broke the kiss, he said, "I planned to light the candles before I brought you up, but I guess I was a little too eager. If you want to wait in the bathroom, I can light them and bring you out."

"Maybe I should take a shower?" I said, suddenly unsure. "I smell like coffee."

He bent his head to kiss my neck. "And I told you it's one of my favorite scents. Don't take a shower on my account."

"My hair's in a rough ponytail. I don't have any makeup on. I'm not dressed up enough to warrant this..." I gestured to the room and lifted my wine glass.

"Madelyn Baker," he said, holding my gaze. "You are the most beautiful woman in the world to me. That's all window dressing. I want *you*."

"I want you too," I whispered, tears burning my eyes again.

He turned serious, lowering his arm and carefully dropping my feet to the floor. He took the wine glass from my hand and set it on my bedside table. "Stay there."

Grabbing a lighter, he started lighting the candles. When he reached the table with the lamp, he turned it off and the room was lit by the soft glow of candlelight.

"This means so much to me, Noah," I said, my voice tight.

He walked over to me and brushed stray hairs from the side of my face. "I love you, Maddie. I plan on spending the rest of my life showing you just how much."

I stared at him in shock. He'd just told me he loved me. I'd figured he'd need another month or two before he'd be able to admit it to himself, let alone tell me.

I must have hesitated too long.

"It's okay if you don't feel the same way yet," he said softly. "I know it's pretty early—"

My heart overflowed with emotion. "No," I laughed. "I love you too."

Then I proceeded to show him.

Noah and I lay in bed, naked under my covers. The candles still glowed around us, some of them now dangerously low, giving the room a magical feel. Or maybe making love with Noah had been magical and I was still in the afterglow. I'd been worried about his injured arm, but he'd told me he wasn't concerned about it and I shouldn't be either.

I was cradled against him, my head resting on his chest while his right arm wrapped around me. His hand curved possessively around my hip, as though he was worried I had suddenly changed my mind and was about to get up and walk away from him.

"Tell me more about what happened tonight," he said lazily, but I could feel his body tense slightly.

I knew what he was really asking, but I wasn't ready to lose this cocoon of contentment.

"If you've already forgotten about feeding me dinner, wine, and dessert, and then seducing me, then maybe you and Aunt Deidre can share a room at St. Vincent's."

He laughed and rolled onto his side to face me. "I tried to make light of it when you called, but I don't like the implications of that guy showing up."

"If getting me a police escort home is making light of it, then I'd hate to see outright concern."

He stroked my cheek with the backs of his fingers while staring at me intently. "I mean it, Maddie. I'm worried."

"Good thing I have a handsome bodyguard," I teased. "One who can spend all weekend with me, locked up in my house."

"You're supposed to work on Sunday."

"I'll be fine. He probably wasn't there for me. I mean, I don't usually work nights. There's a good chance he just walked in for coffee."

"I wish Petra would take my advice and put damn cameras in the place," he half-growled. "Then I could at least see what he looked like."

I kissed him and grinned. "I'm okay."

"But you very easily could *not* have been."

I placed my palm on his cheek, our faces inches apart. He'd lost people he loved to violence, but then again, so had I. Maybe that was one of the reasons we understood each other's flaws and fears. Because we shared the same darkness too.

I gave him a mock serious look. "There are no guarantees in life, Noah, but I vow to live as long as I possibly can so I can see if you're capable of topping what you did in here tonight."

He grinned, and warmth flooded my body. He brought happiness into my life, and I loved that I did the same for him. It felt like a gift that he'd let me in when he was so stingy about allowing people to see the real him.

"I'm going to warn you right now, Maddie. I'm going to be a worrier. I've seen too much, lost too much to be anything else."

"That's okay," I assured him. "I'll do my best to make sure I do everything I can to relieve your worries as long as you do the same for me."

His face froze. "Do you want me to quit the force?"

I jutted my head back in surprise. "What? Why would you ask me that?"

"Because it's dangerous."

"So is driving a car, but I'm not going to ask you to stop doing that."

"Don't be flippant, Maddie," he said, but his tone wasn't harsh. "It's a very real danger."

I turned serious. "I know, but I also know that being a detective is part of who you are. You love it, and you're damn good at it. I would never ask you to quit. Besides," I placed a kiss on his bare shoulder. "I've been in more danger than you have the last few months."

"Don't remind me," he growled, then rolled me onto my back, and leaned over me, his eyes bright with emotion. "Have I told you I love you?"

"You may have mentioned it," I teased. "But I definitely don't mind hearing it again."

His hand slipped between my legs, and I gasped as need washed through me again.

"I love you," he murmured, kissing my neck and moving down.

"And I love that you're a firm believer in showing in addition to telling."

"Always."

Chapter Twenty-Five

"Then why do the police wanting to bring

My ringing phone woke me, and I needed to take a moment to orient myself. I was in Maddie's bed, with her naked body spooned against me.

How had I gotten so goddamn lucky?

Not lucky enough to escape my phone ringing while it was still dark outside.

She released a soft moan, and I kissed her cheek before rolling over and grabbing my phone to silence the call. The screen flashed up at me with the time, 6:46, and Lance's name on the screen.

That wasn't a good sign.

I carefully slid out of bed and headed into the bathroom as I answered. "What's up?"

"Howard Bergan is dead."

My chest tightened. *Fuck.* "What? How?"

"The nurse found him this morning. He was sitting in his chair with the TV on. It looks like he died in his sleep, but Neil told me about what happened at Déjà Brew last night, and well...it seems possible it was homicide. Especially since Maddie talked to Bergan twice, and the both of you have been asking questions around the area."

"Agreed." I cast a worried glance at Maddie, who seemed to still be asleep, then shut the door. "Someone on the staff must have alerted you."

"Actually, Bergan had a note in his file to call the police to investigate his death whenever or however it occurred."

"You're kidding." I ran a hand over my head. He'd obviously known more than he'd told us, and I'd blown an opportunity to talk to him yesterday. Would Maddie forgive me for putting off reinterviewing him? "On second thought, I'm not surprised. He was paranoid as hell. I suppose with just cause." I sat on the edge of the tub. "Are you there? Have you seen his body yet?"

"I'm on my way, but I figured you might be interested in checking it out with me."

"I'd love to, but I can't be involved in an active investigation."

"Sure, you can't be the investigator," Lance hedged. "But if you happened to stumble upon the crime scene while checking out rooms for Maddie's aunt..."

I was tempted. While I trusted Lance, he didn't have as much experience with murder investigations as I did. I was worried he might miss something, and I didn't trust anyone else on the force to figure it out.

"I can't bring Maddie."

"Of course not. There's no reason to involve her in this. Do you feel comfortable leaving her alone?"

Shit. I peered through the crack of the door. She was still lying on her side, sleeping.

"I'll tell her to keep the doors locked and not let anyone in. Maybe we can have a unit do some drive-bys while I'm gone."

"Let me know when you're leaving, and I'll make sure it happens."

"Thanks."

"Of course."

I took a quick shower, realizing I was going to smell like

Maddie's jasmine soap, but I didn't want to shower at home. I always kept a spare change of clothes in my car in a duffel bag, along with a toothbrush. I'd brought the bag in last night, so I brushed my teeth and changed into my jeans and long-sleeve thermal.

When I came out of the bathroom, Maddie was awake but still in bed. The lamp next to her bed was on, casting its glow on her. With her hair fanned out on the pillow, she looked like a goddess.

"I thought you were staying with me today." The disappointment in her voice broke me.

I sat on the edge of the bed. "I wouldn't leave unless it was important." I considered keeping the reason from her, but she'd made it clear she wanted to know the truth—however hard—and this directly involved her. Besides, if she was going to be pissed at me, I wanted it to be out in the open. "Howard Bergan is dead."

Her mouth parted as she gasped and sat up. "Murdered?"

I ran a hand over my head, my anxiety brewing. "Honestly, I don't know, but if I had to bet, my marker would be on yes. Lance pulled the case, but I'm going to drop by and give him my opinion."

"Won't they call in the crime lab?"

"Probably, but I still want to see for myself." I paused and my voice broke. "I'm sorry, Maddie."

Confusion filled her eyes. "Sorry about what?"

"That we didn't try to talk to him yesterday like you wanted."

She shook her head. "We had no idea if he'd even talk to us. You were right to wait." But regret still filled her eyes.

"We'll find who killed your mother. Especially if the murderer took out Bergan to clean up his tracks. We'll catch him, Maddie. I swear."

She gave me a soft smile. "I know you will."

"It's okay if you're mad at me. I understand."

Bewilderment covered her face. "How can I be mad at you, Noah? You're doing everything in your power to find out who killed my mother. If anything, I'm grateful. And I'm glad you're going to St. Vincent's. I don't trust anyone but you and Lance to look into Bergan's death."

I kissed her, meaning for it to be a quick peck, but her lips were warm and inviting, and I let it go further than planned.

"I'm not sure I should leave you," I admitted, holding onto her arms a little too tightly.

"You're worried they'll come for me next."

"It had occurred to me."

She drew in a breath and wrapped her arms around my upper back, hugging me tightly. "We'll stay inside, and I'll call 911 at the first sign of trouble, even if it turns out to be nothing."

"Are you sure you're okay with being alone? There's not enough manpower to have someone park outside."

"I'm sure." She flashed me a grim smile. "This isn't my first time barricading myself inside my house."

"Let's hope to God that it's the last." I gave her another kiss. "Keep your phone close so I can text you periodically and make sure you're okay."

She reached for it on the nightstand. "Got it."

"I love you," I whispered, amazed I could say it so freely. But once I'd told her, it was like there was no holding it back anymore. It kept gushing out.

"I love you too." She gave my shoulder a soft push. "Now go already and hurry back." Her brows lifted playfully. "Did I mention Aunt Deidre takes naps after lunch now?"

I hopped off the bed. "I'll be back as quick as I can."

Her laughter followed me out the door. "I'm counting on that. And Noah?"

I stopped in the hall and leaned back to look into the room.

A grin spread across her face. "You smell like my aunt's flower garden in June."

I laughed, unsure when I'd ever been this happy. I could definitely get used to this.

We had prearranged for me to enter St. Vincent's via the side entrance, and when I arrived, Lance was already holding the door open. "The crime scene team's on standby."

"And the coroner?" I asked, walking in through the door.

"He's waiting to see what you find." He took the lead, bringing me down the hall, but I already knew my way to Bergan's room.

Neil was standing by the door with a crime scene log.

"Figured we should start one, just in case," he said with a sheepish shrug.

"Good thinking." Even though I wasn't here in an official capacity, we still had to have record of me walking into the potential crime scene. Otherwise, if it went to trial, my undocumented presence could potentially lose the case for the prosecution. I signed in and put on a pair of booties.

"What time did the nurse find him?" I asked as I entered the room.

Lance had put his booties on too, so he signed his name and followed me in. "About six-thirty. She found him in the chair and thought he was sleeping, but when she tried to wake him, she realized he was cold and listened for a heartbeat. When she couldn't hear one, she called her supervisor, who called the station."

"She didn't try to resuscitate him?"

"He had a DNR."

I nodded as I studied Bergan's body. He was slumped in his chair as if he'd fallen asleep, but his hands were resting too perfectly on the arm rests. It looked like his body had been staged. "Anyone other than the nurse been in this room?"

"Her supervisor and me," Lance said. "They called the station and Neil came out and sealed the room."

Thank God. I knew a few officers on the force who would have trampled all around before bringing in a detective.

"Did the nurse or the supervisor disturb his body at all? Try to roll him to his side or anything?"

He shook his head. "No. They said they didn't touch him other than the first nurse taking his pulse on his neck. That's how she knew he was cold."

I leaned closer to Bergan to get a good look at his face, then took out my phone and turned on the flashlight. "Look right there around his eyes," I said to Lance. "Those little red dots." I glanced back at him with a questioning look to see if he picked up on what I was hinting at.

A grim look settled on his face. "Shit. Petechiae."

I gave him an equally grim nod as I stood upright. "He was likely asphyxiated. Strangled or smothered." I gestured to a throw pillow on the sofa that hadn't been there when Maddie and I had dropped by the day before. "I'd go with smothered with that pillow, especially since I don't see any bruising on his neck, but that's for the coroner to decide." I stood next to him and put a hand on his shoulder. "Looks like you get to be lead on your first homicide."

His face paled, but his jaw hardened. "Okay. Let's get started."

After Lance called the crime scene team and the coroner, he called the chief to let him know that Bergan had most likely been murdered. Chief Porter said he'd be at the residential center within the next thirty minutes, but he arrived in fifteen.

The crime scene unit had just arrived when the chief walked down the hall wearing jeans and a T-shirt. His face was covered in an uncharacteristic stubble, and he looked like he still had bed head.

"Well, imagine my surprise seeing you here," the chief said dryly when his gaze landed on me.

"He was checking out a room for his girlfriend's aunt," Lance said in a rush.

"At seven o'clock on a Saturday morning? Bullshit," he grunted as they peeked into the room through the open doorway. "You called him."

"He did," I said, "but in his defense, this is his first murder and I—"

"Can it," he said, crossing his arms over his barrel chest as he studied the apartment. "I was going to call you in anyway."

Relief washed through me. I would have had a hard time skirting around this investigation without being actively involved. "Well, in that case, I should probably tell you that I talked to Bergan on Wednesday."

"You did what now?" he barked, turning to face me. "What in God's name for?"

"In my defense, I was only accompanying my girlfriend."

"Maddie Baker," he grunted, then shrugged. "I hear things."

I shot a glance at Lance, who gave me an apologetic look that suggested he was the source of at least some of those things the chief had heard.

"Let me guess why Maddie Baker was talking to Howard Bergan," the chief said dryly.

"In *her* defense, she was looking at the apartment down the hall for her aunt earlier this week. When she walked by his place, his door was open, and he was struggling with the remote. She had no idea who he was when she walked in to help him. Then she introduced herself, and he started saying some ominous shit about her mother. Their conversation was cut short, but it got her thinking. So when she told me she was coming back to talk to him, I offered to join her." I held out my hands, palms up. "It wasn't an official investigation. She only asked questions."

"So you started poking around about Andrea Baker's case, huh? Did you get anywhere?"

"We did. Bergan suppressed information about her murder. He destroyed evidence and purposely thwarted the investigation."

The chief looked around, then asked a nurse who stood in the hallway staring at us for a place we could have a private conversation. The nurse led us to an empty apartment down the hall.

"This room is vacant," she said as she opened the door. "Feel free to use it as long as you need." We started to walk past her into the room, and she looked up at me with fear in her eyes. "Was Mr. Bergan really murdered? Should we be worried? Is there a serial killer on the loose like before Christmas?"

I paused and turned to her, giving her a reassuring smile. "I don't think you have anything to be worried about, but I promise I'll let you and the staff know if you're in any danger."

She nodded, the tension draining from her face. "Thank you."

I pulled my wallet out of my jeans and handed her a business card. "If you have any questions or concerns or think of anything that will help with the investigation, feel free to call me on that number."

She glanced over the card and her eyes widened as her gaze lifted to mine. "You're the guy who was shot a few days ago. People are talking about the editorial in the paper about you bringing trouble to Cockamamie."

My back stiffened. "That's me."

"That paper's full of shit," she said emphatically. "Everyone I know is grateful you're here, cleaning up the bad things in this town." She pressed the card to her chest. "I know I feel a whole lot better knowing you're handling this case."

I started to tell her that Lance was lead on the case, but she'd already started walking away. I was beyond grateful everyone I'd encountered so far had been on my side.

"Are you joining us, Detective Langley?" the chief barked from inside the apartment.

"Yeah." I walked in and noticed he and Lance were sitting on the sofa.

I sat in an armchair, then told the chief about our chat with Bergan and everything he'd told Maddie during both visits.

"And you didn't think to tell me about any of this?" he practically shouted once I'd finished.

"Andrea Baker's case was closed. Bergan was retired. I was helping Maddie look into it, but she was taking the lead on most things."

His face reddened. Getting defensive on her behalf, I added, "She didn't do anything wrong. It wasn't an active case, so she wasn't impeding any investigation."

"I'm pissed at *you*!" he shouted.

"I wasn't investigating an active—"

"Cut the bullshit, Noah! We both know what you were doing."

There was a good chance he'd fire me for this, but I wasn't sorry. Maddie deserved to know the truth about her mother, and we'd obviously struck a nerve.

"I did," I admitted, steeling myself for his reprimand.

He shook his head, his lips pressed into a tight line. "Well, start by telling us who you talked to and what you found out. One of them either did this personally or ordered it done."

"I will," I said, pulling out my phone, "but first I need to check on Maddie. If they felt the need to kill the detective, I'm worried they'll go after her next."

"They have no reason to," the chief said. "Bergan knew things, she was just asking questions." His brow rose. "Unless you two dug up anything specific?"

"We did," I said as I got to my feet, "and I'll tell you everything we found. After I call her."

"I'll have some marked cars drive by her house while you're

working on the case," the chief said as he stood too and headed for the door.

"I already asked Busch to drive by a short bit ago," Lance said. "He texted that everything looked good."

"Doin' my damn job, boy?" the chief grumbled on his way through the door, but I heard the pride in it too.

"Thanks," I said to Lance as I pressed the speed dial for Maddie's number and walked toward the window.

She answered immediately, saying, "Everything is quiet here. In fact, Aunt Deidre is still sleeping, so I'm enjoying a cup of coffee in my room, reading a book."

Relief washed through me. Logically, I knew she was likely okay, but it turned out that my heart wasn't very logical. "You can concentrate on a book?" I teased.

"Okay," she conceded, "so I've been reading the same page for the past ten minutes, but it seemed like a good idea at the time. Plus," she added, "it gives me a good view of the front of the house." She paused. "Detective Bergan was murdered, wasn't he?"

"Yeah," I said quietly, then turned my back to the chief. "Likely smothered with a throw pillow that wasn't on his sofa when I dropped by with you."

"He didn't have any pillows on the sofa the first time I was there either."

"I'll look into it," I said, then added, "This is all confidential."

"I won't tell a soul."

"Be careful," I said, my heart in my throat. "I'd come back to the house, but the chief is bringing me in on the case. I have no idea when I'll be back, but the chief has assured me he's gonna have a marked car make regular drives down your street."

"Well, if it makes you feel any better," she said with a smile in her voice, "I've seen a police car drive down the street within the fifteen minutes I've been sitting here, so we're fine."

"You can attribute that one to Lance."

"Tell him thank you."

"I will. Let me know if anything changes." Then I added, "But call 911 first."

"I will. I promise."

"I love you, Maddie."

"I love you too."

I hung up and tried to ignore the smirk on Lance's face, but my irritation got the better of me. "What?"

"So you finally admitted it," he said, trying to hide his grin with his hand.

"Yes, I told her I love her, and she said it back," I grumped. "Are you happy?"

His hand dropped and his face lit up. "Very."

The chief came back in and announced the crime scene investigators had gotten to work but hadn't found anything exciting yet, and told me to bring him up to speed as quickly as possible.

I told him about the evidence Bergan had stored with his friend in Galena. How Andrea Baker had a boyfriend named Gordon, possibly Gordon Somato, who'd been convicted of drug possession a decade before her murder—and had allegedly testified against his boss. Then he'd gotten out and allegedly rekindled his romance with Andrea about three years before her murder. I added that the neighbor had seen him multiple times at the Baker residence and he and Andrea had engaged in a public disagreement the morning of her murder.

"So the boyfriend could have done it?" he asked.

"Possibly," I said. "But the note is throwing me. Why meet at the school? I can't imagine she'd agree to meet him there given she'd gone to such lengths to keep their relationship secret. If he sent the note, it was to throw Andrea and the police off."

"Does Maddie remember the boyfriend?"

"No. He was only there when she wasn't. Andrea told the neighbor she wouldn't introduce her to him until she was eighteen."

"That seems weird," the chief murmured.

"Andrea was protective of her," I said. "The neighbor also said she thought Andrea went to Mad Hatter's on occasion."

His brow shot up his forehead. "Mad Hatter's? I thought she was this quiet, altruistic English teacher."

"She was," Lance said. "But I suppose she could be capable of both."

"And did any of Andrea's friends corroborate this?" he asked.

"No. The two we spoke to had no idea either."

"Can we trust the neighbor's memory on this? Could she have gotten it wrong?"

"I might be able to dismiss it as faulty memory or an active imagination, only she's nowhere close to being senile. Also, a woman who joined the women's club months before Andrea's murder, Gina Moore, was allegedly the bookkeeper at Mad Hatter's. Another member of the club, Connie Smelton, said that Andrea had invited her. I guess Gina got kicked out of the women's club by the new president shortly after Andrea's murder."

"Did you talk to Gina Moore?"

"We tried late yesterday afternoon, but her receptionist was playing gatekeeper."

He drummed a finger on the table. "Did she know you were a cop?"

"Not at first, but the lady seemed extra protective of her boss once she found out that piece of information."

He gave me a smirk. "Not an official investigation, huh?"

I grimaced. "I may have played that card a time or two. I left my business card and told her that Maddie and I needed to talk to Gina as soon as possible."

"I take it she hasn't made that call yet?"

"No."

The chief sat back. "So the question is which person you interviewed raised the alarm? Then, did they murder Bergan themselves or get someone else to do it?"

"Annemarie's husband has a record, but most arrests were over a decade old," I said. "Still, she didn't seem like she had anything to hide. And, as far as I could tell, her husband didn't have anything to do with Andrea. Annemarie started dating him toward the end of their friendship, and it sounds like Andrea was already involved with Gordy. I don't get the sense there was bad blood."

He laced his fingers over his gut. "My guess is it was the guy in Galena who was storing the evidence or this Gina Moore."

"But we visited the guy in Galena several days ago. Seems like he or the person he told would have acted sooner."

"He could have stewed on it for a bit," the chief said, "then decided to cover his tracks."

"Maybe," I admitted, but it didn't feel right.

"What about this Gina Moore?" Lance asked. "She's being evasive."

The chief nodded. "We need to find out more about her past. The Mad Hatter's connection is suspicious."

It was, particularly since no one seemed to know about it. We were so damn close I could smell it.

But I didn't like leaving Maddie alone.

Chapter Twenty-Six

Maddie

Aunt Deidre woke up about twenty minutes after Noah's call, and her confusion was worse than usual. She had no idea who I was and insisted I leave her house immediately, threatening to call the police. I was practically in tears by the time I fed her breakfast and got her settled in the living room with a game show on TV.

Noah kept sending check-in texts, and I lied and told him things were going great. He had enough to worry about.

Shortly before lunch, my phone rang with a number I didn't recognize, and I answered with a hesitant, "Hello?"

"Maddie Baker?" a woman asked.

"Yes."

"You're stirring up a lot of shit I really don't need," she said through angry tears.

"Gina?" I asked, taking a guess.

"Why can't you leave the past in the past?"

"I just want to know the truth about my mother. I didn't mean to upset you. I only want to ask you some questions, and that's it."

"*That's it?* I have the police trying to track me down. My husband said they showed up at our doorstep while I was at the grocery store. Now I have a trunk full of frozen food that's about to melt thanks to you."

"I didn't send the police after you," I said.

"Oh, yeah?" she demanded. "Then I guess it's coincidence you showed up at my business with a *detective*, asking for me, and then a uniformed policeman showed up at my door the next morning?"

I suspected they wanted to talk to her because of Detective Bergan's murder, but I couldn't tell her that. "Look, I promise you, the only reason I wanted to talk to you is because you knew my mother. Noah, the detective I was with, is my boyfriend. The police knocking on your door has *nothing* to do with me." Then a stupid idea popped into my head. Actually, it was *incredibly* stupid, but I decided to pursue it anyway. If the police picked Gina up, she'd likely *never* talk to me. "To prove that I wasn't trying to trick you, you can lay low at my house for a while, if you want. I can help you with your frozen stuff. I have a big chest freezer in my garage."

"How stupid do you think I am?" she demanded. "You just got done saying your boyfriend's a detective. For all I know, he's gonna be there, waiting to arrest me."

"I doubt they want to arrest you," I soothed. "Only talk. But Noah's not with me, I promise. He's working on a case, so if you come over, you'll be safe. It's just me and my aunt here for the entire day."

"And why would you help me?" she demanded.

"Because you knew my mom, and she obviously liked you enough to invite you into the women's club."

"So, your mom *was* Andrea Baker."

"Yes."

She was quiet for a long moment, then seemed calmer when she said, "I wondered when Susan said your last name was Baker and you were asking questions about your mother."

"So will you talk to me? For my mom? I promise, I won't tell the police you're here. My boyfriend doesn't live with me, so I probably won't see him until tonight."

"You promise you won't double cross me?"

"Gina, I only want to know more about my mom."

"Then why do the police want to bring me in for questioning?"

She seemed on the verge of changing her mind, so I said, "I think I might know why, but I don't want to discuss it on the phone. I'll tell you if you come over to my house."

After seconds of silence, she finally sighed. "Okay. Give me your address."

I gave it to her, then said, "When you get here, pull into the driveway. You can park in the garage. My freezer's out there so you can take care of that too."

"Why do I feel like I'm going to regret this?" she whined.

"I promise you won't. Call me when you're almost here so I can open the garage door for you."

She hung up, and I grabbed my car keys. I had multiple reasons for asking her to pull into the garage. True, the freezer was in there, but I also wanted her to come through the back door. I wasn't sure Aunt Deidre could handle a new face showing up today. She was barely tolerating *me*. But Noah was having police cars do regular drive-bys, and if they were observant, they'd notice a new car in my driveway or in front of my house. And if they were extra diligent, they'd run the plates. If they were wanting to bring Gina in for questioning, they might be looking for her car. I'd promised to help her, so that meant I had to keep it hidden.

Noah would likely have a fit when he found out, but I'd deal with him later. I got the sense Gina would clam up the second the police got a hold of her.

After checking to make sure Aunt Deidre was still watching TV, I headed out the back door and went through the detached garage side door. I'd been working on getting it cleaned out so I could park inside, but it didn't seem fair to park in the garage when

Mallory's car was either in the street or the driveway, so I hadn't finished.

There were a few items scattered around, so I moved them out of the way and went back inside the house. When Gina called, I'd open the garage door, move my car, follow her back into the driveway, then shut the door.

Easy peasy.

And it was. She called and everything went according to plan. Once she turned her engine off, she got out, giving me and the closing garage door a wary look. She looked like she was in her mid to late forties, with blond hair. She had on a track suit, but she was wearing full makeup. Thankfully, she didn't look threatening, just pissed and scared.

"You know you've trapped me in here, right?" she asked.

"I didn't trap you. I hid you. I could get in trouble for this so give me some credit. Now let's get your groceries taken care of."

Shaking her head and muttering something about a bad idea, she opened the trunk of her sedan and pulled out two grocery bags. "I hope you have enough room in your freezer."

"I do." I gestured to a chest freezer in the back and opened the lid. "It's only half full."

She set both bags inside and I closed the lid.

"Come inside the house," I said, heading for the side door. "I'll make you some lunch."

"I'm not hungry."

"Well, my aunt probably is and given the mood she's in today, I can't risk her getting hangry."

She stopped in her tracks. Her wary look was back. "There's someone else here?" She shook her head. "I shouldn't be here. What if she turns me in?"

"First of all, as far as I know you aren't on America's Most Wanted list, and second, she has dementia. She doesn't even know who *I* am today." My voice hitched a little as I admitted the words out loud.

Some of her apprehension faded. "If you're Andy's girl, is your aunt's name Deidre?"

"Yeah," I said, opening the door. "That's her. Come on." I didn't wait for her. Instead, I walked across the back yard and went through the kitchen door. I'd left Aunt Deidre alone in the house for too long.

When Gina hadn't come in after nearly a half minute, I thought perhaps she was going to back out of my garage and drive through the grass to get around my car in the driveway, but she walked in a few seconds later and shut the door. She had a cell phone in her hand and a sheepish look on her face. "I called Artie to let him know I was somewhere safe for now."

"So you changed your mind about me?"

She shrugged. "I figure if you're anything like Andrea, you'll keep your word."

I gave her a long look. "Thank you." Her statement struck a chord, and it took me a moment to recover. I'd heard how much I looked like my mom, but this was the first time my character had been linked to hers.

"Thank *you*," she said. "Artie's grateful too, by the way." She slipped her coat off and draped it over the back of the chair before she sat down, setting her purse and phone on the table next to her.

"I'm sure the police just want to talk to you," I said, "not arrest you. You haven't done anything wrong."

"You don't know what I've done or haven't done," she countered. "If *you're* asking questions about your mom knowing me, then they have to be digging into the same things. Things I don't want them digging up."

That sounded ominous. "You know, hiding from the police isn't going to make them stop looking for you."

"Yeah, well, I need some time to figure out what I want to do." She propped her hands on her hips. "That's why I agreed to come—to buy more time. So tell me why you're suddenly asking about your mother and why the police are suddenly lookin' for me. It can't be coincidental."

"Do you like tuna salad?" I asked, ignoring her question. "Aunt Deidre usually likes it, but lately it's been hit or miss. I could also make some mac and cheese."

"Maddie," she said in exasperation. "Why are they lookin' for me?"

"I promise, if you're hungry you're gonna want to eat first." I settled on tuna anyway and started pulling the ingredients from the refrigerator and cabinet.

"That bad, huh?"

"I'll let you decide." I grabbed the can opener, popped the lid on the tuna, then added it to the bowl. "How did you know my mother?"

She shifted in her seat. "From the women's club."

"Connie Smelton said that my mother invited you to the group. She also said that Everly Barton kicked you out soon after my mom died."

Gina rested her hands on the table, twirling her wedding ring around her finger. "That Everly is a downright bitch."

"I have to agree with you there."

She looked up with a grin. "Met her, huh?"

"At the November women's club meeting." I opened the jar of mayo and turned toward her. "Let's just say she's not too fond of me, and the feeling's mutual."

"Your mom was trying to change that group. That's part of the reason she invited me. To make it more accessible to the average women of town. Not the rich bitches."

"But your husband is a business owner," I said, then hastily added, "I mean, you probably are too."

"I am, but I wasn't then. We were just engaged. And in Everly's eyes, I was and still am just a bookkeeper. It didn't help that she caught wind of my past."

I scooped some mayo into the bowl with the tuna and started stirring. "That you were a bookkeeper at Mad Hatter's?" I shot a glance at her to gauge her reaction.

Her face paled. "Where did you hear that?"

"Connie, but she doesn't believe it for a minute, so your secret's safe."

"Not if she's goin' around tellin' everyone."

"She's not," I said, pausing to add some spices. "I practically forced it out of her."

"Why?"

I stopped stirring and turned to face her again. "Because I wanted to know what Everly had on my mother to force her to resign so suddenly."

"Did *Connie* know why?"

"No, she has no idea, but I figured it out after talking to a few people and piecing things together."

"Whatever you're thinking, I can assure you that you're wrong."

I put my hand on my hip. "So tell me what I'm thinking."

She slowly shook her head, fear in her eyes. "You need to let this go, Maddie."

"Let go of finding out more about my mother? Do you still have *your* mother, Gina? Do you still get to talk to her and celebrate holidays together?"

She took a deep breath and seemed to settle herself. "I do, and I know you lost your mother at a young age, but she'd want you to let this go, Maddie."

"She was mixed up in something dangerous, wasn't she?" When she didn't answer, I continued. "I know she was with Gordy."

Shock covered her face. "How do you know about Gordy? She said she didn't tell you about him."

"I know. I know she dated him when I was little, he was arrested for drug possession and intent to sell. I know he testified in the head drug guy's trial." That was a guess based on what Dawn told us, but I figured it would be better to sound confident. "She started seeing him again years later. What I don't know is where Gordy was for all the years between his arrest and when he started seeing my mom again."

She frowned, obviously not happy. "He testified, but he never went to prison. Gordy went into witness protection."

I stared at her in surprise, but then again, I wasn't sure why I was shocked. It made total sense.

"Gordy wasn't even his real name. Andy said he told her his name, but it was so loud in the bar that she couldn't hear him. She thought he said Gordy, and even though she heard wrong the name stuck."

"So what's his real name?"

"Why are you digging this up?" she demanded. "It sounds like you have an ugly picture of her, but she wasn't involved of any of that shit. It was just happening around her."

Any of what? But I couldn't directly ask her. I was pretty sure she thought I knew more than I did. If she continued to think so, she might accidentally reveal something. So I shifted the conversation. "Then why was she frequenting the Mad Hatter's? That's how you know her. You met there."

"I don't know what you've heard..."

"Pretty much what I told you, but I've talked to a lot of sources, and my mom was apparently pretty good about compartmentalizing the many parts of her life so that most people only knew bits and pieces. No one knew everything about her."

"Gordy did."

"That's bullshit," I snapped before I could think better of it. "I never met the man, which means he didn't know me, and I used to think I was a huge part of her life."

"You *were* a huge part of her life, Maddie," she pleaded. "You're the reason she wouldn't go into the witness protection program with Gordy. She didn't want you to lose your aunt and uncle."

Good Lord, the shocks just kept coming.

"*What?*"

"He asked for you and your mother to come with him, but she didn't want to take you from your family, so she turned him down."

I rested my hip against the counter, trying to take it in. "But he obviously came back into her life."

"He did. He couldn't live without her, so he left the protection program."

"Did he move to Cockamamie?"

"No," she said, twirling her ring again. "But he moved to some small town in Alabama, near the border. That way he could drive up to see her when you were staying with your aunt and uncle or a friend."

"So why were they going to the Mad Hatter's?"

"The bar owner knew Gordy from Chattanooga. He happened to see him on his bike when he was driving out of town. He had someone watching for him the next time he arrived, then he invited Gordy to pay him a visit. And when I say invited, I mean forced. He threatened to hurt Andrea if he didn't go."

I felt sick. "So my mom went with him?"

"Hell, no. Gordy never told her. Not until she found out he was trafficking drugs again. She swore she was done with him, but he told her that he was being forced to do it. Billy had told him that if he didn't cooperate he'd tell Reed's people—that's the guy Gordy turned in—where to find Gordy and his girlfriend."

I swallowed hard. "So why did my mom start going to the bar?"

"Because she got it in her fool head she could convince Billy to let Gordy go. She was hoping she could work something else out that would make him more money, which was the only way he'd agree to such a thing."

"What was it?" I asked warily.

"Honestly, I'm not sure, but I met with her a few times so she could look at the books. They had a couple of meetings and, sure enough, his revenue started increasing from all his various businesses."

"All of them? How?"

"Like I said, I don't know, but I suspect she helped him figure out a way to launder his drug money."

"*Why?*" I demanded. "Why would she do that?"

"Like I said, she wanted Billy to agree to let Gordy free." She paused. "And he did. Your mom also helped convince me to leave Billy and get a job with Artie. Artie knew about my past employer but didn't care. And she invited me to join the women's club, and everything was going well until Everly kicked her out of the group."

"What did Everly have on my mom? Did she know about Gordy or that she helped Billy?"

She snorted. "No. Everly found out about my past and threatened to tell the group. She seemed pretty smug about the prospect of ruining me and your mom by association. Your mom agreed to step down, but I could tell that she was anxious about something else. When I asked her about it, she said she wasn't afraid of Everly, but she didn't have the energy to deal with her right then. She had a bigger fight on her hands."

"What fight?"

"She wouldn't say, but I suspect she was referring to Billy. Men like him don't stick to their word. I suspect he got greedy and wanted more—either for Andrea to work more magic for him or for Gordy to come back or both."

"Do you think Gordy killed my mother?"

She snorted again. "There ain't no way. That man would sooner have killed himself."

"The day she died...someone left her a note telling her to meet them at the high school. Do you think it was Billy?"

She hesitated. "I don't see how. Billy would have told her to meet him at the bar."

"What if she refused?" I asked. "What if he caught wind that she suspected one of the teachers was molesting students so he knew she'd think the note was from that teacher, not Billy?"

"I don't know," she said. "The underhanded approach wasn't really Billy's style. He was more into intimidation, not shock and awe."

"So you don't know who killed my mother?" I asked.

"No, darlin', but even if I did, I'm not sure I'd tell you. Billy might be dead, but there are plenty of other people connected to him who are still around to finish you off."

My blood pooled in my feet.

"I'm hungry!" my aunt called from the living room. "Where's my food?"

I glanced down and realized I'd finished making the tuna salad and toasted two pieces of bread while on autopilot. I slathered the salad onto the toast, cut the sandwich in half and put the halves on two plates. I added some crackers to my aunt's plate, then piled some chips onto the other and set it in front of Gina.

"I'll be right back."

Aunt Deidre turned away from the TV as I walked into the room. She took one look at the plate and her upper lip curled. "What is this?"

"It's your lunch, Deidre," I said sweetly. "Tuna salad on toasted wheat bread. One of your favorites."

"I hate tuna salad."

"Really? Because Albert said you loved it." I blinked to ease the burn in my eyes. Her behavior wasn't her fault, but this wasn't the woman I knew and loved. She'd be horrified to know she was talking to me this way.

She glanced around the room. "Where *is* Albert?"

"He got tied up with a church committee. He'll be home soon." It was my standard excuse, but it always seemed to work.

Tears welled in her eyes. "I miss him."

My heart broke. I sat down next to her, wrapping an arm around her back and cupping her shoulder. "I know you do."

"I miss Andrea too. She hasn't come by to see me in ages. Where is she?"

"She's busy too," I said, swallowing the lump in my throat. "With Maddie."

She turned to face me. "I think she's seeing him again."

I held her gaze. "Gordy?"

She nodded. "She's being secretive and gives in too easily when I ask for Maddie to spend the night."

"Maybe Andrea loves him."

"I know she does," she said disgust. "She says she's going to stop seeing him at her house because Maddie almost saw him the other day, but I don't think I believe her."

"I'm sure she's doing the best she can," I suggested, then stood. "I'll be in the kitchen if you need me."

I started to head back to the kitchen when she called out, "You're not so bad for hired help, but I still prefer the other lady."

"Thank you," I said, equally insulted and amused.

Gina was standing in the doorway watching my aunt as I reached her. "She really does have dementia."

"I'm probably going to have to put her in a facility. In fact, I toured St. Vincent's a few days ago."

Her face paled, and she turned to face me.

"Why does that make you nervous?"

"What did you do?" she asked.

"I saw Howard Bergan. But from the look on your face, you already knew he was a patient there."

"What did you do?" she repeated.

"He told me he hid evidence and stalled my mother's case

because a man threatened him. A skinny man. We have the evidence he hid. She had a key on her when she died. A gold house key. Do you know what it could have gone to?"

"Her house?" she asked sarcastically, but I saw the fear in her eyes.

"What did it go to, Gina?" When she didn't respond, I moved onto the more incriminating piece. "Do you know why my mother was holding a pendant with an eagle on it when she died?"

"You need to let this go, Maddie," she spat through her teeth. "You're gonna get yourself killed."

"Where's Gordy now?" I pressed. "Did he come to the funeral?"

"Of course he came, wild horses couldn't have kept him away, and Billy was counting on that. He nabbed Gordy on his way out and told him the deal was off. He had two choices. He could either go back to being Billy's mule, or he'd kill the second most precious thing to him."

"His motorcycle?" I asked in disgust.

"No, you ungrateful girl. It was you."

"*Me*? I've never met the man!" I felt light-headed. So much of my mother's life had been a lie. Had my parentage been one too? "Was Gordy my father?"

"He didn't meet your mom until you were in preschool."

"Then how could I be the second most precious thing to him?"

"Because he loved your mother, and you were the most precious thing to *her*. He'd do anything to protect Andrea's daughter. Even sell his soul to a devil like Billy Hauser."

"I didn't even know him!" I protested, angry at the rush of guilt. "Why would he do *that*?"

"For your mother."

"Wait," I said, as my brain started connecting pieces. "Billy was murdered about a week later."

"Yep."

"Oh, my God, did Gordy kill him?"

"Let's just say the police never investigated it too hard, but if I were a bettin' girl, I'd put down a thousand bucks that he did."

"Because he thought Billy might have killed my mother?"

"I don't know. When I asked him about it, he told me it was to protect you. He said the fact that Billy had threatened you was enough to take him out." She made a face. "Not that he admitted to doing it. He made it all sound hypothetical."

"Wait," I said. "Billy was murdered about a week after my mother's death. You saw Gordy again after the funeral? After Billy was murdered?"

"Hell, I see him all the time."

"What? *Where?*"

"He's living in town now. Damn good mechanic. But he goes by a different name now. George. He owns George's Garage." Her cheeks reddened. "Now tell me the real reason why the police are looking for me."

"Howard Bergan's dead."

Her eyes went wide with fear. "No."

"Noah thinks we pissed someone off by looking into my mother's death and they're...I don't know. Wrapping up loose ends?"

She shook her head. "You've really done it."

"Who's doing this?"

She shook her head again, determination filling her eyes. "Nope. I already told you too much. If you want to know more, you need to go talk to George."

She rushed over to the kitchen table and snatched up her coat and purse. "I have to get out of here. For all we know, they're comin' for you next." She threw the back door open and rushed out toward the garage. She disappeared through the side door, and seconds later the garage door opened. She was already getting in her car.

Yep, she planned to drive in the grass.

I grabbed my keys and ran out, thankful she had to pause long enough to grab her groceries because it gave me time to back my car out onto the street before she pulled out. She peeled out of my driveway, and I watched her blow through a stop sign.

Who was she so terrified of?

I parked my car in the driveway and headed to the garage to close the door. Just as I reached overhead for the handle, I felt a sharp pain in the back of my head and then everything went black.

Chapter Twenty-Seven

Noah

It took all morning and into the afternoon to work the crime scene. Surveillance footage showed a man entering the building through a side door at 10:03 the night before. He'd stood outside for a good ten seconds before opening it, presumably because he was picking the lock. There wasn't much to see—he'd had on a hoodie that completely covered his head and knew enough about surveillance cameras to keep his face down. He headed straight for Bergan's room and entered at 10:04. Three minutes later, he emerged and then exited the building the same way he'd come in.

We were in the process of talking to the night staff and residents to see if they'd seen or heard anything. We questioned the custodian about why the alarm hadn't gone off. He claimed there had been a faulty connection, but the security system company said they'd fixed it.

Had the killer been behind that, or was it a lucky fluke?

I texted Maddie a little after noon to see how she was doing. She didn't answer right away, causing me a moment of panic, but she sent a text about five minutes later.

Everything is fine.

The wording seemed odd. It wasn't like her, but someone grabbed my attention with something connected to the case. We still hadn't found Gina Moore, and her husband claimed he hadn't seen her since she'd left for the store around ten. Odds were, we'd shown up at his door before she'd gotten home, and he'd warned her off.

The staff found more surveillance footage of the parking lot. A pickup truck had pulled in from the west side of the building at 9:59. The driver was the murderer, that much was clear. When he left the lot nearly ten minutes later, we got a glimpse of his license plate, but it wasn't a clear read. Lance sent it to the crime lab to see what they could come up with.

Around three, I got a call from Margarete, who was in a state of panic.

"*Noah?* I was driving home from a long lunch with a friend, and I found Deidre wandering down the street, about two blocks away from the house. I tried calling Maddie, but she's not answering. It took quite a bit of convincing to get Deidre in my car. She doesn't remember who I am, and she claims she doesn't know Maddie."

My vision tunneled, and I lowered down into a nearby chair. I needed to treat this like any other case, but that was impossible. Especially when I felt like my life was about to be ripped apart again.

"Other than confused, is Deidre okay?" I motioned for Lance to come over.

"She's wearing her house shoes and no coat, but she doesn't seem worse for wear."

Lance stood in front of me, and I pressed the mute button on my phone. "Send a car over to Maddie's house. *Now*. Deidre was wandering down the street, and Margarete can't get ahold of Maddie."

"Shit." He turned and made a call on his phone.

"Noah? What should I do?" Margarete was asking.

I turned off the mute button. "Can you take Deidre to your house? If not, I can get someone else to pick her up."

"Don't you want me to take her home and see if Maddie's there?"

"*No*. I'm sending some officers over to the house to check things out." My voice broke, and I took a deep, slow breath to control it.

"What's going on, Noah?"

"I don't know, but I'm on my way. I'll be there in a few minutes." I clicked off the call, my ears buzzing.

I refused to let my mind consider the possibilities, because none of the alternatives I was coming up with were good. Maddie would have realized that Deidre had gotten out by now, and she would have accepted Margarete's call, or at the very least called me.

I had to get out of here. I had to go see for myself. "I'm going to check on Maddie," I announced, then bolted down the hall.

"I'm coming too," Lance called out from behind me, and I heard him telling the chief we were leaving, but it barely registered.

I had nearly gotten to my car when Lance said, "We're taking my car. Get in."

In a stupor, I climbed into his passenger seat.

"Don't think the worst, man," he said as he peeled out of his parking spot.

He was right. Maybe Maddie had gone to the bathroom and Deidre had gotten out then. Or maybe they'd both lain down for a nap. I tried to focus on those possibilities as I called her number. It went straight to voicemail, and panic flooded me again. I felt like I was going to be sick.

"I never should have left her this morning. I should have stayed with her."

"She'll be fine," Lance said. "She's resourceful."

I started to hyperventilate. If the man who'd killed Bergan tried to smother Maddie, could she stop him? Lance was right, she *was* resourceful, but if she had gotten away from her attacker, why was her phone going to voicemail?

"Her phone's going straight to voicemail," I said, blankly realizing Lance needed to know that piece of information. "Which means it's turned off. She doesn't turn off her phone. Ever. She keeps it close by in case someone calls about Deidre."

"Take some slow deep breaths. I'm sure she's okay."

"I told her I love her," I said, my vision tunneling again. "What if I cursed her?"

"You didn't curse her," he said. "And thank God you finally manned up and admitted to your feelings. I've been hoping for it." When I didn't answer, he said, "You can have your freakout. You're due, but as soon as I pull up to her house, you have to snap out of it. I need you to focus. I'm good, but I'm not as good as you."

When I didn't respond, he shook his head. "You're in worse shape than I thought if you didn't take that bone I just threw you." He sped around a corner then turned to me. "Noah. Will you be able to get it together?"

Leaning forward, I covered my lower face with my hands. "Yeah."

"She's not dead, Noah. I promise."

I sat up, outraged. "You can't promise me that."

"Well, too damn bad because I just did."

I took deep breaths, trying to focus. Reminding myself if Maddie was in trouble and I wanted to help her, I had to pull it together.

When Lance pulled up to the curb across the street, two cruisers were already parked in front of the house, their lights flashing. One officer stood in the middle of the yard, and another was on the porch. The front door was closed.

I hopped out of the car, relieved when my control slipped back into place. The first thing I noticed was the open garage door. The second was that Maddie's car wasn't in the same place it had been when I'd left this morning. "Have either of you been in the house yet?" I asked the officers.

"No," they said in unison.

"Did either of you do any drive-bys earlier?" Lance asked. "Was the garage door open?"

"I did the drive-bys," one of them said. "At least one an hour, sometimes more often. The garage door was open when I drove by around one."

"*And you didn't think to let us know?*" Lance shouted.

I ignored them as I reached the porch, pulling out my gun. I had no idea what I'd find, but I planned to be prepared. But first I had to get through the front door. I lifted my foot to try to kick it in, but Margarete hurried over. "Wait! Wait! I've got a key!"

Lance took it from her and bounded up the steps. It took him all of a second to unlock the door and push it open.

I took the lead, shouting inside, "Maddie?"

No answer.

Lance followed me in. "I'll take the upstairs."

"Okay," I forced out, my mouth dry, then entered the living room. "The living room's clear."

And so was the dining room and kitchen, but the back door was wide open.

That answered how Deidre had gotten out.

I checked the powder room and, heart in my throat, the basement. All clear.

"Nothing upstairs," Lance called out.

"Nothing down here either," I said. "Her purse and coat are on the hall tree, but the back door was wide open."

"Did Deidre open it or Maddie?" he asked when he reached me.

"Good question." Something on the kitchen table caught my eye. I walked over and picked it up.

I felt sick again. "It's the business card I gave Gina Moore."

"Are you *sure*?"

"Positive. I wrote Maddie's name and number on the back. I'd messed up one of the Ds." I lifted it to show him.

"So Gina was here?" Lance asked.

"Either that or she told someone and gave them the card."

"Detective Langley," one of the officers called out. "I found something."

I dropped the card back on the table and ran out the door. The officer was at the back of the house, pointing toward the ground.

Lance and I stopped a few feet away. "Her phone," I said.

"You sure?" Lance asked.

"Check out the case. It has stars." I had the sense to follow some semblance of protocol and snapped a few photos of it before I carefully picked it up with my bare hand and turned it over. The screen was shattered like it had been hit hard with something in the center.

"Someone destroyed it," Lance murmured.

My nausea returned.

"So she was kidnapped?" he added.

"Most likely."

This is just a normal case ran through my head. *You have to treat it that way.*

Unlike I'd done with Caleb.

My father had always taken joy in pointing out my failures. From the lost Little League games to my 3.9 GPA in high school, to the fact I hadn't caught on that the kid I was mentoring had gotten hooked on drugs and killed a convenience store clerk in a robbery. It had taken him killing my dog, and then nearly killing me, to catch on. He'd told me I'd never be a good detective because I was incapable of keeping a clear head and blocking out my emotions when it really counted.

Part of me believed him.

But Maddie needed me now. I couldn't afford to fuck up.

I stuffed every bit of fear deep down and focused on the case in front of me.

"Why would they take her?" Lance asked, glancing around the yard as though he'd find the answer there. "For what purpose?"

"I don't know. If they were going to kill her, they'd do it here and get it over with. Just like with Bergan."

"Detective Langley?" the other officer called out. "I found something too." Only he sounded more apprehensive than the first officer.

He was standing in the driveway, a few feet from the front of Maddie's car. "Careful." He pointed to the concrete, splattered with multiple drops of blood.

I closed my eyes and took a deep breath. Lance put a hand on my shoulder and squeezed.

This is just a normal case.

I opened my eyes and examined the blood.

"It might not be hers," Lance said. "It could be someone else's. Like I said earlier, she's resourceful."

I nodded but didn't say anything. My gaze followed the small drops of blood to the end of the driveway and out onto the street, where there were more. It looked like whoever was bleeding had stayed there longer than they had on the driveway.

"Whoever was hurt was walked or carried down the driveway and put into a car."

Lance gauged the distance from the curb to the location on the street. He grimaced and gave me a grim look. "Or a trunk."

Fury blazed through me. I'd find the son-of-a-bitch who did this and make him wish he'd never been born.

I turned to the officer closest to me. "I want every officer in this city tracking down Gina Moore. She was likely here and could have taken Maddie. The sooner we find and question her, the better."

Maddie's life depended on it.

Chapter Twenty-Eight

Maddie

I woke up with a terrible headache. My stomach was churning, and I could feel the bile rising in my throat. It took me a few moments to orient myself. Moving vehicle. Confined space. Stale and musty smell.

A trunk. I was in a trunk.

My head was fuzzy and there was a constant ringing sound. Something wet and sticky covered the back of my head and neck. I struggled to stay awake, but I forced my eyes to stay open. I needed to take stock of my surroundings. I wasn't sure what was going on—my last memory was of Gina backing out of my driveway—but I needed to try to get out of here.

I was in a car, in the trunk, facing backward, where the taillights would be. Daylight seeped through the cracks enough for me to get a dim view of my surroundings.

Something floated into my memory, telling me that I could get out of this trunk. That newer cars had cords you could pull to escape. Only I didn't see a cord and my arms were tied behind my back. My feet were secured too.

What had happened? It all felt surreal, but I wasn't scared, just confused. It was like I was out of my body, removed from the situation. But I was here in my head, very much in it.

Focus, Maddie.

I racked my brain to remember how I'd gotten here. I remembered the pain in my head and now I was in the trunk of a car.

Obviously, I'd been kidnapped!

What was the ringing? It was piercing my ears.

Focus on Noah. He was going to be devastated when he found out I was missing. Then, for the first time since waking up, pure panic washed through me.

Aunt Deidre.

Everything returned at once, and I realized that Aunt Deidre must have been left unsupervised. Mallory wasn't coming home until Sunday night and who knew when Noah would be back. What would my aunt do all alone?

Oh God. The back door was still open!

Tears streamed down my cheeks. She'd eventually find the open door and get out. She wasn't dressed for the cold weather. How far would she get before someone found her?

If someone found her.

Had Gina set this up?

The car turned a corner, sending my body sliding toward my feet.

Right turn. They'd made a right turn.

I knew I should keep track of the turns so I could tell Noah, but I had no idea how many turns they'd already made, plus my head was still groggy and that ringing was giving me a headache.

Then I realized the ringing was in my own head.

I could hear the murmur of voices, but I couldn't make out any words. It would probably help if the ringing went away, but I had no way to fix that.

I tried to turn my head so I could get a better look of the area where the light was coming through. Yes. They were taillights.

Maybe I could kick them out, but probably not since my feet were bound.

I tried to figure out why they'd taken me. Obviously I had some purpose, or else they would have killed me. But what?

Gina thought the man who'd killed my mother had also killed Detective Bergan, but I wasn't so sure. Gina also didn't think Gordy killed my mother, but she did think he killed Billy, and no matter her reasoning, it seemed more logical that Gordy/George would kill Billy to avenge my mother's death. Not to protect *me*.

If my mother's murderer was afraid I was turning over too many secrets from the past, it made more sense to kill me like Bergan, not kidnap me. But if Gina was right about George protecting me in the past, did that mean the person who'd kidnapped me was doing it to get leverage on George? I couldn't make sense of it, though. I'd never even met the guy. There had to be another reason.

The car made two more turns and then pulled onto a bumpy road. Less than a minute later, we came to a stop, and the engine cut off.

The ringing in my ears had dulled enough that I could hear what the voices were saying.

"Get her out and bring her in," a man with a deep voice said. "Now that we have her, we'll invite our guest."

The car doors opened, and seconds later, light flooded the trunk. The sky was overcast, but I could make out the faces of the two men. One was young, but the other was in his late thirties or early forties. Both had multiple tattoos, but neither had the eagle wings I'd seen on the guy who had come into Déjà Brew.

I cast a glance to the right and saw the sign over the building we were parked next to. Cock of the Walk.

Fear shot through me. Did that mean these guys were with the Brawlers? I'd heard horror stories about them and this place. It was run by a motorcycle club that was rumored to make people disappear. They were allegedly hardcore into drugs—both selling and using—and no woman in her right mind would step inside the place. Not if she didn't want to run the risk of being violated.

If the Brawlers wanted me, there was a good chance the only way I was leaving was when they carted me out into the woods to bury my body in a shallow grave.

"Come on, Sleeping Beauty," the older guy said with a laugh. He reached in and grabbed my arms, wrenching me into a sitting position.

My world began to spin, and as he started to haul me out, I leaned forward and vomited.

"Goddamn it!" he shouted, shoving me back into the trunk. "She threw up on my new shoes!"

My head hit the lid, and I could see stars as pain shot through every nerve ending in my body.

When the younger guy laughed, the older guy punched him in the gut. "You think it's so damn funny, Murphy? You bring her in by yourself."

Murphy doubled over, clutching his stomach while his cohort stomped away, his feet crunching on the gravel.

I took a second to try to absorb my surroundings. We were in a nearly empty parking lot that had been covered with fresh gravel. A two-lane road was next to it, and trees were across the street. If I could get away from Murphy, I could potentially run across the street and into the woods.

"Why do you want me?" I asked, but my tongue felt too heavy to enunciate clearly.

Murphy looked up from his crouch. "What?"

I tried to swallow to coat my dry throat. "Why am I here? Why do they want me?"

"Don't care," he said, still hunched over. "Just do what the boss man tells me to do."

"And who's the boss man?"

He let out a nervous laugh. "You sure don't know much, do you?"

"I'd know more if you told me anything," I said, hoping it didn't sound as sarcastic as it did in my head.

"Come on," he groaned, then leaned over the trunk and swung my legs over the edge.

I needed to escape, and I couldn't do it with my feet tied together. "You're either gonna have to untie my feet or carry me inside. I probably weigh one-ninety, one ninety-five. I don't want to hurt your back."

He narrowed his eyes. "You're lying. You don't weigh that much."

Then, just to prove me wrong, he pressed his shoulder into my stomach and lifted me up. "Don't barf on my back."

"No promises," I said, trying hard not to, although it would serve him right. I glanced back at the open trunk as he carried me away, taking in the plate-sized blood stain on the carpet. I told myself not to be alarmed. Head wounds bled a lot.

Based on the blood dripping on the ground, mine was still bleeding.

I considered trying to get away from him, but I couldn't run away with my feet and hands trussed up. If I tried, I'd likely just piss him off and get another wound for my effort. As hard as it was, I needed to cooperate for now and look for another way to escape.

Murphy was carrying me through the empty bar. Pictures of roosters were on the walls, confirming what I already knew, although I'd hoped my head wound had made me misread the sign. This definitely was Cock of the Walk.

I was in deep, deep trouble.

"Take her to the back," a man over by the bar said. "They're calling him right now."

Who were they calling? Part of me wanted to ask, but my head was throbbing from hanging upside down.

"Hey, there's blood dripping all over my clean floor!" the bartender called out.

"What are you talkin' about?" Murphy asked with a laugh. "Your floors ain't never clean."

"You're cleaning up the mess before we open at five!"

Ignoring him, Murphy headed down a hall and through a door. Then he turned down another hall and opened a door, flicking on a light. Shelves lined the walls of the small room inside, and a wide array of cans and boxes covered the shelves.

"This place doesn't seem very hospitable," I said, my words slurred.

He laughed. "Not up to your standards?"

"I doubt it'd be up to anyone's standards."

"At least it's not the walk-in freezer." He dropped to a crouch and unceremoniously dumped me onto the tile floor, then headed for the door. "That's where we kept the last guy."

I started to panic. My hands and feet were still tied. "I have to go to the bathroom."

He shook his head. "Nope. No way."

"If you don't take me, I'll pee my pants."

"So pee your pants."

He turned to leave, and I called out, "Can you untie me first?"

"Nope. No one said I could."

"Please? My arms really hurt, and I presume you're locking me in here. I can't get out."

He hesitated.

"*Please?* That way if I get sick again, I can make sure I throw up somewhere in the middle of the floor." I winced. "I doubt you want to clean *that* up."

Groaning, he came back inside. "*Fine,*" he grunted, then untied my hands. I didn't press my luck and ask for my feet. With my hands free, I could manage that one myself.

He left me on the floor and walked out, shutting the door behind him.

I gave myself a moment to let the room stop spinning. I tentatively reached my hand to the back of my head, jumping from the pain as soon as I touched the large lump. Blood matted in my hair and coated the back of my shirt.

I needed to untie my feet.

I set to work and managed to finish it despite a whole lot of fumbling, but then an overwhelming fatigue settled in on me. I didn't have the energy to even consider what to do next. I laid my head down on the floor, the cool tile on my cheek giving my throbbing head some relief. I closed my eyes and then jerked awake a few seconds later when I realized I'd fallen asleep. I couldn't fall asleep. I had to find a way to escape.

It sounded like a good plan, but my eyelids felt too heavy, and my arms and legs were like blocks of concrete.

Get up, Maddie!

I knew I should.

I knew I had to—and I *would.*

Right after I took a little rest.

Chapter Twenty-Nine

Noah

I watched the two officers take off in a hurry while Lance studied me.

"Maybe you should sit down, Noah. You're looking a little green."

Panic flared through me, with nowhere to go. "I have to find her, Lance!"

He put his hand on my arm. "I know. I know. Just take a moment."

My eyes burned and my throat was clogged.

I was failing her. Just like I'd failed when dealing with Caleb.

"What if she doesn't *have* a moment?" I choked out.

He didn't say what I was already thinking. She'd been gone for at least two hours. Ten seconds wasn't going to make much of a difference.

I took a deep breath in and held it for several second before releasing it. My panic settled, making room for my professional side to slip back into place. "We need to see if any of the neighbors have surveillance footage. I doubt we'll catch what happened since the two neighbors across the street don't have cameras, or at least they didn't the last time we pulled footage from the block. But others might have captured the vehicle or, please God, a license plate."

"On it," Lance said, pulling out his cell phone.

I walked over to Margarete, who was standing on the side of her yard, horror written on her face.

"What time did you leave for your lunch?" I asked.

Her gaze darted to the driveway, then back to me. "Where's Maddie?"

"I don't know," I said, my voice breaking again. I cleared my throat. "I'm trying to figure it out. What time did you say you left?"

We both knew she hadn't told me, but she didn't correct me. "A little before noon."

"Did you see anything unusual going on?"

"Well, there was *something* a little weird. Just as I was about to leave, I saw Maddie back her car into the street. A green car pulled into the driveway, then Maddie pulled in behind her and parked. But when I drove past on the way to lunch, Maddie's car was in the driveway, and I didn't see a green car at all."

"When you left for lunch was the garage door up or down?"

"Down, definitely down. I noticed right away it was up when I brought Deidre home."

"Where is Deidre now?"

"My daughter was with me in the car. She took Deidre into the house."

"I think I should call an ambulance to take her to the hospital," I said, glancing over to her house. "Maddie's going to be worried when she finds out she was a few blocks away without a coat."

"Noah."

I grabbed my phone and started to dial the number.

She put an arm on my arm. "Noah."

I lifted my gaze from my screen to her face.

"Deidre is fine. I promise. She doesn't need to go to the hospital. I think it would only make things worse."

I nodded. She was right, of course. I wasn't thinking straight, which was bad news.

My father had been correct—I was incapable of holding it together when it really mattered.

No. I could keep it together. I had to.

"The green car," I said. "Did you see who was driving it? How many people were in the car?"

"It was a woman, and from what I could tell, she was alone."

"What did she look like?" I asked, searching my phone for the photo of Gina that we were circulating.

"Blond hair. Middle-aged, I'd say. Her car was nice but nothing fancy."

I held up my phone and showed her the photo. "Did she look like this?"

Margarete leaned closer then nodded. "Yep, that's her all right."

"Lance," I called out. He was standing next to one of the marked cars, talking to an officer. He glanced up at me.

"Gina was here a little before noon."

He walked over and listened to Margarete repeat her story, and when she finished, his face set. "We really need to talk to her now."

"Agreed. For now, let's ask the other neighbors if they saw anything."

"On it."

A half hour later, we had footage that showed Gina's car driving toward Maddie's house shortly before noon, then leaving about twenty minutes later. The footage also showed a dark sedan drive toward the Baker house and then stop a house away, on the opposite side of the street. The car pulled away from the curb, pulled into a driveway two houses down, backed up, then drove toward the Baker house. About three minutes later, it was seen on a camera farther down on the opposite side.

"Look at the time stamp," Lance said. "12:32."

It fit...but it also drilled in the fact that Maddie had been taken three hours ago and we were no closer to finding her.

"They found her," an officer shouted at us.

My heart jumped. "Maddie? Where?"

"No," the officer said, with a grimace. "Sorry. Gina Moore. She's down at the station."

Lance and I jumped into his car and hightailed it to the station.

She was sitting in an interrogation room when we arrived, vacillating between looking pissed and scared.

"I'm Noah Langley," I said in a no-nonsense tone as I sat in front of her. "I'm Maddie's boyfriend. I know you were at her house this afternoon. Tell us where she is."

Her eyes widened. "She's missing?" She closed her eyes and cursed under her breath. When she opened her eyes, her jaw set. "I *told* her to leave it alone."

"Leave *what* alone?" Lance asked.

"Her mother. Everything to do with Gordy."

"Did Gordy take Maddie?"

"Gordy?" she asked in disbelief. "He wouldn't hurt a hair on her head."

"Then who took her?"

"I told you I don't know!" she shouted. "But I suspect I know why."

"Then why?" I barked, getting pissed she wouldn't just spit it out.

"They're trying to punish Gordy, and they're using her to do it."

"Why would using Maddie hurt Gordy?"

"Because of Billy Hauser. Or whoever killed Andrea. I don't know."

"Wait," I said, shaking my head. "Billy Hauser owned the Mad Hatter's. He was murdered a week after Andrea Baker was killed."

"She'd worked out some deal with him to keep Gordy from

having to work for Billy. But I caught wind that he was reneging on the deal. He wanted Gordy to start working for him again."

I leaned forward. "I'm gonna need you to start from the beginning."

She did, telling me about how Gordy and Maddie's mother got connected to Billy.

"Do you know where Gordy is now?" I asked.

"He's here in Cockamamie under all y'all's nose," she said in disgust. "He goes by George now, and he has a shop."

My eyes flew wide as I glanced at Lance. I could tell he'd also made the connection.

"George's Garage?" I asked.

"How many are there in town? *Yes*, George's Garage."

Lance got up. "I'll send someone to the garage and his residence to bring him in for questioning." Then he exited the room.

"He ain't gonna be there," Gina said. "They probably already had him come see Maddie so they could get whatever pound of flesh they're wanting from him."

"And you have no idea who's wanting their pound of flesh?" I asked.

"Not a clue."

"Noah," Lance said, his voice tight. "I need to speak to you in the hall. Now."

I glanced up at him, surprised by the anxious look in his eyes, and followed him into the hallway.

"You know something," I said, forcing myself to stay calm.

"You know we've been watching George's Garage."

"Tell me something I don't know," I grunted, getting pissed. "I was there the first day we did surveillance."

"Well, I got one of those kids to finally talk a little bit last night, and a familiar name popped up."

"Joe Kipsey," I said. Finally.

"The kid said it's like Kipsey has some kind of vendetta against

George Dempsey, but we can't figure out why. As far as we know, Kipsey has never lived in Cockamamie."

"But he has a vendetta?" I asked, my blood running cold, because Kipsey was ruthless.

I knew where they'd taken Maddie, and I was more terrified than ever.

Chapter Thirty

Maddie

I woke with a start when someone called out, "Come on, Sleeping Beauty. You're late to the party."

I didn't recognize the man's voice, but I murmured, "Just one more minute."

Two men grabbed my arms, and I was hauled up off the floor, my head bobbing forward.

"Jesus," another man said. "How hard did he hit her head?"

"It don't matter," said a voice I recognized. "She don't need to do any talking. Just seeing her will be enough."

I fought to stay awake as they started dragging me out of the room.

They're going to kill you, Maddie. Snap out of it!

That roused me. I lifted my head to take in my surroundings. My feet weren't working yet, but I couldn't keep playing along. I had to *do* something.

"Wait a minute," I said. "I think I'm going to be sick."

I was nauseated, but not enough that I felt like I would throw up. Word must have gotten around about the other guy's shoes, though, because they took a step back while still holding onto me.

I took several breaths in through my nose and out through my mouth to keep up the nausea ruse. We were in the same hallway Murphy had brought me through but headed in the opposite direction.

"Ready to go now?" one of them asked. I didn't recognize him, but the other guy was an orderly I'd seen at St. Vincent's. In Detective Bergan's room.

Oh God. Was he the person who'd smothered Bergan with a pillow? Only he hadn't seemed like a murderer. He'd been nice.

"I know you," I said, trying to picture him holding a pillow over Bergan's face.

For the first time, I wasn't sure I was going to get out of this.

He at least had the good grace to look guilty. "Sorry."

"You were spying on Detective Bergan."

He gave me a sheepish look. "Nothing personal, Maddie."

"It sure seems personal."

"Now that we've all had a nice chat," the other guy said, "let's get going."

We continued down the hall, and I walked instead of being dragged, but I purposely moved slowly, trying to buy myself some more time. I was feeling more coordinated than when I'd woken up, but I was in no condition to take on both men. Especially since they were both armed. The unnamed guy's weapon was in the back of his pants, and the orderly had a holster at his side.

What if I could wrestle a gun away?

I wasn't sure I was with it enough to try. In the end, it didn't matter, because we turned a corner, and we walked through a door into a massive garage that looked big enough to park four big RVs or tractor trailers.

The man who had walked into Déjà Brew last night was present. His arrogance made it clear he was in charge of whatever was happening here. Several armed men were with him, including Murphy and the guy I'd barfed on, who didn't look thrilled by our reunion.

Standing across from the man in charge, unarmed, stood a man who looked vaguely familiar. He was older and had a head full of gray hair. I'd seen him before, but for the life of me, I couldn't figure out where.

The man in charge commanded the room, all eyes on him...until I walked in. When he saw me, he grinned, releasing a little chuckle as he swept an arm toward me. "*Here* she is."

"What happened to her?" the gray-haired man asked, outraged. He took a step toward me, but Murphy and the guy I'd barfed on pointed their guns at him.

"She gave my guys a little trouble," said the man in charge. "But she's perfectly fine. Completely alive."

The gray-haired man was still pissed. "She's covered in blood, Kipsey!"

Was the gray-haired man George? How did I know him?

"It's a minor head wound, George," Déjà Brew man—Kipsey—said. "They tend to bleed. She's fine, and I suggest we keep her that way. It's time to get down to business."

Some of the anger faded from George's face. "What do you want?"

"You already know what we want."

His anger was back. "I ain't dealing with stolen cars. I can't. The police are already breathing down my neck. I've seen them parked down the street, watching me."

"We can probably back off with the cars," Kipsey said, extending his hands in a sign of peace. "See? I'm not totally unreasonable, but we can still work with the junkers you ship to Dallas. All you need to do is add a little extra cargo and we're all good."

"By extra cargo, you mean you want me to cart your drugs for you."

The man in charge gave an exaggerated shrug. "Semantics."

"And if I agree?"

"Then Andrea's little girl gets to live her life. And if you don't, she doesn't."

George's face paled. "What did you just say?"

Kipsey's eyes lit up. "Andrea. Andrea Baker. Wasn't she your girlfriend?"

George started to say something, then his gaze shot to me and then back to Kipsey. "How do you know about Andrea?"

"My brother told me about her," Kipsey said. "I think you knew him." When George didn't take the bait, he said, "Billy Hauser. Ring any bells?"

I didn't think it was possible, but George looked even more shocked. "Billy didn't have any brothers."

Kipsey laughed, but it sounded wrong.

George licked his bottom lip and shifted his weight. "Okay. Fine. Done. You didn't need to take her to get me to agree to this, Joe."

"Funny, I've been trying to get you to agree for months now, so I figured I needed to step it up a notch."

"Point taken," George said. "Now that that's settled, how about we let her go and you and I can work out the details."

"I could do that," Kipsey said, taking several steps toward me. "But where would be the fun in that? I wanted to see your face when you saw me hurt her."

I gasped and tried to take a step back, but the two men holding me kept me in place.

"But I agreed to your deal!" George shouted.

Pure evil radiated from Kipsey's eyes as he approached me. "I said she'd *live*. I never said what shape she'd be in."

I gritted my teeth and spat out, "If you try to touch me, you'll regret it."

Kipsey chuckled. "Oh? You think you're going to hurt me? You're a fucking mess."

"Why are you doing this, Kipsey?" George pleaded. "I said I'd do it, and I won't break our deal. I swear."

Kipsey turned to face him. "I know you killed my brother, *Gordy*."

George stumbled a few steps backward. "What?"

"I knew someone in this shithole did it, and I needed a place to set up base after I got out, so I figured I might as well come here and find out who killed him. Imagine my surprise when I found out it was you."

"You have no proof of that," George countered.

"Oh, I think I've got all the proof I need. You took my brother, so I figure hurting *her* will hurt you way more than outright killing you." An evil grin spread across his face. "Let's get started, shall we?"

Chapter Thirty-One

Noah

Lance insisted on driving out to Cock of the Walk. I called one of my sheriff's deputy friends on the way and told him the situation, asking him to arrange for several deputies to meet us out there.

"We're going to make it in time," Lance said, shooting me a nervous glance.

"Yeah," I said absently, but I couldn't help thinking about how long Kipsey and his men had kept her and what they could have done to her.

I had to believe she was still alive. I had to believe she was safe.

Lance's phone rang, and he put the call on speaker. "Forrester."

"Hey, Lance. We've gone to George Dempsey's house and his garage and there's no sign of him," Neil said through the speaker. "One of his employees said he was working in the garage. He got a call and they say he started acting weird, then he took off."

I shot a glance to Lance. "Neil, how long ago was that?"

"About an hour ago."

My stomach sank. If he'd been summoned by Kipsey an hour ago, there'd been more than enough time for Kipsey to use Maddie as his leverage and then be done with her.

"Should we keep looking for him?" Neil asked.

"No," I said. "Dempsey's already on his way or at the location Kipsey's called him to." I turned to Lance. "Do you think he'd be brazen enough to hold a meetup at Cock of the Walk?"

"Yeah," Lance said. "I think so."

My throat tightened. "If we make the wrong call, and she's not there when we show up, he might kill her."

"I know. Which is why it's your call. If you want to take some time to dig in so we can be certain, just say the word."

I took a breath and considered my options, forcing myself to look at the situation with my head, not my heart. I shook my head. "No. We stick with the plan."

My anxiety ratcheted up with every mile we grew closer to the bar. We were going without a search warrant, which meant we couldn't force our way inside the bar.

How was I going to search the property for her?

We'd figure out a way.

It turned out to be easier than I'd expected. The property had an eight-foot-tall barbwire chain link fence, with a large gate to the right of the building that led to a large gravel lot with several outbuildings. The parking lot had a handful of cars, but I was most interested in the gate. I was ready to tell Lance to plow through it—a legally gray move—but it was partially open.

I could see two sheriff's deputy cars, lights flashing and sirens blaring, coming from the opposite direction.

Lance reached the lot first, and he must have read my mind, because he headed for the gate. "Drive through it," I grunted.

He held on tight to the steering wheel. "That's the plan."

He sped through the too-small opening, barely slowing down.

The gate bounced off the car and slammed into the side of the bar as Lance drove down the side of the building.

"What next?" Lance asked.

"Find Maddie." It was pretty shitty as far as plans went. I shook my head to clear it. "We'll go in through the back door."

Chapter Thirty-Two

Maddie

Kipsey lifted his hand to slap my face, and instinct took over. I dropped into a squat and pulled free of the men who were restraining me, then kicked Kipsey hard in the groin with the heel of my shoe.

The two men beside me had been too shocked to react, but now they both reached down for me. I rolled over so my back was to them, then grabbed the nearest arm and tugged hard, flipping the guy onto his back. His head hit the concrete floor with a loud thud, and he didn't move. The other guy grabbed me around the waist and pulled me off the floor. But I hadn't taken all those self-defense classes for nothing. I wrapped a foot around his leg and twisted my body, throwing him off balance. He started to fall, and I gave his thigh a hard shove. He landed on top of his buddy, the orderly.

Kipsey was still doubled over, but pure rage covered his face.

"Stop her!" he shouted, then hastily added, "But don't kill her. I'm going to really make her suffer now."

The two guys with guns had been pointing them at George, who was watching the scene unfold with horror. But Vomit Shoes Guy gleefully pointed his gun at me. I was standing in the open, several feet from Kipsey and the two men on the floor. I had no cover, and I suspected he would shoot me out of spite for vomiting on him.

"If you kill her, you might as well kill me too," George said in a broken voice.

"Maybe that can be arranged," Kipsey growled as he started to stand more upright. He slipped a knife from a sheath on his belt and held it out toward me. "But first I'll make her suffer, just like I did with her mother."

I gasped in shock, but George let out a bellow of anguish and fury. "*You* killed Andrea?"

Several shots rang out. It took me a second to process that George had tried to run over, and Murphy and his friend had shot at his feet.

"You stay where you are," Kipsey said with a grin, starting to circle me. "*You* get to *watch*."

"NO!" George shouted. More gunfire went off, but I had my gaze locked on Kipsey. I was starting to see two of him, which was going to make dodging his six-inch blade difficult.

Kipsey jabbed his knife toward me, and I jumped backward to evade it. I'd had some training in evading an aggressor armed with a knife, but my head was so scrambled it wasn't coming back to me.

I moved to my left, heading toward the open entrance to the garage. There were woods off in the distance. If I could get outside, maybe I could make a run for it. Then I realized I couldn't leave George behind. Maybe we could both run?

There were grunts and gunshots coming from the group, and a quick glance told me they were bunched up and physically fighting.

Kipsey used my moment of distraction to thrust the knife at me. I caught the glint of the blade at the last second, so I spun to the side, and it ran across my bicep instead of slashing my core.

I didn't feel it at first, and then my arm was on fire as blood ran down my forearm.

Kipsey laughed. "You're putting up more of a fight than your mother."

"I don't know about that," I shot back, trying not to let him goad me. "She got your eagle necklace." I gestured to his chest. "Replaced it with a tattoo, huh?"

"It was a gift from my daddy. I didn't realize it was gone until I left. By then the cops were swarming the place. That damn janitor."

"So you were partners with your brother?" I asked. We were practically dancing in a circle as I tried to evade him.

He laughed. "Fuck no. He was my older *half*-brother, and he thought he was too damn good for me. But I dropped into town to pay him a visit and heard about his dilemma with Andrea Baker. He said he had it covered, but I was still trying to win his trust. I told Billy he needed to show the bitch who was boss. So I sent her a note and got her to meet me at the school. Told her it was in her best interest to help my brother out with his business ventures and maybe there would be a little something in it for her. I figured I'd convince her one way or the other to cooperate."

"But she didn't cooperate, did she?" I prodded. I was moving us closer and closer to the entrance, a good ten feet away from the wrestling men. I didn't dare spare them a glance.

"No, the bitch actually spit in my face. Can you believe it? So I showed her she wasn't as high and mighty as she thought she was. Funny thing is, Billy was *pissed* that I killed her. Said she had a key he needed. The asshole was so mad he sent me on a mission to Knoxville a few days later and gave the state police a tip that my car would be carryin' drugs. I was in jail when Billy was murdered. But when I got out, I saved up my money and called in a few favors and convinced the owner of the Cock of the Walk to sell it to me. I wanted to find out who killed my brother and I figured living here was the best way to do it. Might as well make a little money while I was at it. I've been biding my time, sussing things out, and then you started stirring up shit."

"You threatened Bergan's family," I said.

"It wasn't hard to get him to stop. He actually peed his pants when I met him the first time. I didn't give him a chance to pee 'em the second."

"You smothered him with a pillow."

"With Jimmy-boy's help over there." He gestured in the direction of where the orderly still lay. "I was in and out with no trouble at all."

"So why kidnap me? Bergan was dead. There wasn't any threat to you."

"Because, by process of elimination, I'd figured out that old George here killed my brother and decided to use that to my advantage."

"If you hated Billy so much, why did you care who killed him? He set you up to get arrested."

"Maybe so, but he was still my brother."

He must have decided he was done bragging about his exploits because his eyes shifted from amused to deadly in the split of a second. He started to lunge for me, and I realized I'd boxed myself in. I was three feet from the wall.

Kipsey gave me a self-satisfied look as he took a step closer. "Got nowhere to run, little girl."

He wasn't prepared when George tackled him from the side, throwing him sprawling to the ground. The knife was knocked out of Kipsey's hand and went skittering across the floor.

George grabbed Kipsey by the hair on the back of his head, then slammed it onto the unyielding floor. "*You* killed Andrea? I'm going to kill you, you son-of-a-bitch!"

I looked up to see if the men with the guns were about to shoot at George or me, but they were all sprawled on the ground.

George continued to slam Kipsey's head, and it was clear he was either dead or unconscious. I slowly approached them. "George? You can stop now. He's not going to hurt either one of us anymore."

George stopped and looked down at the blood on the floor and Kipsey's broken face and released his hold.

I held my right hand out to him. "Come on."

He stared down at Kipsey and a new fury filled his eyes. If Kipsey wasn't dead, George planned on finishing the job.

"George," I pleaded, realizing that I'd started to cry. I moved a little closer, my right hand still extended. I was trying to ignore the pain in my left arm as I held it at an angle against my stomach. "Please? I want to go home, George. I want Noah."

My words seemed to shake him out of his stupor. He climbed off Kipsey and got to his feet, only to wobble a bit.

That's when I saw that the front of his shirt was drenched in blood.

I stared at him in horror. "Did you get hurt?"

He shook his head, but his eyes were becoming glazed as he reached down to his right side in confusion. "Maybe I did."

I rushed over and helped him down to a sitting position, putting his back against the wall. I started to look for a phone, but I could hear the wail of sirens outside. I hoped to God they were coming here. Had Noah put it together and figured out where I was being held?

"Let's just sit here and wait for the ambulance," I said as I squatted next to him, terrified by the amount of blood on him.

He shook his head. "They're gonna arrest me for murder." His gaze landed on the pile of men. "A whole pack of 'em."

"You killed those men in self-defense," I protested. "They won't charge you for that."

His gaze lifted to mine. "Not with Billy."

"You thought he killed my mom." It was then I realized how I knew him. He'd been in the coffee shop multiple times.

"Nah," he said with a short laugh. "He liked her too much. She was a spitfire. You take after her. He never would have killed her. I've always known that."

"Did you know Kipsey did it?"

"I never laid eyes on the man until a few months ago when he walked into my shop and tried to convince me to become partners in a stolen auto parts ring. I turned him down, not that it stopped him from tryin'."

"Then why kill Billy?" I asked.

He smiled up at me. "For you."

I shook my head, tears falling in earnest. "Why? You didn't even know me." Why would he sacrifice so much for *me*?

"I may not have met you while your momma was alive, but I felt like I knew you. She loved you something fierce."

I choked out a sob. "George."

"All these years, I've been trying to keep you safe. I knew your momma's killer was still out there, and I had an irrational fear he'd come after you too—or maybe *not* so irrational. So I was equally relieved and terrified when you moved back."

I stared at him in shock. "You knew I moved back?" I knew I should have been horrified that a man I didn't even know had been keeping tabs on me, but I found it endearing.

He grinned again, but this time it was more playful. "At the risk of sounding like a stalker, I always knew where you were." He coughed and blood sprayed from his mouth.

The sirens were getting closer. "Just hang on, George." I took his hand and squeezed.

Please God, let them be coming for us.

He sank against the wall, and even though his face was white from blood loss, pure joy lit up his eyes. "Nah. You can take care of yourself now. I think I'll go see your mom."

"Don't die!" I pleaded. "Please don't die! There's so much I don't know about her, and you have so many answers."

A tear slid down his cheek. "All you need to know is that you were her true north."

Why didn't that feel like enough? "Why did you come here?" I cried, starting to sob. "Why did you try to save me? You don't even know me."

"If she could love *me*, then how could I not love you too?" He coughed again, but it was weaker this time. "You're her baby girl, and I swore to her I'd protect you with my life. Even if that meant stayin' away from you when your mom and me were together. I failed you last November and December, but I swore I wouldn't do it again." He looked up at me, his eyes unfocused. "Forgive me?" he whispered.

"For what?" I asked in dismay.

"I put your momma in danger. I was the one who ultimately got her killed. I should have stayed away, but she was my everything and I lost her. And so did you." His face crumpled. "Forgive me?"

I squeezed his hand tight and brought it to my chest. "I forgive you, George."

He smiled then and the light left his eyes as his grip on my hand relaxed.

Noah found me minutes later sobbing over a man I'd never known—a man who had willingly sacrificed himself for me out of love for my mother.

I didn't feel worthy.

Chapter Thirty-Three

Noah

When Lance pulled behind the building, two commercial-sized garage doors stood open, and multiple people were lying on the floor.

"Maddie!" I shouted as I bolted out of the car before Lance could come to a full stop. I frantically scanned the space. I didn't see her at first. But then I heard her gut-wrenching sobs and found her huddled over a man who was slumped against the wall. My heart skipped a beat when I saw the back of her shirt, her arm, and her hair were covered in blood.

"Maddie!" I cried out and rushed toward her, dropping to my knees beside her. My first thought was to triage her and find out how badly she was injured. I gently pulled her off the man and turned her to face me. She held her bloody arm against her chest. "Where are you hurt?"

She looked up at me with bloodshot eyes. Her face was streaked with dried and fresh blood. She looked like she'd been to hell and back. "Noah."

I cupped her cheek and choked out, "I'm here."

"I hoped you'd come."

My eyes and throat burned. "I'll *always* come." My gaze

dropped to the front of her shirt, which was spotted with blood. "Where are you hurt, Maddie?" I asked again, my voice rising in panic. "Your arm?" I gave it a quick glance and saw something had sliced her bicep. She'd need stitches. But her cut arm didn't explain all the blood covering her clothes and body.

She looked down at her shirt, then shifted her gaze to the man she'd been draped over. "It's not all mine. Some of it's George's."

"George?" His face was ghostly pale, and the front of his shirt was drenched with blood. I felt slightly better knowing the blood on her shirt wasn't from her. Still, there was no doubt there was a shit ton of dried blood on the back of her shirt and in her hair.

"He died," she said through fresh sobs. "Trying to help me."

"Maddie, I'm sorry."

"Where's the rest of the blood from?"

She nodded then winced. "They hit me in the back of my head when they kidnapped me at the house."

The sirens outside were very close, but I wasn't sure they'd sent an ambulance. "Lance?" I glanced over to see him going from body to body, checking pulses. "Maddie needs an ambulance."

"I don't," she said, trying to get to her feet. "It looks worse than it is."

I nearly told her to stay on the ground until the ambulance arrived, but I knew better than to suggest it. Maddie didn't stay down. She got back up. That's who she was.

I stood and helped her up, gently wrapping my arms around her back and pulling her to my chest. "We're going to get you checked out anyway."

Sheriff's cars pulled up next to Lance's, and several officers got out, guns drawn.

"Some of them are still alive," Lance said. "I've handcuffed a few of them, but they need ambulances too."

I looked around the room in shock, realizing I was so focused on Maddie that I'd barely noticed the chaos spread around the room.

"Too?" one of the officers asked, then a knowing look filled his eyes as he took in Maddie.

"Can you tell me what happened?" I asked her, but she shook her head and started to cry again.

I LEFT Lance in charge as I rode to the hospital with Maddie. They put staples in the back of her head, stitched up her arm, gave her a pair of scrubs to wear, and said she could go home after they'd observed her for another hour. She still hadn't told me what happened, and the sheriff's department was growing impatient for her statement. I could tell she was still traumatized, though, and I refused to press her.

I left her in her exam room to get an update on the suspects. Joe Kipsey had a head injury, but the doctors expected him to recover. Several other men had gunshot wounds, but they were also expected to recover. One of them—an orderly at St. Vincent's—had agreed to talk in exchange for a reduced sentence. He'd tied Kipsey to the car parts ring, his plan to coerce George to transport drugs to Dallas in junk cars, and also shared some of Kipsey's distribution routes.

When I made it back to Maddie's room, a deputy was sitting in a chair next to her bed, taking her statement. My ire rose. "I told the chief I'd let him know when she was ready to give a statement."

"It's okay, Noah," she said. Her face was still pale and dark circles underscored her eyes. "They need to know what happened."

I needed to know what had happened, too, but I also realized she might have felt more comfortable talking about it when I wasn't there. A fear that she'd been harmed in other ways besides the wounds on her head and her arm hung over me like an anvil. If I found out any one of those men had violated her, I'd kill them. And if they were already dead, I'd revive them and kill them a second time.

I waited in the hall until she was done with her statement, and the ER doctor discharged her shortly after. Lance had arranged for my car to be dropped off at the hospital, so I drove us back to Cabbage Rose House.

She was quiet on the drive home, but she clutched my free hand. She was so unlike herself, she was scaring me.

I parked my car in front of her house and turned off the engine. "Maddie, before we go in..." I kept my gaze out the windshield, careful not to look at her and make her uncomfortable. "I just want you to know that no matter what happened, I'm here for you in any way you need me. If they..." I swallowed. "...touched you, I'll support you in any way I can."

"They didn't touch me," she said softly. "At least not like that. They kidnapped me, put me in the trunk of their car, stored me in a supply closet for most of the day, then hauled me out so Kipsey could try to torture George by hurting me. But they didn't touch me like you're thinking. I'm fine."

"Maddie, any one of those things would be enough to traumatize you. Let's get you inside."

I walked around and helped her out of the car and into the house. Margarete had agreed to take care of Aunt Deidre overnight so Maddie could get some rest. After I unsuccessfully tried to coerce her to eat some reheated leftover spaghetti, I took her upstairs to bed and helped her take a shower. Once she was clean and dry and tucked into bed, I curled up next to her.

"Can I do anything else for you?" I asked, worried about how withdrawn she'd become.

"No." She rolled partway to look up at my face. "I'm upset about this afternoon—I'll probably have nightmares for years—but I'm most upset because I watched George die right in front of me."

She held my gaze. "He died for me, Noah. He fought all those men and attacked Kipsey to protect me. I didn't even know him."

"I know," I said, brushing a few stray hairs from her face. "I don't pretend to understand what he's done in the past or today, but he must have cared for you very much."

A tear rolled down her cheek, and I wiped it away.

"He killed Billy Hauser to protect me. He said he knew Billy didn't kill my mom, but he didn't trust him not to hurt me." More tears fell. "He killed a man for me, Noah. A man who'd only threatened to hurt me. While part of me feels grateful, I also feel so guilty. Like I caused that man's murder."

"Hey," I said gently but firmly. "You had nothing to do with it. If George had really wanted to help you, he would have told the sheriff's department about the threat. Not enacted his own vigilante justice."

She didn't look convinced.

We were quiet for several long moments before she said, "I know who killed my mother. Joe Kipsey admitted he did it to convince his brother Billy to let him into his business. Only Billy wasn't happy he'd killed her and set Kipsey up to go to prison."

"Wow."

"But I finally know," she said. "For the first time since she died, I know who killed her and why, so why do I still have this gaping hole in my heart?"

I wrapped my arm around her, holding her tight while she cried herself to sleep.

Chapter Thirty-Four

Maddie

When I woke up, I was aware of two things. One, I was cocooned by Noah's body and felt more loved and protected than I ever had in my adult life. And two, I felt like I'd been run over by a truck. My head hurt, my arm hurt, my eyes felt swollen, and my entire body ached.

I'd been a basket case after Noah found me and brought me home, but this morning I felt lighter than I'd felt in ages. I still hurt, inside and out, but I felt less burdened. Maybe it was the good long cry I'd had last night before bed, or Noah holding me all night. Maybe it was the knowledge that my mother had been loved deeply, and that I'd found someone who loved me that way too.

"Good morning," Noah murmured in my ear, then placed a kiss on my shoulder.

"Good morning."

"How are you feeling today?"

The worry in his voice touched someplace deep in my heart. "Better."

"You don't have to tell me that, Maddie. You don't have to tell me what you think I want to hear."

I rolled onto my back and looked up into his concerned face. "I do feel better."

He gave me a dubious look.

"Truly. I do. I got answers about who killed my mother. I can let that go. And yeah, there's still a hole in my heart, but you're helping me fill it, Noah."

His eyes widened.

"My mother's my past, and maybe that hole is there because I couldn't let the past go. Not without getting answers. But now that I have them, I can fill it with something in my present." I gave him a soft smile. "I can fill it with a life with you, Noah."

He kissed me, then we made love, and he treated me so gently that I could feel myself falling more deeply in love with him.

I could see a future with this man, and it filled me with joy.

Mallory came home by lunchtime. Noah and I were snuggled up on the sofa while Aunt Deidre sat on the love seat, watching yet another game show. She burst through the door, took one look at us, and demanded, "What happened?"

I was tempted to downplay it, but Noah gave me an understanding look and took Aunt Deidre into the kitchen so they could make lunch together.

Mallory sat down next to me, and I gave her an abbreviated version of what had happened since she'd left for Chattanooga. When I was done, she was furious.

"Why didn't you call me?

"I didn't see the point," I said. "You couldn't have done anything. I came home from the hospital and went to bed."

"You still should have called me."

"I know. You're right. I'm sorry." Then I narrowed my eyes. "What are you doing back so early?"

"What are you talking about?" she asked defensively. "I told you I was coming back today."

"You said you were coming back *tonight*. You're about six hours early. What happened?"

Exasperation spread across her face. "Lance is what happened."

I shook my head. "What does *that* mean?"

She ran a hand over her head in frustration. "I was trying to have fun with my friends, hanging out a bar, and one of them was trying to set me up with a really cute guy. All I could think about was Lance." She grunted in frustration.

My eyes went wide. "*Oh*."

"What if he *is* the one?" she asked with tears in her eyes.

I picked up her hand and squeezed. "Is that bad if he *is*?"

"I'm scared, Mads."

"And what about that scares you?"

"Now you sound like a shrink," she teased, then turned serious. "What if I screw it up? What if he *is* the one, and I get itchy feet to move on to the next guy?"

"Well," I said, "if that happens, then he isn't really the one, now is he?"

She sat back into the sofa and sighed. "Being a grownup sucks."

I sat back with her. "Tell me about it. I still haven't decided what to do about Aunt Deidre. I need to talk to the director of St. Vincent's. I don't have much more time to decide before they move onto the next person on the list."

"Do you really want to put her in a residential care center that had a murderer as an employee?" she asked in disbelief.

"The orderly wasn't a murderer. He only aided and abetted."

"Well, there you go," she said as though I'd said the most logical thing in the world.

We were silent for several long seconds.

"She could just keep living here," she said. "Then you don't have to sell Cabbage Rose House and we can all keep living here together."

"Eventually she'll have to go somewhere else."

"Exactly. *Eventually*. But for now, let's just hire someone to help at night." She grinned. "And then you'll be able to have an actual social life."

I snorted. "A social life."

"It wouldn't hurt to *try* to have one," she said with a shrug.

"We could always move to Chattanooga like you'd mentioned," I said. "They have multiple care centers there."

"Yeah, I know, and while I was the one to suggest it, now I'm not so sure."

"Really? *Why?*" I asked with mock innocence.

"Do you want me to say it?" she demanded then released a heavy sigh. "Because I don't want to leave Cockamamie, and neither do you."

"I don't," I admitted. "And neither does Noah."

"Speaking of leaving Cockamamie, did you see the Chattanooga newspaper article about Noah today?"

"There's an article about Noah?" My stomach in knots, I picked up my phone and started searching for the Chattanooga newspaper website. "You could have led this entire conversation with that little fact."

"There's no fun in that," she teased, but she put her hand on mine before I could properly freak out. "Chill, Mads. It's good. Really good."

I found it and sure enough, it was. It basically said the Cockamamie newspaper editorial staff was a bunch of morons who should be praising Noah instead of tearing him down. In fact, it said if the city of Cockamamie was too stupid to recognize what a jewel they had in their midst, then the city of Chattanooga should try to find a way to bring him there.

"See?" she said. "Noah already has a job in Chattanooga if he wants one."

I lifted my brows. "Shouldn't you be calling Lance?"

She laughed. "Not yet. But I will."

After we ate lunch, I took Aunt Deidre upstairs to take a nap. Mallory said she needed to run an errand, but I noticed she'd freshened her makeup and touched up her hair before she left.

The temperature was in the upper fifties, so I put on a heavy sweater, and Noah and I sat out on the porch swing. He rested his arm on the back of the swing, cradling my shoulder as he pushed off the floor. The swing started to sway. Gently.

"I think Mallory's headed for Lance's apartment," I said as I rested my temple on his chest.

"Really?" he asked in surprise.

"Yep. She and I had a talk about Aunt Deidre, and I've decided to keep her home for now. I'll just hire another aide to help at night. That should buy us more time both in keeping her at home and keeping Cabbage Rose House.

"It's been in my family for generations," I added, tears stinging my eyes. "It doesn't feel right to sell it."

"It's only right if you want to sell it," he said after a moment's pause. "You shouldn't feel obligated to keep it if it's too big or too much to maintain. But if you love this place, then you should do everything in your power to keep it. No matter what."

I looked up at him and smiled. "Thank you, because I want to do everything in my power to keep it."

"Then I'll do everything in my power to help you. This house is special to you, and it feels like a forever house, Maddie." He hesitated, then said, "You know, I never believed in love at first sight until I met you."

I laughed. "Not the first time you met me, and not even the second."

"Okay," he conceded with a chuckle. "When I eventually came to my senses."

We were silent for several minutes, Noah pushing against the floorboards every few seconds to maintain the gentle sway.

"This seems like a great house to raise kids in," he said softly. "It's too bad Aunt Deidre and Albert couldn't fill it with children."

"I was here a good bit of the time," I said. "But I always wanted a brother or sister. Or even one of each."

"So you would want two kids?" Noah asked, hesitation in his voice.

I sat up and turned to face him. "Noah..."

His eyes locked on mine. "Because I was thinking that if I have kids, I don't want just one. I'd want at least two. And if all goes well, maybe three."

I stared at him in disbelief. "Noah, you don't have to tell me this. I want to be with you. I know you're still on the fence about having children."

"Part of the reason I didn't want to have them is because I was convinced I'd be like my father, but lately, I've begun to realize I'm not like him at all. And I have to admit that the thought of having a little Maddie running around has a certain appeal."

"What about a little Noah?" I asked, telling myself not to get too excited about this conversation, but I was getting excited anyway.

"God help us if we have one," he said with a grin.

I smiled at him like a fool. "I love you, Noah."

"I love you too," he said, then lowered his lips to mine and proved beyond a shadow of a doubt that he meant it.

When he lifted his head, I grinned. "Don't you think we're getting ahead of ourselves, talking about kids before we've even talked about marriage?"

"I plan to marry you, Maddie Baker. Not yet, but I do. And then we'll have three kids and maybe a dog." A hopeful look filled his eyes. "I miss Sarge. At first, it didn't feel right replacing him, but I've been thinking—"

"You can get a dog if you want one, Noah."

"A dog is a commitment, and if we're eventually getting married, it only seems right to make sure you're on board with this."

"I'm more than on board with this. I've always wanted a dog. Besides, there are studies that pets are good for Alzheimer patients."

He kissed me again, his face radiating happiness. "I'm looking forward to forever with you, Maddie."

I liked the sound of that.

Thank you for reading Half Baked, the final book in the Maddie Baker Mystery series.

To find out more about Denise Grover Swank's book, join her newsletter.

Printed in the USA
CPSIA information can be obtained
at www.ICGtesting.com
LVHW091303060924
789970LV00008B/721

9 781942 439004